The Fishers

An Amish Life Collection

By Amos Wyse

&

Laura J. Marshall

Perhaps some of you are familiar with Amish tradition and customs. For others, this may be your first exposure to them. Like the population around them, the Amish are not uniform in practices, dress, nor dialect. Some keep to the ways of old while others may be more progressive.

Some *Englishe* still think of Amish as Dutch. That comes from the mispronunciation of Deutsch, the German language and heritage of most Amish. The words they use are either German or a derivative colloquial variation. Below is a compiled list of words in German or near-German to clear any confusion. Many German nouns pluralize by adding an "e" to the end. The various dialects and spellings of these words that are found speak to the nature of closed communities, as well as to the Swiss heritage of some Amish communities.

Bann - Shunning, **complete** *avoidance of a person*

Bobbel/e - baby/babies

Bruder - brother

Daed - dad

Dochder - daughter

Eldere - parents

Englishe - non-Amish people

EnkelKinder - grandchildren

Familye - family

Frau - Mrs

Freund - friend

Gott - God

Grossdaed - grandpa

Grosseldere - grandparents

Grosshaus - common smaller home on same farm for grandparents

Grossmutter - grandmother

Grossmutti - grandma

Grossvater - grandfather

Gut - good

Haus - house

Herr - Mr

Jah - yes

Kind/er - child/ children

Mein - my

Mutter - mother

Mutti - mom

Newehocker - Side-sitter 2 men and 2 women who witness the Amish wedding/ bridal party

Ordnung - Strict rules governing the Amish society.

Rumspringe - The time after a young adult leaves school but has yet to formally join the church. It is sometimes used to see the ways of the Englishe world.

Schwager - brother-in-law

Schwagerin - sister-in-law

Schwester/e - sister/s

Suh - son

Und - and

Vater - father

Viel Gluck - good luck (much luck)

Was - what

Planting Seeds

The Fishers

(An Amish Life 1)

1

Spring was upon the land. Caleb reached out his arms, stretching his broad shoulders. If any had seen this, they would have thought he was hugging the air and the land, and they would not be far off from what was in his mind. He knew better than most that even in the chill of the early morning, the rising sun was warming the earth and getting it ready for seeding. He could smell the rich loam waking up all around him. The smell of *Gott*'s promise is how he thought of it.

He had spent a good number of hours over the winter months making sure his leather hitches were strong and oiled so that his plow was as eager to turn the soil as he was. Today was that day. He would take the team of Belgians and start an early hay field.

Caleb, being a man of nineteen, was no stranger to the workings of horses, hitches, and plows. He had been working this land for as long as he could recall. He'd grown up listening to his *daed* and *grossdaed* tell him stories of how they worked it in their youth as well. Caleb was a rarity in the Amish community. He was the only son of Jacob and Ana Fisher, so he knew this land would likely come to him some day.

Now Caleb was not an only child, he had four *schwestere*. Sarah was two years older and now lived with her husband on his farm in nearby Lancaster County. They had just welcomed their second *bobbel* and had honored Caleb by giving the boy his name. Then behind him were the twins Lizzie and Emma. Many could not tell the seventeen-year-olds apart. He had no such problem.

Lizzie was the more daring of the two and had ventured into the nearby town for a day during her *rumspringa*. She came home less impressed with the *Englishe* than what she had been previous. Both went to Sunday evening youth meetings, but neither had yet been driven home by anyone other than Caleb or their *daed*.

The last of the girls was Naomi, and while her name meant pleasantness, she was a rather headstrong little girl. This was presenting itself currently as she was insisting on helping Caleb plow the field.

"Naomi," Caleb pleaded. "The horses don't know your touch. They'll not pull straight for you. I just do not have the time to do this over and get it planted today."

Naomi looked him in the eyes, measuring his green eyes with her brown. "*Gut*. Then tomorrow you can show me on the south field," she replied.

He looked at her and smiled. There were few things on the farm he enjoyed so much as the plowing of the fields in spring. He could not help but feel for her. There were, however, more suitable tasks for a thirteen-year-old girl to be doing on a spring day. *Mutti*, no doubt, had other chores waiting for her to be done. He watched her amble back to the *haus* in resigned discontent.

Caleb lowered his head and said a prayer before beginning the work. He prayed this way throughout his day. This particular prayer centered around the verse from Ecclesiastes. *Plant your seed in the morning and keep busy all afternoon, for you don't know if profit will come from one activity or another — or maybe both.*

After his prayers were sent, he walked the horses over to the plow and moved to where he had chosen to begin. He then made the plow ready and began the season with the sun on his face and a smile in his heart.

He checked in front and behind, keeping the lines straight and watching for the rocks that made their way to the surface each spring. He would take extra care near the edge of his field that was closest to the road. He would occasionally find things there thrown from cars to make his work harder.

The minutes fell away to hours and his mind began to drift. His thoughts briefly went to the one thing he had done in *rumspringa* that had surprised him. He had gone to a neighboring Mennonite farm and plowed a field with a tractor.

He had seen them for years and always wondered what they would add to the joy of farming. What he learned from that day was this: They took away the ability to hear the ground opening and to feel the blade work its way through and up into the reins.

It also added the stench of diesel smoke to the task, which pleased Caleb not at all. He was glad he had done it. He would no longer think it was a better way.

Gott made farmers to tend the land as He made the land to tend the farmers. Caleb liked being part of that pairing.

His shadow shorter, his mind and stomach agreed that it was time for lunch. As close as the house was to this field, he was able to tie the horses up in the shade and head back to have some of the stew that *Mutter* had promised to make that morning.

Few nearby cooked so well as his *mutti*. He had been offered baskets and been polite about their contents, but none held a candle to his *mutti's*. As he came closer to the *haus,* he saw a strange wagon outside. He knew most of the local families and unless they had reason to buy another, this was none of theirs.

Upon entering the *kich,* he saw three strangers. The man appeared his age with the tell-tale beard of a last-fall groom. But there were two women with him, each looked to be the same age, perhaps eighteen or nineteen.

One of the women sat talking with *Mutti* while the other made herself useful stirring the stew. It was as if his eyes played tricks upon him. His *mutti* letting control of her kitchen into another woman's hands?

Each woman wore the apron of a joined member of a community, but they wore different kerchiefs than the women here. Clearly this was the stranger's bride who was working, but who could the woman be that sat talking?

"Ah, you must be Caleb," the man said to him. "I am Samuel King. I have heard you are a good man with a forge and hammer. I am hoping you can help me with my plow." He stopped and restarted, "Forgive me, Caleb, where are my manners? I just this week came to own the Lapp farm down the way and am a half season behind in being ready." He dragged a hand through his beard. "I went today to the barn and found the tip of the plow is pointing opposite the curve of the blade. I've no forge nor tools of my own to make the repair. I've not much, but I could pay you in trade or in coin."

Samuel had all this out of his mouth without having breathed in once. Caleb tried not to chuckle at the clearly distraught man.

"So," Caleb started. "We're to be neighbors then?"

Looking the man over, like himself, he had the shoulders and arms of a man who worked the earth.

"My *daed* is at market and I've a team hitched waiting for me in the field."

He saw Samuel's shoulders slump. It was a telling thing that he was both introducing himself and asking a favor at the same time. It said he was either lazy or in great need. The man did not look like a lay about.

"I will need to get them brushed down from their labors before I could look at your plow." Caleb offered. "As for payment, perhaps a meal at your table to get to know our new neighbors."

Samuel smiled for the first time, and the smile suited him more than the dour face he began with. It appeared he was about to speak when Caleb heard a soft female voice offer, "I could unhitch and tend your horses. It would allow you to eat your lunch and then have light left to see to work, if that would suit you." It was the woman at the pot speaking.

Caleb raised an eyebrow and replied, "I could not ask you to do that, Mrs. King. You should be with your new groom."

At this, the woman seated next to *Mutti* laughed and said, "I am Mrs. Rebecca King. My husband was so concerned to get things moving he has forgotten his manners for introduction."

Samuel blushed, but did so looking at his wife with love. This was clearly their way, teasing each other.

"That," she continued, pointing to the woman at the stove who had curls of red hair falling out her kerchief, "is my twin, Ruby. She is good with horses, so perhaps it is a good idea?"

Caleb gave it a half-second thought and said, "No, giving it thought, I'll need my team with me to bring your plow back for working on. I know the Lapp farm, from years back, had a forge but if you've not the tools, it would be quicker for me to work it here."

Ana, his mother broke in, "I'll not have you running off unfed. Forging is hot and hungry work. Sit and eat. There is time enough to see if it is a quick fix or a couple days work."

Caleb loved his *mutti*, as the bible told him to, but he also respected her ability to run the farm in *daed's* absence. She was, of course, correct.

Mutti stood to bring the food into the dining room for lunch, but Ruby smiled, putting a hand up, and said "You all go and sit, Mrs. Fisher. I am no stranger to serving stew to hungry men. Let me help."

Caleb felt his smile slip a bit at her words. Surely a woman so handy had a husband. She must be helping her *schwester* get settled before returning home. He was not sure why he was affected by that and did not stop to analyze it.

Shortly after, they prayed together then ate the stew. Caleb noticed this batch was extra good. It was clearly his *mutti's*, but something had been added. They prayed again after the meal was done and Mrs. King stood to help with clearing the table and washing the dishes.

Ruby and Samuel offered to help swap the horses out of the plow and hook them to the wagon. "Many hands," they said, and Caleb smiled at the truth of it.

It took nearly no time to set the horses to the wagon and Caleb more than once saw Ruby display the strength and skill her *schwester* had described. He thought it odd that her kerchief was that of a single woman. Perhaps their previous community did things different. He had not been many places, but he knew some held other ways.

2

The trip to the former Lapp, and now King farm was a mere fifteen minutes by wagon. He had not been this way for a few years as he had no business on the other side of it. The trip was pleasant with little traffic from the *Englishe* and only the clopping of the horses' hooves to be heard. The sun shone brightly now, warming Caleb's shoulders on the early spring day.

The farm had the look of a place being rescued from itself. The Lapps had no heirs that wanted the land for farming and *Herr* Lapp would not sell it to developers. He wondered how it came to the King family and found himself instantly liking Samuel and happy that *Gott* had led them here.

Caleb drew his team next to Samuel's and then they walked toward the barn.

"Here she is," Samuel said, with some measure of uncertainty in his voice, pointing at the plow.

"Ah, this has hit one rock too many. The point will need to be heated and hammered straight," Caleb replied. "Let us see what shape the forge is in." He walked around the outside of the barn. "I see the anvil is still here. That may mean …"

He continued looking. Under a wooden table in the forge shed, he saw it. "Yes, here they are. *Herr* Lapp's forging tools."

Samuel looked at him in wonder. "How did you know what to look for and where to look?"

"I was taught to shoe horses on this anvil."

Herr Lapp was a man who kept mostly to himself, but loved to teach the willing how to "make iron bend," as he called it.

"I see the bellows are still good and there is some coal. Here, let us get this project going, shall we?"

Caleb lit the forge and the coals began to glow. The two men removed the wooden parts from the plow and lifted it up to be looked at better. The plow showed its age, but like most well-crafted things, had many, many years left in it.

"Samuel, how much experience do you have with a hammer and forge?" he asked.

Samuel did not want to look as useless as he felt and offered, "I could probably do this if you'd like to get back to your fields."

"That's nae what I meant," Caleb replied. "I am here as a neighbor to help. We will do this until it is done right before we move on." He stated this as if any other option was not worth considering. "I can show you and teach you what I am doing or, we can do this together."

"Truth be told, I am not much with a forge," Samuel replied. "I'd be grateful for any instruction you might share."

Then and there Caleb knew he was right to like this man. It was not an easy thing to ask for help. Nor being shown what to do on your own farm. Whomever this Samuel was, he was not a vain nor boastful man, and Caleb wanted him as a friend, as well as neighbor.

Caleb walked him through how to ignite the forge and how to check the steel. He heated a couple of rods in the coals, showing Samuel what color to look for and how the steel changed as it became more orange. They went on like this for a while, then moved the plow tip to the coals to heat.

Caleb let Samuel decide when to pull it and was impressed that he pulled it at about the same time he would have. A man who could learn was a man he was willing to teach. They took turns hammering the point and welding a crack they found. Samuel took to it quickly.

While the men worked, the women went about their day. There were cows to milk and feed, a meal to be made, and a seat to be set for an extra man at the table.

As Ruby began making bread for the meal, she found herself looking out the window toward the two men who were working between the barn and the small shed. They were men from the same mold. While Samuel was a bit taller, Caleb's shoulders were a bit wider. From this angle, they could be brothers and from the animated way they moved and talked, it was clear they were bonding as friends.

"A handy man to have close by," remarked Rebecca to her sister. "He appears a good farmer, a good smith, and perhaps a good husband?"

Ruby immediately looked away from the window and spun towards her sister. "He is a *Godly* man to put neighbor ahead of self." She walked swiftly to the cupboard to take down some plates. "But, I am sure a man such as this has captured the heart of a local girl. I'll hear no more of your marriage talk." She caught her sister's eye and shook her head. "You will not mention this to him and ruin the friendship Samuel and he are starting with this nonsense."

Even as she said these words, Ruby saw the truth in her *schwester's* words. This was a *Godly* man, a hard worker and a farmer like their father had been before the accident had cost him his wife and his farm. He was all the things she came here hoping to find for herself.

It was like storms were rolling across Ruby's mind. She could see the reflection of it through her *schwester's* eyes as she watched her speak of this man.

They went about the chores of the afternoon until done, speaking little more until the dinner was ready and the men needed to be gathered. Rebecca stated her intent to fetch them and appeared surprised when Ruby quickly offered to go with her.

The clanging of struck steel rang out from the back of the barn, but stopped when they came around the corner to the forge shed. The men looked to be holding a large, red-hot bird's beak between them and over a barrel of water. Before either woman could ask what it was that they were doing, the men lowered it into the water with a loud hiss.

The man named Caleb is indeed good with a hammer and forge, Rebecca said to herself. It would be wise to pay attention to his words at dinner regarding his place within the community.

As the men quenched the plow to harden it, they were surprised to find two extra sets of eyes watching. They realized the women had come out at some point and stood watching their labors.

Caleb took the blade out, drew a file across, and saw that the steel had done as requested. Samuel drew a file across his side of the newly cooled steel and it did not cut into that side of it either. Both men smiled and reached out to clasp hands. All that was left was to let it cool and put the parts of the plow back together.

"You are a good worker, Caleb Fisher. I am glad to call you neighbor," exclaimed a grateful Samuel.

"You are a hard worker, yourself, Samuel King. I would be honored if I might call you friend, as well as neighbor," Caleb replied.

"Come, you two," Rebecca said cheerfully. "You have both earned a decent meal for such fine work."

Each of them, deflecting their part in it, started to say, "It was mostly Caleb … Samuel's work" at the very same moment, setting the two of them to laughter and not for the first time that day.

Caleb made sure that Samuel was able to put the pieces back together when they cooled, and volunteered to come by in the early hours to help him when he seemed less than positive.

"You will want to be at the fields early. Maybe have someone walk it to check for stones. We don't want to make a habit of this," Caleb suggested.

"*Ach*, that is a *gut* idea. I can have Rebecca look for them ahead of the horses while Ruby finishes unpacking."

Confused, Caleb closed his mouth in reply. Usually the woman of the house did the unpacking and setting up. Why would her sister do this which would then leave them not knowing where things were? He would never ask such a thing, but he could not help but wonder.

The women led them to the *haus* and the men first washed themselves suitably clean at the well pump outside, then made their way to the table. Samuel led them in prayer before the meal, and then they got to eating.

The ham and potato meal was delicious, but Caleb was won over by the bread. It was lighter and sweeter than what he was used to. It was *wundebar*. As the meal wound down, he offered his thanks to his hostess, complimenting her specifically on the bread.

"I have never tasted such bread," he gushed. "You are a lucky man to have such a *gut* cook for a wife, Samuel."

"The Lord has shown me much favor in my life, Caleb," he replied. "I will need to keep working hard or she will make a fat man of me." He laughed heartily.

"I'll not let you get fat, Husband. You need a *gut* meal to make *gut* work," Rebecca replied. She then turned to Caleb. "But the bread was not my doing. Ruby made our *grossmutti's* bread for us this day."

"*Ach*, it is nothing but a bit of honey in the dough." Ruby's cheeks pinked at the compliment.

"Perhaps you could teach *meine schwestere* how to do this so that they might find good matches," Caleb remarked. As he said it, he saw her face fall slightly. But then the frown was gone so fast he thought he might have imagined it.

"I'll gladly teach them, but I should hope the local men are not won over by such a slight thing as sweetness in their bread," Ruby said.

"No, I should think not, but they have sweetness in their souls as well and though only seventeen, they have their hearts set on finding a man each this season," offered Caleb. "I tell them there is no hurry, but they tell me it is different for them. Perhaps you could inspire them with the truth of the value of waiting, Ruby? Coming from a twin might mean more to them as they are twins themselves."

Ruby's heart felt heavy. Had he just mocked her for being twenty without a man? What value of waiting did he speak of? Being a burden on her twin as she tried to make her new home with her husband? How rude was this man? She decided at that moment, Caleb Fisher was a fool and she could not tolerate fools.

The room had fallen silent. Caleb, the foolish man, used that as an opportunity to take his leave, promising to return early to help assemble the plow.

As the women started clearing and cleaning up, Samuel went out to finish the work of the farm. Ruby stared from the window. The cows had come up from grazing and waited to be let into the barn.

She turned suddenly, knowing it was now just she and her sister. ""Who does that man think he is?" she vented.

Startled from clearing the table, her sister asked, "Who? Samuel?"

"No, not your Samuel. He is a kind man. I am talking about that Caleb! Mocking me in our home for not having a man. That was as unkind a thing as I have had said to me in all my days. 'Perhaps I could teach his *schwestere* the value of waiting,' he said. 'Perhaps sweet bread might serve them better than it has me,' he said."

Rebecca clearly held back a chuckle which caused Ruby's head to heat even further. She banged a dish against the counter with too much force. Rebecca came up beside her, placing a calming hand at her back.

"I heard no such things from him. I heard him compliment your bread and invite you to his home. Besides, did you not say earlier that you had no interest in him?"

"I said no such thing … earlier," Ruby caught herself. "But I am surely saying it now."

Ruby was tempted to continue, but was already embarrassed over the unkind words and temper that had left her mouth and caused a commotion. Why should she care of this man's opinion of her?

3

Caleb rose as usual somewhere around four in the morning, should he have bothered to keep a clock, which he did not. He got up when he awoke, he ate when the sun was high and again when it was low. He knew some kept clocks, but his brief experience with one had left him feeling that the clock was telling him when to do everything and that was not the job of a machine to do.

He dressed and breathed in the still air of morning. It had the decided smell of coffee to it, and this drew him to the source.

In the k*ich*, *Mutti* and *Daed* were starting their day together as they had done all of his years. They sat and prayed over the coming day. This, to Caleb, was what home looked like and what he wanted his k*indere* to grow up knowing.

He nearly tripped over his feet as he walked, making such a commotion that both *eldere* looked up at him before continuing in prayer.

What has me thinking of kindere, he wondered. *I must make time to see my oldest schwestere Sarah and her husband and their fine son.* Clearly this was why he was thinking of k*indere und bobbele.* *What* other reason could there be, after all?

He poured himself a cup of coffee from the pot and cleared his mind in prayers. He added a prayer for his new friend, Samuel, before he finished.

"*Daed,*" Caleb began. "We have new neighbors, Samuel and Rebecca King. They are taking over at the Lapp farm across the brook."

"So, they have arrived then," his *daed* replied with no surprise in his voice. "*Gut.* May the Lord show them peace here."

"No surprise that you would know of them sooner than I," Caleb grinned. "I was not aware that the Lapp family had made a choice on that land, but am glad it did not get sold to the *Englishe*. I would have thought, though, that there would be one in our own district to buy the farm."

"*Herr* Lapp offered it to me in his last years," Jacob responded. "But, as I told him, I have but one son and this is farm enough for a man and a family. He spoke of a district on the other side of the hills that had lost much of their land and he felt called by *Gott* to make it available to them. This man was ready, able, and willing to make the travel to join us. We will have to make his acquaintance soon."

"I met him yesterday. He, his wife, and his wife's twin were here." Caleb took another sip of his warm coffee. "Samuel had found neither the forge nor the tools *Herr* Lapp left behind. He and I did a repair on his plow that he might get those fields tamed in time for planting. I'm headed there this morning to help him finish the job."

His m*utti* turned to look into Caleb's face. "You seem eager to help this man, or is it being eager to see that *schwester?*"

Caleb looked struck. Why would his m*utti* think him desiring another man's wife? He sat there with his mouth opening and closing like a fish taken from the brook. The world seemed an odd place this past day, he decided and then stood.

"*Daed*, would you like to come with me this morning to meet our new neighbor?"

"*Nein*, they will be our guests for dinner in two nights and I will meet them then," came the reply. "I will have Lizzie & Emma tend the milking this day and I will finish plowing the hay field." He quickly added, "You did right to be helping this man, Caleb. I am happy the Lord resides in your heart."

Pushing up from the table, he laid a hand on his mother's shoulder then quickly walked outside. The air was warmer than usual for spring and, knowing his father would need the Belgians, he started the walk to Samuel's farm.

As much as Caleb respected *Herr* Lapp, he was no longer thinking of the land as anything but Samuel's. The walk took him a bit over an hour and he replayed some of the words he had heard the last few days over in his head.

His thoughts centered around Ruby despite himself. Why would his *mutti* say that about him this morning? Did he give an appearance of impropriety? He would have to speak of this with Samuel and apologize. It would be no good reflection on him nor the community to have a man appear untoward to his sister-in-law. It was decided in his head, he would speak to Samuel and make amends. He felt better for having thought it through.

It was about this time that he came to the entrance to the King farm. Caleb walked up the path with the sun at his back, seeing Samuel out on his porch with a cup of coffee in hand. He smiled at Caleb as he drew closer.

"Come, friend," Samuel offered. "Let us drink a cup of coffee and then start our labors."

Caleb usually only had a single cup, but was glad for a moment to speak with Samuel without having to pay attention to the work at hand.

"Samuel," he said hesitantly. "I fear I may have offered offense to your family. Your *schwagerin,* Ruby."

Caleb blushed red as he spoke. In Samuel's face he saw a smile break out and began to hope for the best.

"I'd not planned to mention it, but you did seem to get a bit under her skin," Samuel replied.

Dread and embarrassment wrapped themselves around Caleb's insides. He had thought himself making a *gut* friend and instead he was deserving of no such thing. Clearly his words or actions said something he did not intend. He was so embarrassed he wanted to run all the way home like a *kinder* and hide in his room.

So mortified was he that he failed to see the smile on Samuel's face or the twinkle in his eyes.

Caleb admired Samuel's ability to hold back any anger felt towards him. He hoped if tested so, he would show this restraint.

"Do you think I should apologize to Ruby in person then?" Caleb offered.

"Nae, I think leaving her be is the best approach at the moment. She is a Godly and forgiving woman, Caleb. Give her time. Let us get this plow finished so that you can get back to your fields. I have kept too much of your time already."

Caleb was grateful to be able to finish this task to make up for his unforgivable actions. They walked silently to the barn and prayed before starting the work.

They made short order of putting the plow back to right. Caleb noted aloud and thanked Samuel for the obvious care he'd taken of the leather harness they had removed the night before. It was freshly cleaned and appeared to have been oiled.

"You do have a way of thanking the wrong people," Samuel said with a laugh in his voice. "That is also the work of Ruby. I will lose much when her husband comes to claim her."

To Caleb that was as bad as a horse kick. So, she did have a husband and he now had another person to apologize to. What a mess he had made of the friendship with his new neighbors.

Caleb's voice was slight as he said to Samuel, "My *daed* has told me that your family is to be his guest in two nights."

Samuel broke in, "Yes, indeed. Rebecca is eager to meet him. *Herr* Lapp spoke of him as a *gut* man with a *gut* family. When he came out to offer us this farm, he said that your *vater* was helpful with his decision to do this thing, giving us a chance to live as our Lord intended. I've not met him, but I too feel a debt to your *vater.*"

"Would it be better for Ruby if I were not present?" Caleb asked, looking at his feet.

By looking at his feet, he missed the shocked look on Samuel's face. "Nae, Caleb. I think it best that the two of you put this little thing behind you, don't you?"

He wondered how Samuel could think this a "little thing". He now had to tell the Bishop and church E*ldere* that he had offended this woman, a guest in their midst. He had shamed himself, his friend, his family, and his entire church district. This was clearly the worst thing Caleb Fisher had ever done.

"Well then ...," his voice trailed off. Caleb reached his hand out slowly wondering if it would be accepted. "I will see you again then."

He was relieved that Samuel took his hand and rather surprised that he seemed genuine in his statement, "Fare well, friend."

Ruby watched some of their exchange from the garden she was weeding, having fed the chickens earlier. She told herself she was not trying to overhear them, but was rather frustrated by the fact that she could not hear a word they spoke.

After Caleb left, she found an excuse to make conversation with Samuel, thinking herself much cleverer than she appeared.

"So, that man has left, has he?" Having decided not to speak his name further. "Did he not have the decency or the courage to apologize, or perhaps neither?"

Samuel raised his eyebrows and replied that, in fact, the offer to apologize had been made, but he had suggested that Caleb give her time before making it.

Ruby looked for another to focus her anger on, but could not bring herself to be angry with Samuel. He had been saintly to her *schwester* and in truth, to her as well.

Their farm had been the glue holding their previous community together. Now that it was becoming a h*ause* for *Englishe*, there would be no future for her nor the district itself she feared. If this Caleb had thought to apologize, perhaps she would have to rethink him. She decided it would take a right *gut* apology.

4

Caleb walked home with the weight of the world upon his shoulders. He would pray about this and *Gott* would help him fix it. And so, he began praying as he walked home.

He prayed as he plowed, prayed as he seeded, and he prayed as he ate. It felt *gut* to speak with *Gott* so much, but he had not yet found an answer. He would pray more.

After the dinner prayers were said, Caleb chose not to read with his youngest *schwestere*, Naomi, a pastime they shared most nights, and said an early *good-night* to the twins as they worked on yet another of their beautiful quilts.

It amazed him that they finished any with as much giggling as they did while sewing. And finish them they did, enough that their chests were full and several had been sold in town where they purchased their sewing supplies. They dutifully gave those earnings to their *daed* who, without telling them, kept it for their future.

Caleb could usually get them giggling in fits, but this night he did not seem to have it in him. He was eager to bed so he could pray for his answer.

"Ana, what is with Caleb?" asked Jacob. "He ate little, said less, and looked lost. Has he a sickness about him?"

"It is altogether possible," smiled Ana. "He has been this way since meeting Rebecca King's twin."

Jacob's eyes grew wide and joy crept into them. "Has he said this to you?"

"I am his *mutti*. When has he had to tell me what I have clearly seen?" Ana replied. "I spent time with this Ruby and she is a strong and Godly woman. She would make him a good match if he would pursue her."

"Do you think then that he will pursue her?" Jacob asked his wife. This was no small matter. His son had not found a woman he felt a fit with in the last three seasons.

"I think you watched him wrestle with that decision today. I can see him praying for guidance. It is *gut* that he does this. *Gott* will show him the right path to take. He managed to get us together, did He not?" Ana asked, the last with a light laugh in her voice.

"That He did, Ana. *Gott* is *gut*."

Caleb woke earlier than usual. He knew this as there were no sounds or smells coming from the *kich*. He dressed and made his way in the dark to the stove. There were still hot coals and he stoked them to a blaze, adding more wood to both warm the *kich* and make the coffee.

When the coffee began to steam, Caleb took the pot and poured himself a cup. No sooner was it poured then he was joined by his *vater*. He poured his *daed* a cup, handing it to him. Caleb opened his mouth to speak, but before he could, Jacob interrupted.

"Caleb, your *mutti und* I have noticed you praying deeply for *Gott*'s answers this past day. You are right to be doing so. Some questions can be answered by men, but the important ones should be prayed upon for *Gott*'s guidance. We are glad you are giving this much thought."

Caleb's world seemed to tilt. Did his parents then know already of his error? How had his quiet life become so confusing and loud?

He sighed deeply. Breathing back in, he responded, "*Vater*, I must go today to set this right. I am sorry to take time from my chores again, but I feel I must do this thing."

Again, Caleb's eyes were so lowered that he failed to see the surprise and perhaps joy in his *daed's* face.

"Do you not think it wise to wait for the Sunday youth meeting to speak to her?" Jacob asked, his voice rising in question at the end.

"No, they are to be guests for dinner in your home tomorrow and I would like this resolved before then," Caleb said with conviction.

With that and his *daed's* nod, the coffees were finished, and the day's chores begun. Caleb would be able to get a few things done before going to beg forgiveness.

The sun seemed to take forever today to show itself and, as eager as he was most days to see it, the sun offered no joy today. He brushed off the hay on his clothes and began the walk to Samuel's *haus*.

From the porch, Jacob watched his son's back as it disappeared down the road. Ana drew up beside him. He spoke into her ear, "I've never seen a man so determined to do something it looks like he does not wish to do. We spoke this morning and he is going to speak to Samuel about Ruby this day."

"I heard you two but felt it not my place to disturb this talk. I wonder if he is going to speak to her directly. You are right though, he does not have the face of a man in love."

At the King farm, the day started with gathering eggs, milking the cows, and feeding the animals. This was their routine. With Ruby's extra hands, Rebecca could either help with the animals or make their breakfast. She and Ruby seemed to take turns, knowing as twins seemed to when the other wanted to swap.

Ruby had a bounce back in her step today. Having slept the night on it, she decided she would accept Caleb's apology (assuming it was worthy), and she might even let him drive her home from a Sunday Youth Meeting after Community, since it would be so close by and of course not wanting to make her *schwager and* Samuel drive her to and fro.

If others thought it meant more, it was a risk she would suffer. She caught herself blushing at this and, to no one but herself, admitted that Caleb seemed a right *gut* match indeed.

No sooner had she convinced herself of this did she see a man coming up the road from Caleb's way. As he got closer she saw it was Caleb himself, walking deep in thought. She saw him wave to Samuel, and go to speak with him.

She moved to the door to eavesdrop, despite guilt niggling at her.

"I have come to speak with Ruby, Samuel," Caleb said flatly.

"It is customary to ask to speak to a woman, is it not?" Samuel replied smiling.

"Ach, I am an oaf. Yes. Samuel, might I have your permission to speak to Ruby?"

"I believe she is willing to speak with you, Caleb. I wish you *viel gluck*.
"

Peeking from around the open door, Ruby saw Caleb shake Samuel's hand like a man condemned, then head toward the door. Ruby stepped back and turned away from it to not appear eager. She hid away her smile also, and awaited his words.

He knocked lightly then entered the home. Seeing her near the table, he spoke softly, looking into her eyes as she turned. "Ruby, I have come to apologize for the offense I have given you."

Ruby thought to herself, *he can stop there, that is all I need to hear*, but he did not stop there. Eyes at his feet he added, "If I have done anything to make you think I would pursue you, I regret it so very, very much. I did not realize myself to be doing it, truth be told."

Ruby stood dumbfounded for a moment then erupted, "Oh, no Mister Fisher! You have made yourself perfectly clear, now haven't you?" Her voice grew louder as she went. "Clearly you feel you have not humiliated me enough and came to do it again today? Have you no decency?"

She sniffed and turned away. Rebecca came in unexpectedly then, assessing the situation quickly and wrapped her arms around Ruby, giving Caleb a look that would have frozen water in summer.

He backed away, saying over and over, "I just came to apologize. I don't know how I keep making this worse."

Samuel entered, seeing his wife and his *schwagerin* in tears. Caleb was not wise to the ways of women, but he knew when to back away.

"Caleb, I think it best you leave," Samuel said softly. "This was not what I expected or I'd have not let you speak your mind."

Caleb nodded, "I have gotten what I deserved. Not more, not less." He turned, condemnation falling around his shoulders.

5

Caleb made the walk home with Ruby's pained voice in his ears. It made no sense. She seemed calm until he had apologized. He poured over his apology, again and again, and found no fault in it. Why had she not accepted it?

What bothered him most, was that he could not stop thinking about the woman. He thought well of her. Enough so that when he had imagined what his future bride would be, Ruby fit that mold. Perhaps a bit less temper would be *gut*, but he had brought that out in her, hadn't he?

He returned home for lunch but ate only a few bites. His parents saw that it had not gone well for him and let him be. The Lord would find his match in His due time. There was no rushing the hand of *Gott*.

Caleb went about his plowing in silence. For perhaps the first time, not even that brought him peace. The singing of the birds seemed to mock him and the swiftly racing clouds across the afternoon sky reminded him of the impending visit from the Kings.

He kept switching his eyes from back to front, yet still had a hard time keeping his rows straight. He did manage to miss a rock in the field, but it was more from the sound of the horse's shoe hitting it than any attention he had been paying.

It was not *gut* for man nor plow to work this way. He stopped the horses under a tree and got off the back of the plow. Caleb fell to his knees and prayed. He prayed for forgiveness, he prayed for calm, he prayed for strength. Nearly an hour went past on his knees.

He saw his *vater* from afar at one point, but he disturbed him not. Caleb and *Gott* needed to speak and his *daed* let them be.

Caleb rose, noticing the sun had moved far across the sky, and got to finishing up the field. The lines after he prayed were straighter than before, but still showed his troubled mind.

"Finished plowing then, have you?" asked Jacob after the pre-dinner prayer. "Plant your seed in morning ...," Jacob started.

"And keep busy all afternoon, for you don't know if profit will come from one activity or another – or maybe both," Caleb finished.

Jacob nodded.

Shortly after, Caleb was a bit more himself, reading verses with Naomi. He did not know what the twins were up to, but they were not giggling at all tonight. He was tempted to get them going, but he just hadn't the energy to do it.

He gently kissed Naomi's head and said aloud, "Good night and sweet dreams."

He took his leave of his *familye* and went up the stairs to his room. He wasn't sure, but he thought he heard the twins giggle just as he closed his door to pray before sleeping.

At the King farm the morning started badly, and the air was tense the whole day. Samuel left the twins to work out the problem and went about the chores he could do solo. He got a good part of his main field plowed, finding many of the rocks that used to be fence near the edges. They were not so much thrown into the field as they were knocked over. Checking both sides he saw paths that deer had made. Samuel liked a good venison stew.

Back in the house, Ruby had finished crying by midmorning. She had fooled herself into thinking that Caleb was interested in her, but he had made it clear he was not. Why would he do such a thing?

She had been pursued by a couple of merchants' sons and had politely let them know her disinterest when it was clear that they had no intention on farming. She could think no other life fitting for her. That the first farmer she saw did not want to speak kindly to her was not the end of her world, she decided, even as she wondered why he would not at least want to get to know her better.

Clearly, if he was concerned about her being led on, there was another girl for him already. *He probably would have gotten to that had I not stopped him*, she thought to herself.

She spent the rest of her day doing chores and wondering who the woman was who had captured the attention of the man. The longer she thought about it the more it felt like another had beaten her to her Caleb.

My Caleb? Why would I think him mine? I have known him for all of two days and I am clearly suffering from the long trip here.

The rest of the day went the same: Convincing herself he was not the right man for her. She put up a valiant fight, but by night time prayers she found herself asking *Gott* for yet more guidance and understanding.

Thursday morning broke overcast. The clouds were high enough, Caleb thought, that they would not have to worry much about rain. Well, at least today.

"Could be rain headed this way for Friday?" Caleb asked his *vater*.

"*Ja*, I think it so. We will plant our seeds this morning and they will be watered in by *Gott* himself."

"*Gott* shows His blessings for those who look," Caleb remarked.

Jacob smiled.

Caleb could remember his *grossdaed* saying this often before he passed. His eyes diverted to the *grosshuas*, empty now four years. Caleb decided to check on it as he had not been in there himself in months.

"A rainy day is a good opportunity to clean up the *grosshaus, ja?*" Caleb remarked, standing near the barn and looking towards it.

"Planning to push your *mutti und* I into there so soon?" his father teased. "I should think you could wait for your *schwestere* to be married off first."

Caleb smiled sadly. How far off his idea was. Caleb was likely to be married after Naomi at this pace. The first woman he'd found as a suitable match was married to another.

The two men went about the planting and finished it early afternoon.

"I think it best not to plow the next field today. We'd not finish it before the morning and it looks of rain." Jacob said. "Humor your father with a task. Come with me."

Caleb followed his *daed* to the pile of canvas in the back corner of the barn.

Barn cleaning, he thought, then began to think what he might be able to do with more room in here and set his eye on getting it done.

Jacob grabbed a corner of the canvas and began to pull it back, revealing a courting buggy, an open-air wagon for giving a special girl a ride home from Sunday youth meeting.

"Let us take this outside for the rain to wash away the dust. The wood still seems *gut*. We can bring it back in tomorrow and make sure it is ready for use," Jacob said to his son.

"*Ja, vater,*" Caleb responded.

What girl would have him after he had explained himself to the church council? Still, it was a wagon and if not cared for, would lose its usefulness. *Gott* gave them all the bounty they could steward over properly.

Caleb and Jacob cleared off the wagon and parked it alongside the barn. There was a good twenty years of dust on it despite being covered. Rain starting the job was a right *gut* idea.

By the time they had cleared out the corner of the barn, Jacob turned to Caleb and said, "It is time to go to the *haus* and get ready to welcome our guests. I trust that despite your spurning you can be a *gut* host, Caleb."

Vater thinks I was spurned by Ruby. Perhaps he is not aware that she has a husband waiting for her return, Caleb thought. It made sense now that he looked. It was clear his *vater* had no idea what a fool he had made of himself. He now looked forward to this meal with even more dread.

6

Entering the *haus*, Caleb smelled the meal being prepared. No doubt Lizzie and Emma had made noodles today. He also smelled potato boiling. The aroma stopped him from his path and led him into the *kich*. Sure enough, all the Fisher women were chopping, stirring, or prepping dishes.

Caleb admired the girls and knew that *Mutti* would have them ready when the time came for them to make their own homes. These were fine matches for any man worthy of them. Naomi saw him and squealed, "I made the noodles myself today!"

Caleb replied, "I did not think you old enough for such an important task. Are you sure they are fit for guests?"

He held his face stoic as Naomi hesitated in doubt.

He continued, "I feel it my duty to check them before we share them with our new neighbors."

"You will not be eating all the noodles before the meal, Caleb," came his *mudder's* voice. "Rest assured, I supervised the noodle making. They are sure to be as good as mine."

Caleb winked at Naomi, teasing, "Well, it was worth a try."

"Now get your dirty self to a wash bowl and make yourself presentable," Ana chided him. "I'll not have a man dropping dirt into my meal."

He turned and went to the washroom. An urn with hot water was awaiting him. He scrubbed himself clean as if it were a Sunday, then got himself dressed.

As he came out, his *mutti* met him and said, "You still clean up well. Perhaps I might have *enkelkinder* yet."

He replied, "You have two already. I'd not think you eager to add more."

She replied simply, "More family is always *gut. Gott* shows us no greater blessing than family, Caleb."

Nodding in agreement, he again sniffed appreciatively. He was looking about the kitchen counters overfull with abundance when his *mutti* tapped him on the shoulder and pointed, "I also took out two jars of the creamed spinach. And," pointing to another set of jars, "we will have the last of the peaches as cobbler."

He thought wistfully that this was as good a last meal as anyone could want. The sound of horses broke that thought and announced their guests' arrival.

Ruby sat behind Samuel and Rebecca while getting another good look at the Fisher farm. It was a sizeable spread with cattle and pigs. The fields looked kept and the barn sturdy.

That was when she saw it. The courting buggy ready to go, just needing horses. She was right, Caleb had another he was courting. She would just avoid him as much as possible tonight and not make a further fool of herself.

That is what she thought anyway.

Samuel stopped the wagon, hopped out to tie up to the post, then helped the women out of the wagon. Upon alighting, Jacob opened the front door and said, "Welcome neighbors, come in, come in."

Rebecca and Samuel spoke with the elder Fishers, thanking Jacob for his part in having *Herr* Lapp travel so far and offer up his farmland. Ana, unaware that Jacob had a hand in it, beamed at her husband.

"*Ach*, you make too much of my part. I told him to seek *Gott*'s guidance and have the courage to do as He directed." Jacob would not let himself be praised. "*Gott* led him to you and you to our table. Come let us break bread and become good neighbors."

During this exchange, Ruby looked about. Everything about the home said *sturdy* to her. The furniture, the walls, the family. All of it. These were good people, she decided. Clearly Caleb did not get his ways from his parents.

At about the time she decided to not think anymore of him, he came quietly into the room. It was then that she realized that she also thought of her Caleb as solid. *He is not 'your' Caleb*, she chided herself. *Be a good guest and do not make a scene.*

"You have a right *gut* farm, *Frau Fisher*," she spoke, turning purposely away from Caleb's direction. "You can see *Gott*'s blessings on the land and your home."

"That is most kind of you, Ruby," Ana replied. "*Gott* has indeed blessed us bountifully. Speaking of which, let us sit and sup together that we can become better acquainted."

She led her guests to the table in the dining room and sat Samuel and Rebecca nearest to Jacob on his right. This put Caleb and Ruby together also on the right with Lizzie and Emma across the table and Naomi beside them.

"Let us pray," began Jacob and he gave thanks to *Gott* for his blessings, for his family, community, and their new neighbors. When Jacob prayed, you could hear the praise in his tone. The words took shape and emanated with feeling. Jacob's love for *Gott* echoed in each word he spoke.

All heads lifted as he finished and joined with a heartfelt *amen*. The girls passed out plates filled with noodles, or potatoes, and large bowls heaped with all sorts of the bounty from the farm. Ana then passed around a plate with fried steak.

Light conversation floated across the table. Despite being obviously uncomfortable sitting next to each other, Ruby and Caleb ate in quiet peace. Right until they passed the bread.

"Lizzie and Emma, Ruby makes a *wunderbar* bread that is so good it will keep you from being spinsters."

Caleb was looking at his *schwestere*. Their faces started to smile, then froze. He had teased them for a year already about being spinsters, so he could not understand their sudden shock at it. He looked around to find everyone had stopped eating, staring right at him. He turned to his left and Ruby was holding her face in her hands, clearly crying but trying her best not to.

"Caleb!" boomed his *vater's* voice. "Apologize at once to your *schwestere* and to my guests. You were raised better than this."

Ruby jumped up and went out the back door, followed closely by Rebecca to console her.

Samuel rose and turned to Caleb, shaking his head. "I know that Ruby rebuked your advances, but that is not good reason to treat her so poorly. I have seen much *gut* in you, but this is unacceptable."

Caleb's head was not keeping up. He had kept his mouth shut the whole meal except once when he praised Ruby's bread and now she was crying. It hurt him deep inside that he had made her cry again. He wished to fill her heart with joy and laughter, not pain and crying. He took his leave from the table with an apology to all.

Emma stood and walked to where Ruby and Rebecca were out on the porch. "Please, Ruby. Do not cry. My *bruder* can be a *donderkopf*, but he means well. He has been teasing us since we finished school that we would grow old with him on this farm. I think it is his way of telling us he never wants us to leave." She placed a hand gently on Ruby's shoulder. "He is a *mann*. He would never say it so clearly to us though. He did come home raving of this bread of yours. I've not seen him that *gobsmacked* since he was a *kind*. I would like to know how you make it. Perhaps I could visit you and you might show me?"

Ruby was now conflicted. She welcomed this show of friendship from Emma, but did not understand why Caleb had spoken so poorly of her.

She gave Emma a quick hug and said, "Emma, I would gladly share the secrets with you."

Now it was Emma's turn to be shocked, "How did you do that?"

"Do what, exactly?" replied Ruby, unsure where the conversation might be going.

"You knew it was me. Emma."

"Of course. I knew who you were. Why?"

"Caleb is the only one we cannot fool. We even get *Mutti und Daed* confused when we try," responded Emma, still agape.

"Perhaps twins are best at knowing twins?" came the only reply Ruby could think of.

Emma knew that she and Ruby would be friends. She then spoke it into being.

"Would you mind terribly if I came by tomorrow? I will need to get permission, but if you are baking for the weekend, I would like very much to help you."

Ruby saw Emma in a new light. She was young, but centered. She was sturdy. That word again. This would be a good friend to have.

"Come after breakfast then. We will make enough bread for the weekend and a few spare loaves for you to take home with you. Feel free not to share them with that *donderkopf bruder* of yours," she added, smiling at the nickname. She laughed a little bit. Her tears had dried during the conversation.

"Let me go speak to *Mutti*," Emma said, then was gone for a moment only to return with a big smile on her face. "*Mutti* said yes! I will bring flour for what I take home. That was *Mutti's* only hesitation. We will not take from you as you are getting upon your feet."

Ruby knew the real reason was that their kind did not like to owe anyone anything. Debt was to be avoided. She could hear it clearly in her own *vater's* voice. "Debt is a bad choice that brings more bad choices into your home." She wondered if Caleb was a bad choice that asking for help with the plow had brought to them.

Ruby gently scrubbed at her eyes and straightened herself up, returning to her hosts. Caleb had left. She was relieved to see that she would not have to face him again.

"I must apologize for ending such a meal with my outburst. I pray you do not hold this against Samuel and Rebecca. They are good sturdy people." There was that word again. It was truly what she wished for. A sturdy life as a farmer's wife. This should not be a difficult thing.

Ana spoke, "I could hold nothing against you or your family. I beg apologies for my son. He is a better man than this. I cannot think of what is going on in his head these last days."

"I am grateful that you will let Emma come to our home. I will be blessed by her friendship, I can tell that already."

"Emma? But Emma was still in her seat next to... *ach schnickelfritz* those two! Always been that way too. They love to make us think they are each other and I confess they do it too often. Emma then will be there tomorrow."

Ruby hoped that she had not gotten Emma and Lizzie into trouble. They had apparently switched seats with no one the wiser. Tricksters indeed.

7

Rain came as expected that night and kept up through the morning. Rain did not stop work on a farm, but made it slower and much more muddy. The cows needed milking, the eggs gathered. A man would come by later to buy them from Samuel.

Englishe were all too eager to buy farm fresh eggs, milk, and cheeses. Ruby disliked the *Englishe* more than most, but the accident could not hold all the blame for it. They presumed too much and did not respect themselves nor their women. They were *not sturdy*. She had long since decided.

This was a *gut* arrangement for all. It meant they did not have to man a stall in the market to sell their goods, and that meant *she* did not have to man it. Rude people taking her photo as if she was something unusual. Some of the boys were too forward, some of the men were worse.

She had worked briefly after the accident to help with expenses. Her *vater* did not want it, but came to accept that it was needed. Ruby hated every moment of it. The city was tall, closed in, and stunk of waste and garbage. She felt that smell might never leave her. No, she shuddered, this was a much better place for them all.

As the dawn broke as clearly as it would on this wet day, a wagon came up the path. She was pleased to see Emma step out. She was pleased until she saw that it was Caleb who drove her. It made sense, she supposed, but that didn't mean she had to like it.

"Emma," she called and waved. As she approached the girl, she gave her a quick once over and said, "Good, I thought you two might try to fool me. As nice as Lizzie seemed, I am glad it is you, Emma."

Emma laughed, being led into the warm *haus*. "I've worn Lizzie's kerchief, her dress, and still cannot fool you! You must promise not to teach anyone else how to do that." She balanced her bundles of baking staples. "It would put an end to years of fun."

Ruby made a solemn promise to not share. Not that there was any one thing that made Emma different, but it was as clear as day for Ruby.

"Come let us get our hands clean so that we might get them truly dirty with flour."

Emma smiled in agreement.

Into the *kich*, heart of the home, they went. While the oven heated, they worked together mixing and kneading the dough. Over a cup of tea, they waited for it to rise, talking of the area, the nearby farms and people, and of course they talked about the community.

Ruby had many questions. She had been a member of her former community, would she have to make her profession again? What were the customs of dress for Sunday prayer services?

Eventually Emma steered the subject to boys. She confided that she had her eye on John Beiler. He was the youngest child and that assured him land to farm. He was kind and smiled at her often.

Ruby enjoyed Emma's enthusiasm. They talked and talked, or perhaps Ruby listened and listened would be a better way to put it. Emma had opened up to her new friend and wanted to share all with her.

"It looks ready to put in the oven, Emma," Ruby said, seeing as the dough had since doubled in the pans.

In they went and when they were done, the next batch behind them. They did this until all of the bread was baked and then sat down together for a glass of water. Ruby had done what she always did, making a mini loaf at the very end. She broke it in two and offered half to Emma. Emma bit in and her face lit up.

"Caleb was wrong!" she exclaimed. "He said this was the best bread he had eaten. It is the best bread *ever made*. Something as simple as a bit more yeast and some honey has made this praise worthy." She continued gushing.

Ruby laughed. Having grown up with this bread, it was not a special thing for her. It was one of the few things left that tied her to her *mutti*. And that did indeed make it special, she reflected, taking another bite of the light sweet fare.

The two cleaned up and Ruby continued to talk of joining the community. Officially she would speak with Bishop on Saturday to find out what was needed and expected.

Samuel and Rebecca had come out to see the land and joined last Sunday, but as landholders, she suspected their joining might be different. Emma did not have all the answers Ruby sought, but she was reassured by her confidence in the church leadership's helpfulness and acceptance.

The two, now fast friends, looked over the *kich* and saw there was nothing left to do. The cleaning had been done quickly with many hands. Emma wrapped up the loaves she was taking home in a towel and peered out the window.

"Look," she said to Ruby. "I wonder how long *dunderkopf* has been out there waiting on me. You are an amazing woman, Ruby. I've never seen Caleb afraid of anyone before."

They both laughed as Ruby walked her out to the carriage.

"Come on, Lizzie," said a clearly agitated Caleb. "I've things to do myself this day."

Emma turned to Ruby and they both laughed at Caleb. Then they spoke at the same time, "*Donderkopf.*"

8

Caleb was not sure how everyone made Ruby laugh so easily. He need but open his mouth and she would run away in tears. He decided to ask Lizzie when she shared that heavenly smelling bread with him.

During the ride home, he tried to start the conversation, only to be met with giggles and silence. He was not sure which bugged him more. He loved his *schwestere*, but he often failed to understand them.

Home arrived before any answers from the giggling Lizzie. She ran into the *haus* with her bread to be met at the door by a giggling Emma. Wait, no, that was Lizzie, he was sure of it.

"*Ach,*" he said loud enough for them to hear him. "It seems you have gotten me. As I am seeing a pair of Lizzies today."

He now at least understood the giggling ride home a bit better and found himself chuckling along with them.

"Ruby saw right though us," Emma said. "She took a quick look and knew it was me."

For some reason, Caleb did not like that. He was the one who could tell them apart when no others could. He was not sure he wanted to share that with anyone. Especially with someone that seemed to despise him so.

Emma brought the bread to *Mutti* before Caleb could get his hands on it. She smelled it and smiled. "A loaf of this with dinner tonight will be a treat."

Caleb did have much left to do today. He wanted to get into the *grosshaus* and make sure all was well there.

He left the women, went across the property to the *haus* and opened the door. It always happened that when he opened the door he expected his *grosseltern* to be on the other side, as it had been for so many years.

The air was musty, but smelled dry. That, he thought, was *gut*. He lit the lights and looked around. It was as it had been the last time he inspected it. Empty except for the echoes of the happiness he had felt here.

He finished his walk around the inside noting where the glazing on a window needed fixing, but found no other problems. He would repair that glazing the first day the rain let up so it did not become a problem.

Turning off the lights, he closed the door and walked back towards his home. From this distance, he could see the lights and smoke from the chimney rising. It called to him. The house looked like it belonged here and it was happy. Caleb felt the same.

Since he was already wet, he went to the barn and cleared the stalls. He stacked the manure and the hay into a pile that would compost into this fall's fertilizer. The milk was not the only benefit of the cows. The smell, as bad as it was, did not bother him. This was part of who he was. He was a farmer. Sometimes a farmer stinks.

Finishing up, he took a look at the wagon they had placed outside yesterday. Sure enough, the rain had washed away the dust and what was left was a work of beauty. The wood he recognized as mahogany. It glowed as if a dark red fire burned somewhere inside it. The wagon had held up well. He would grease the wheels tomorrow and take it for a quick ride before putting it back away.

It was a fine courting buggy, but he felt it was bolder and more brash than he would be while driving it. Not that he'd be doing any of that soon.

Satisfied that the wagon would be fit to ride when called upon, Caleb turned and walked his soaked-to-the-skin-self back towards the *haus*.

Stepping into the mud room, his *mutti* was waiting for him with a washbowl and pitcher of hot water.

"I've got your *schwestere* on the other side of the house. Strip off those clothes and bathe yourself. I'll not have you tracking that mud through my home."

He noticed a pile of fresh, dry clothes next to a towel on the small table and thanked *Gott* for his *mutti's* love again.

"If you need more hot water, knock on the door and I'll get you a new pitcher," Ana said to the mud pile that vaguely resembled her only son.

Caleb looked at his hands and arms, realizing that not even two pitchers of water would get him clean. He took off his shoes and stepped out into the rain again, letting it soak him. He rubbed his hands up and down his sleeves, torso and legs getting most of the mud off himself, then went back to wash off and warm up.

Even having gotten the majority of the mess off, he found need for that second pitcher of hot water, covering himself as it was handed through a nearly closed door to him. When finished, he poured the remaining water over his head to rinse and toweled himself off.

Putting on clean dry clothes made him feel better than he had in a week. He opened the door, found his *mutti*, and gave her a kiss on her forehead.

"There is my son," she said. "Where have you been these past few days?"

"I was off my path for certain, *Mutti*, but I know my path now and I am ready to walk it."

Later that night, with the sound of rain on the roof as a background, Ana spoke of this with Jacob. "He seems resolved to do something. I do hope that he does not anger that girl further. I can't understand a girl not wanting my Caleb."

"Our Caleb," Jacob interrupted, "has not been acting like our Caleb as of late."

"It is truly odd," Ana agreed. "Those two seem such a perfect fit to each other, and they can't be in the same room. It just doesn't make sense."

"If there is a path, the Lord will lead them to it, Ana," Jacob said as he rolled over to sleep.

Ana said yet another prayer for her son and her own understanding, then slept as well.

9

The rain did not let up until late Saturday afternoon. The fields too wet to plow meant the girls were quilting, and Caleb and Jacob were in the barn taking the wheels off the wagon and checking them for rot. Finding none, they greased the axles up and put the wheels back in place as the sun began to set.

"It will need to be driven still before we put it away," Jacob commented. "Take your *schwestere* to services in this tomorrow. I will follow in the closed wagon in case there are any problems."

Caleb did not want to go to services in a courting buggy, but he would never say no to his *vater*. He steeled himself to the snickers he would get arriving in this and leaving with only his *schwestere* along for the ride home.

He read with Naomi again that night, letting her pick the chapter and verse. She chose Psalms, one of his favorites, and then as if *Gott* himself had stepped in, she chose Psalm fifteen. As they read verse two and three, he felt convicted.

The one whose walk is blameless, who does what is righteous, who speaks the truth from their heart; whose tongue utters no slander, who does no wrong to a neighbor, and casts no slur on others.

Naomi read this with him at the start and alone by its end. He had wronged his neighbor. His walk was not blameless. He had thought he spoke truth, but he knew in his heart he felt something for Ruby, another man's wife. He must speak to Bishop after services for advice.

Sunday morning broke clear and warm. *Gott's* promise of spring fulfilled in its glory. However, Caleb dreaded the day.

He did as his *vater* had requested and hitched a horse to each of the wagons. Lizzie and Emma were eager to ride on the "new" wagon, but Naomi looked at the sparse room and decided to stay with her *eldre* in the "old" carriage.

Caleb made sure all were ready and led his horse out toward the Troyer farm holding services and his impending doom. Lizzie and Emma were surprisingly proper and did not giggle a single time the whole trip.

They arrived and made their way in. They sang hymns and praised *Gott* for the next three hours, and the spirit of the Lord was with them that day. Caleb, despite his impending conversation with the bishop, found he was singing and praying with extra vigor this day.

As the prayer meeting let out, he dared to cast his eyes about. All the usual faces were there smiling and communing together. Then he saw Samuel, and next to him was Rebecca, and next to her, Ruby.

There was something different about Ruby, but he could not place it. Yet he had no time for pondering it, for he had to put this to an end in the only way he knew how. To be honest and bear the punishment for his sins. He made his way to Bishop Yoder and asked for a private audience.

It was a common thing for youth to need guidance and he was glad to spend the time with Caleb.

Closing the door behind him, Bishop Yoder began, "Speak Caleb. Any can see that there is a weight upon you. Let me help you lift it off."

"I fear I have sinned against *Gott,*" Calen stuttered out. It sounded worse in his voice than it did in his head, and he was aghast at even that.

Bishop Yoder sat down then and looked Caleb square in the eyes.

"Caleb, you have done the right thing to bring this to me. Speak your sin that we might pray together."

"Bishop, I … I was a guest at my neighbor's home and coveted a married woman." He felt both horror and relief having said it. "I did not mean to and in fact, was not aware that I had until it was made clear to me. I have tried to block this out, but I am drawn to her."

Bishop Yoder tried to hide his shock and disappointment. He had known Caleb all the days of his life and would never have thought to be having this talk with him.

"You know that coveting your neighbor's wife is a grievous sin," the bishop replied slowly. "You must cast aside this evil desire, or you face the eternal wrath of *Gott* Himself, son."

Caleb nodded, he knew the depth of his sin. He knew that he could not worship with evil in his heart. He held his head low as he listened.

"It is Rebecca then. Has she given any reason for you to make these advances to her?" Bishop Yoder asked.

"Rebecca? No Bishop, I speak of her sister Ruby. I am drawn to her as if by the hand of *Gott*. Please Bishop, help me to understand and overcome this."

What happened next, Caleb did not expect at all. Bishop Yoder's head reared back and he began to laugh. It was a deep laugh from his toes that put sparkles in his eyes when it got to his head. "You speak of Ruby, you say. Rebecca's twin?"

"*Ja*, Bishop. It is she that vexes me so."

"Caleb, she spoke with me yesterday to join our community. I saw in her a strong young woman full of love for the Lord. She was a member of her old district and we have granted her membership in this one. As such, we have a duty to protect her."

Caleb's heart was racing. Why Bishop would laugh before shunning him did not make sense to him, but surely that had to be what came next.

"Tell me," the Bishop inquired. "What do you know of her husband?"

"I spoke with Samuel and he said that he would miss her when her husband came to claim her. That is all that I know."

Again, Bishop Yoder laughed. Caleb was a peaceful and *Gott* fearing *mann*, but he did not understand this laughter at his expense.

Figuring the boy had been torturing himself long enough, Bishop Yoder stood, walked towards him, put his hand on his broad shoulders and said the very last thing Caleb would have thought.

"Caleb, Ruby has no husband. I think that Samuel might have been testing your intentions with his *schwagerin*. He was seeing if you might be the husband to take her away."

Caleb's head swam yet again. No, this could not be so. All the things said. All the anger. He did not know if he should rejoice that he felt love for a woman who was in fact available, or misery for having made the match impossible to make.

Bishop Yoder patted him on the back again and said to him, "I can see that you have much to ponder. I expect to see you at Youth Meeting this day. You have not sinned against *Gott*, and that is the blessing here. If you find yourself needing more guidance, my door is always open for you."

10

Caleb walked out to the now empty meeting room. His *schwestere* must have gone home with the *eldere*. He drove the wagon slowly home, replaying the scenes in his mind to see how he was so wrong. He arrived at when Ruby burst into tears at his home and berated himself aloud, "I am a fool. No, I am a fool's fool!"

He had called his seventeen-year-old *schwestere* old maids in her presence. He had apologized if she felt he had been pursuing her. He was perhaps a fool's fool's fool. He knew two things for certain at that moment. He could never face her again, and he had to see her to try to make this right.

He arrived at home, leaving the horse and wagon together. He went into the *haus* and found Emma, then asked her to speak with him in the yard privately.

"Emma," he started, "your brother is a fool."

Emma had never seen Caleb this way. She sat and listened.

"I have made a mess of something and I don't know if it can be fixed. I learned today that Ruby is not a married woman."

Emma nodded, waiting for him to get to the point. When he said nothing else, she realized that was his point. "You mean, you did not know her to be unmarried? How could even you be so dense?"

Caleb wished he had that answer, but he did not. "Emma, I went to her home and apologized if I had made her think I was interested in her." He continued, aghast. "I called you a spinster with her in the room, and she older and unmarried."

"Caleb," Emma replied. "You are correct. My brother is a fool. I have a question you have not yet answered though. Why is it that this bothers you so?"

He felt himself grow warm, blushing.

"No! You? Her?" Emma found she couldn't make a fit sentence with the words running around in her head.

"What do I do?" was all Caleb could think to say.

"You need to speak with her at meeting today. There is no other way to be had. You must admit to being a *dunderkopf* and hope she has a soft spot in her heart for lost kittens and stray dogs." Emma laughed with him now rather than at him. "Go! Let *Daed* know he will need to bring Lizzie and I to meeting. You had best ride alone. You don't need us there to laugh at you as you grovel."

He went to his *vater* and did just that. Despite having doubts about Caleb being in the same room as Ruby again, Jacob agreed to take the girls and bring them home.

"Who knows how long I might have this pleasure before some young man grabs their attentions away?" he said aloud.

Caleb left early for Youth Meeting, taking the open wagon and praying for a miracle. When he got there, some had already started the volleyball flying. It was a common way to pass the time for those who arrived before they congregated to pray and spend time together as to the future of the community.

He set the wagon off to the side, facing it away as was the custom, and started scanning the crowd. He found a face he had not expected,

Samuel. These meetings usually did not include the married, but he was glad to see him and walked quickly to him.

Unknown to Caleb, Ruby watched this all from nearby. At first, she could not hear them so she found reason to get a bit closer until she could. The two men walked towards each other cautiously, then Caleb began to speak and wave his hands about. She had missed this part and did not hear their greeting. She did overhear the rest.

They shook hands tentatively.

"Samuel, I am asking your permission to speak to Ruby," Caleb stated.

"I am not sure that to be a wise thing. It did not go so well for you last time, or have you forgotten so soon? I have had two angry and sad women in my home this week and they both blame you. Why would I ask for more of this?"

Caleb explained the mix up, what he had said to Ruby when he thought he had been forward with her as a married woman, and all the details as best he could. When it came to the part where he reminded Samuel of his part in it, Samuel winced and slapped his forehead. Caleb finished and his eyes pleaded with Samuel for his permission.

"I may well be a fool for this, Caleb." At this he reached out his hand in friendship. "But, yes. You have my permission and my best wishes for your success in getting her to listen to this fantastic tale."

Caleb smiled from ear to ear, then realized that the hardest part of his task was upon him. It was at that point that they gathered for their prayer and worship that always began and ended the meetings.

It was common for the young men to ask an available girl to drive her home that they might become better acquainted as a discrete start to a courtship. As the volleyball game went on, he saw a few bold men make their moves, some with success, some with none.

He did try to get Ruby alone to speak with her but, being the new girl, many wanted her attention. To Caleb's consternation, many of those were young men. Caleb waited for his moment and as they began to gather for the closing prayers he saw his chance.

He walked up to her, and led her away from the door gently by her elbow. She had not screamed yet, so that part was going well.

"Ruby," he started.

"Caleb," she replied flatly.

"I … I am a fool, Ruby."

Trying to hold back her smile, she replied, "Well at last, something we agree on."

"More than a fool, I am a *donderkopf.*"

"So, Emma has let me know. Now you see, this is better. We have many things we might agree on, given a chance."

Putting his heart on the line, he looked at her and spoke again, "I would like that, Ruby. I would like to get to know you better. Perhaps I could drive you home after meeting?"

"I feel it would be good to know more about each other, Caleb. I will start. My name is Ruby Stolzfus. I live with my twin and her husband. I have no husband of my own." Ruby could not hold her laugh in any more as Caleb's face fell upon hearing the last of that. "I heard you speak to Samuel. And while I thought there was nothing to explain your behavior, I was wrong. It all makes a twisted sort of sense." She paused, her eyes finding his and they softened. "I am sorry you have agonized these past days. The meeting is breaking up now. Come, let us ride together and talk more of this."

Caleb was not sure he had heard correctly. She was not just going to forgive him, but perhaps give him a chance to court her? He felt *Gott's* love around him and walked her to the wagon.

"Where is the girl who usually sits in this seat?" she asked. "I saw this out when we came for dinner. Am I taking another's ride home?"

Caleb wondered what she was saying, then stopped and had a laugh of his own.

"No," Caleb said to her gently. "We had cleaned the barn and noticed the wagon needed some work, so we left it out to have the rain wash it for us. As for the last girl in that seat, you have met her, I am sure."

Caleb watched her eyes as she thought over the young girls she had met today. Many of whom had mentioned how close she lived to Caleb. She did not see any as someone he would pursue.

"I am at a loss, Caleb. If it is not too imposing, would you tell me?"

"I believe you have met my *mutti, ja?*"

"You mean to say that no woman has ridden in this seat since then?"

It became clearer to her how Caleb felt. She looked at him and thought he looked like a sturdy man, smiling again to herself as they came up Samuel's drive.

"I enjoyed this drive. Perhaps I could drive you again next week if that is not too forward of me," he asked with hope in his heart.

"I enjoyed this ride as well." She swallowed before replying, "Perhaps next week, you might show me some of the other roads and sights about as well, if the weather is as nice as today."

Caleb helped her down and walked her to her door. He saw her inside then turned to go home.

Along his path home, his heart felt light and he lifted his head, thanking *Gott* for the blessing of Ruby and for His good will and purpose.

He wiped down the horse, put the wagon away where it could be accessed easily next week and then he stretched. His *mutti* looked out the window at her son. He seemed to be hugging the air and the land. Had she been able to see inside his mind she would see that was not far off from what he felt.

Pulling Weeds

The Fishers

(An Amish Life 2)

Caleb Fisher breathed in the rich smell of the farmland around him mixed with the sweet early summer aroma of honeysuckle coming in to bloom near the tree line. That alone on most days was enough to put a smile upon his face, but today he had a new reason. His Ruby had agreed to see him. This meant he would be driving her home from meeting, allowing them to see if they would be a fit pair.

His Ruby. His smile widened. The words felt right in his mind. After all that had come before this day, Caleb welcomed the thought of his life going back to the way it had been previously, but with the addition of courting Ruby.

He walked past the carriage his *vater* had used to drive his *schwestere* to meeting earlier this day, his demeanor calm and confident. It lasted to the doorway of the *haus*, but not a moment longer for as the door opened and his *eldere*, Jacob *und* Ana looked out, he witnessed their expressions alter toward disappointment.

Behind them, the youngest of his family, Naomi, stood smirking. "It is good to see someone remembers the way home," she remarked.

This immediately made Jacob tense and Ana turn with a flourish, sending her youngest scurrying from the room. Caleb tilted his head, pondering, as this was a perfectly normal tease from Naomi and yet a rather different reaction from *mutti und daed,* who now stood before him silent.

It was at that point that it dawned on him. The overwhelming silence in the house. He could not recall a time it was not filled with some noise or another, whether it be cooking noises, cleaning noises, or the twins' constant giggling.

And, there it was. The noise that was missing was his 17-year-old twin *schwesetere*. *Vater* had taken them to meeting and he and the carriage were both back. Where could those two have gone off to?

He had looked forward to speaking with Emma about his progress with Ruby. It was a big thing to drive a girl home and have her agree to see you. How excited his *schwestere* would be!

Some day they would have courters driving them home. He wondered how his parents would look waiting for them to arrive. As that thought hit him, he came to a full stop, spun like a loose gate in a strong wind and said aloud, *"Nein...? Jah?"*

1

Lizzie looked in the small mirror over the bureau in their bedroom. Her sister Emma stood behind her. They were identical twins and despite the years of developing separate tastes, dislikes, and personalities, at seventeen, they could still fool their parents briefly and any other they decided to for as long as they chose. This was a source of unlimited amusement.

"Emma," Lizzie said to her twin, who was smoothing her skirt. "Is it true that Caleb is taking the buggy to meeting *und daed* is taking us?"

"*Jah,* Caleb is planning to drive Ruby home today. I think the *donderkopf* has finally met his match," replied Emma, now finishing setting her kerchief upon her head.

"Caleb *und* Ruby?" a puzzled Lizzie said. "She cannot stand to be in the same room with him."

"More like she cannot stand his attitude toward her, which has changed. I trust she will see that and they will have a chance," Emma said, a wistful tone in her voice. "I see the look in her eyes when she speaks of him. It is not just anger I see there."

Lizzie, getting past her original shock, added, "I wish there was one I thought of in that way. I can see none here that want to be men instead of boys."

Emma did not see the trap her sister set and jumped in quickly, "John Beiler is not a boy, he is a right *gut* man. He nearly runs his family's farm already."

With that, Lizzie burst into a fit of laughter and giggles. "You are so taken with that boy, Emma."

Emma, fighting off her own inevitable echo of her *schwester's* giggles, nodded. "I'd like to be taken home by him. Why does he not act now that we are of age? He smiles at me when we pass and trips over his words when we speak."

Lizzie, through her fit of giggling replied, "That makes him a right *gut* fool."

At that, Emma lost her battle and broke into a matching fit of laughter while finishing preparations for Sunday meeting. There would be food and one of the deacons, or perhaps the bishop, would speak to them of the choices before them and help to lead them to *Gott*.

This was also the time when brave young men tried to garner the attention of hopeful girls to begin the courting ritual of driving them home in an open buggy, which served both to keep the youth chaste and to make the declaration public, even as most did not speak of it until it either came to fruition or end.

Emma hoped that one day soon, John would ask her. Lizzie gave it no real thought at all.

Jacob Fisher called upstairs to his daughters, "It is time to be going. Come along."

The giggling died down for the moment and they went out to the covered wagon to be driven to Meeting.

Upon arriving at the Miller's farm, hosts for the day's meeting, the girls waved goodbye to their *Vater* and walked quickly towards the group of youths setting up the game. The girls, being athletic, were always asked to play volleyball even when those asking them to play got the names wrong as often as right.

"*Dochtere!*" Jacob called out, using the same voice he used to call across the farm to them. "I will be under this tree waiting for you."

Being Sunday, Jacob would do no work. As close as he was here to town, he would not go and do the business of tomorrow. It was simply not done. He would do something rather untypical for the Amish, he would rest a spell waiting on his young women. He sat sideways in his wagon, tipped his straw hat forward, and began to pray.

2

As usual, upon the twins' arrival they were surrounded first by their female friends to catch up. They broke free several minutes later to speak with Ruby.

Lizzie sidled up next to her, "We've much to discuss."

Ruby ducked her head and tucked a stray piece of hair into her kapp, eyeing the girls who came to join them. "We should talk soon. Perhaps we could start that quilt we spoke about making at dinner?"

Lizzie took the hint, a gleam in her eye and winked at her sister. The three of them smiled, agreeing on getting together during the coming week should time and chores allow.

Then began the parade of boys to speak with the girls present, some boldly, and others with broken voices.

Many of the them wanted to meet Ruby, the new girl, but despite being mannered, she was clearly not that interested in what they were saying. John Beiler came over and asked Emma to play volleyball. He even got her name right. Off she went, smiling. Lizzie chatted a bit more with Ruby until she felt a tug on her shirt.

"Excuse me," said a deep voice. "I hear that you play well, would you like to join us?"

Lizzie turned and saw a face she did not know.

"That would depend," she said, holding back her natural desire to giggle, "upon who it was that was asking."

"I am Peter Miller," came the reply in a slightly less assured voice. "I'm helping my uncle with his market stall the next few weeks."

Lizzie had heard all she needed to know. Despite being a new face, he was not suitable for her. She would be a farmer's wife and could not imagine her life another way. Not that she had given it much thought yet, but she did know that much.

She turned her back on him and went out onto the small field set up for volleyball. The games were always fun. They tried to keep the teams as even as possible, mixing the boys and girls so that neither team dominated for long.

After a couple of quick games, the twins returned to a small table that had been set with cups and pitchers of ice water.

They glanced around the gathering and Emma remarked, "Where is Ruby? I wonder if Caleb has scared her away. Or can he have won her heart for the moment?"

"I should think neither. There is Caleb there, speaking to Samuel," replied Lizzie, pointing to the pair.

"It is either not going well, or Caleb is trying to describe how a windmill works," laughed Emma.

At that the two fell about themselves with their infectious laughing. Those around them, even the ones who had no idea why they were laughing, soon joined in.

It was shortly thereafter that the deacon got everyone's attention to come inside the great room to prayers.

Usually the girls sat next to each other, but today they ended up about ten feet apart, each at the end of a row of chairs. They sat and listened as the Deacon spoke of the love of *Gott* and the temptations of sin.

Emma was her usual attentive self when she felt her hand being held and a voice in her ear ask if he might have the privilege of driving her home.

"Yes, I'd be delighted," flew from her mouth before she saw his face. This was not John. This was a face she did not know at all.

With her *yes*, Peter pulled her quietly from her seat and put his finger to his lips, reminding her to keep quiet. She wanted to say something, anything, but she was walking towards his buggy and had no idea what to say.

As they got outside to where most of the wagons sat, they came to his open buggy. He reached to help her up just as she gathered her wits about her and asked, "Might I inquire what possessed you to ask to drive me home?"

Peter looked deeply into her eyes and she felt her resolve to stop this fading. "I saw how you played volleyball with such fire and I would like to know what it is that lights the fire in your eyes."

Whatever Emma had planned to say left her head at that moment, never to return.

"I could not accept a ride from a stranger whose name I do not know," she blushed.

Peter nodded and was quick to respond, "Peter Miller, nephew of Moses Miller. I am here to learn the business of his market."

Emma looked him up and down. He was a strong man to be working a market. "Is that what you do now, Peter Miller?" she inquired.

"*Ach nein,*" he replied. "Let us discuss this on the ride, shall we?"

"Give me a moment. That is *mein vater's* wagon there, under that tree. Let me walk over to tell him I will not need a ride this day," Emma replied with a smile.

And so she did, waking her father from his prayers and shocking him with her quick explanation and goodbye.

"So, Peter," Emma began, hopping into the buggy without his help. "Tell me why a farmer would want to sell to *Englishe.*"

"I am not a farmer," Peter answered, then almost immediately added. "Well, I do help out on my family's farm of course. What I am drawn to though is furniture making. I enjoy starting with a tree and making something that will last out of it. The farm will go to one of my younger *brudere.* This is the path I see for myself. Making and selling furniture."

He handled the horses competently and put Emma at ease. She settled back while he continued, "The *Englishe* may have no love for quiet, but they do know quality and pay well for it."

The tree branches danced with the warm breeze of the late afternoon. Emma feasted her eyes on the beautiful day and listened as he pleaded his case to her. She liked his confidence and that he knew where he was headed. This was the way of a man, not a boy.

The more he spoke of making furniture, the more animated and alive he became. Gone were any hesitations or shyness. This is what it looked and sounded like to speak of something with passion and love. Emma liked the sound in his voice. It called to some part of her.

"Did you never think to buy up a farm of your own?" She asked more to add something to the conversation than to suggest she disapproved of his choice.

"I have saved up and I am considering buying a wooded lot near home. I can cut my own trees, have them milled and dried in town, and use them to build my home and barn. I will surely have some cattle and horses there after a time. I'd not know what to do with a morning that did not include milking," he laughed.

Emma smiled and a small sigh escaped. He painted a pretty picture, and she could see herself as a part of it. She was so interested in what he was saying that she lost track of where they were going, paying no attention as they took the right fork where they should have gone left.

It was a good deal of conversation and travel before Emma wondered aloud, "Where are we?"

"What do you mean?" Peter looked at her confused. He pulled to the side of the paved road. "I am taking you home. It is this way, *jah?*"

"No, Peter." Emma looked around to get her bearings. "I believe this is the road to the big city. I live back the other way."

"But – but … you did not say anything," Peter stammered.

"I was too busy listening," Emma said, a giggle forming.

Then the two of them sat there, in a carriage stopped on the road, and laughed until they almost fell off. Each time one of them managed to get control for a moment the other laughed harder until they were both doubled over again. Finally, with both of them holding their sides, Peter turned the wagon and started back towards the road to Emma's *haus*.

3

Back at the meeting, Lizzie looked this way and that, trying to find Emma among the girls present. *She must have gone to daed already.* As she stood to do the same, a rather tentative John Beiler asked to drive her home.

Lizzie could barely contain her laughter. Here was her *schwester's* dream man asking to drive her home. Only he got the wrong *schwester*! Quickly, she hid her sense of hilarity at the irony and agreed to the ride home.

She could only imagine the look on Emma's face when they stopped at *daed's* wagon and she saw her with John. Lizzie would of course allow John to drive home the girl he intended asking at that point. She couldn't wait to see his face when he found out that he was with her and not Emma!

"I will be delighted, John Beiler," she replied as she thought Emma would.

He looked at her oddly a moment, then let a small smile come to his face. They walked out of the great room, past empty spaces where eager suitors had already claimed their intended. They walked over the trampled grass towards his buggy. As they neared his, Lizzie informed him that she needed to let her *daed* know that she would not need a ride.

She allowed him to talk his way into escorting her to her *daed's* waiting wagon, but there was no Emma present when they arrived.

"Let me guess," said Jacob. "You also have a ride home this fine day?"

Lizzie blinked, her head turning this way and that. Also? If Emma already had a ride, who was it with? And then a second thought chased the first away. She had agreed to be driven home by Emma's dream man. How would she ever explain this one?

While Lizzie was trying to get her bearings, John stepped forward to shake Jacob's hand. "Yes, sir. If you wouldn't mind terribly, I would like to spend a bit of time with your daughter, and would appreciate it if you would allow me to drive her home."

Hearing this, Lizzie turned and wondered when John Beiler had become so polite and proper. This was not something he had showed her in the past. This must be how he acts for Emma. This ride may be fun yet, she giggled to herself.

"Get her home safely then," her *vater* said, nodding at the pair.

She and John walked back to his waiting buggy.

"That was rather bold of you, John Beiler, speaking to my father for permission," teased Lizzie.

"I was rather more frightened to speak with you, to be honest," John replied.

Lizzie saw his face go from tanned to flushed and tried to hold back her giggles and laughter. As John's face went to bright scarlet, she lost her battle and let out a belly laugh.

"It isn't funny," John said, before he too joined her in laughter, agreeing it kind of was.

He helped her up into the wagon and set the horses to walk. On the ride home, the more they talked, the easier the conversation became. John was a farmer and as the youngest, the Beiler farm would go to him in time. He had two younger *schwestere* that would need to find their mates or fates before that would happen, but he had a natural peace about him. He was not rushing to be something else so much as he was enjoying who he was at this moment.

When Lizzie asked him if he was eager to be the man of the farm, he replied, "This is the day the Lord has made, I will rejoice and be glad in it."

Lizzie had never thought of John as a smart boy, or really had much thought about him at all, she admitted to herself. She could now see why Emma might find herself attracted to him.

Emma. How will I explain this ride to her? A feeling of sadness fell across her heart as she looked at John. *How can I tell this man that I have deceived him in my schwester's name?*

John must've noted her countenance change, for he asked her, "Is everything okay? You suddenly do not look pleased; did you leave something behind at meeting?"

Why does he have to keep being so nice? She felt even worse that she had tricked him.

"No, nothing of the sort," she replied. "I was just thinking about a quilt I am making."

She found herself displeased that she had lied to him, but could not tell him what she had done. To make matters worse, she was still in the midst of doing so.

Just before her farm, John stopped the buggy and turned to her.

"I've enjoyed our time and conversation. Would I be too bold to ask if I might drive you home next week?"

Lizzie saw a way out. No one needed to be hurt. Emma would love to be driven home by John next week, so Lizzie quickly agreed. "Yes, that would be perfectly wonderful."

He smiled broadly and started the horses towards the Fisher *haus*. From here, they could see the wagon that her *daed* had been using already put away, as well as Caleb's parked beside it.

Another buggy headed toward them in the distance from the other direction.

John arrived first, turning smartly onto the path before the *haus* and stopping. He jumped down and offered his hand to help Lizzie alight. Walking her to the door, he waved to Jacob who stood near the porch throwing feed at the chickens.

"Safely home as promised, sir." He then turned to Lizzie and said aloud, "So next week then?"

Lizzie blushed that he would say this in front of her *daed*, but for Emma's sake replied, "Yes, John. Until then."

He took his leave of Jacob and Ana, and climbed back into his wagon humming a hymn.

Peter and Emma arrived at the same spot that John had just vacated. Emma was slightly shaken to see him driving away from her *haus*. What would he be doing here? However, to her great pleasure, Peter asked her to allow him to drive her home next week, promising not to get them lost next time.

Emma realized that she would prefer they did get lost again. She had truly enjoyed the time they had spent together.

Upstairs in their room and away from prying ears, Lizzie burst out, "Oh, *schwester*, you accidentally got my Peter and I got your John." She laughed at this, but failed to see the hurt look on Emma's face. She continued, "Peter had been talking to me and apparently thought you were me. I'm sorry if he bored you to death. I made it up to you though. I told John that you would ride home with him next week. He never knew I wasn't you the whole ride."

Emma immediately realized the truth in Lizzie's words. Peter had come up as if they were acquainted when he dragged her off. He must have thought her Lizzie. Her heart sank at the thought.

"Oh, what a trickster you are," Emma tried to sound happy saying, "What ever shall we do next week?"

"I have it all worked out so no one gets hurt. You ride with John and I will ride with Peter." Lizzie explained, thinking to herself that she could let Peter know she was not inclined to ride with him after all.

Lizzie felt a twinge of jealousy when she thought of Emma riding with John, but it was her he thought he had asked, and only fair that Emma get the man she had longed for these past months. They would be a *gut* pairing. *So would John und I*, she thought, but kept that to herself.

Emma felt trapped. She had enjoyed Peter's company, but could not be the person that stopped her *schwester* from such a *gut* man. While she had long wished to have John ask her, she now wanted to get to know Peter. She could not see hurting her *schwester*, so she began to resolve herself to riding with John next week.

4

The topic of conversation that week turned out to be Caleb's return to happiness and Ruby having agreed to date him. Lizzie and Emma both adored her and hoped to welcome her to their family. They would get to see her Wednesday afternoon, having agreed to work on a quilt together. This would be a fine way for her to join the Fisher women.

Pride was a sin, but they knew they produced some of the best quilts around. Their *vater* had taken to having them make extras to be sold in a friend's market stall. They were always asking for more of them.

Sure enough, Wednesday came and Ruby was driven to the Fisher's by her *schwager*, Samuel. While the girls gathered Ruby up and off to the nearby sitting room, Samuel came in to say hello also.

"Samuel," Caleb called out upon seeing him, having just returned from the fields. "It is *gut* of you to stop in." He led the way into the kitchen, offering him a warm cup of coffee "Sit, friend, talk with me a bit."

"Ah, about that," Samuel followed then stood awkwardly, looking at his feet. "It seems I am pressed for time and I was hoping it would not be an inconvenience for you to drive Ruby home when the women finish."

Caleb noticed a slight blush to his face and forehead. He then realized this was Rebecca's doing. Samuel could not lie convincingly. Caleb admired him the more for it.

"It would be my great pleasure," Caleb said loud enough for Ruby to hear in the next room over the tittering girls. "Give your wife my best."

They shook hands and both enjoyed a few sips of coffee. The two men walked out the way they had come and stood by Samuel's carriage.

"Do you enjoy fishing? The stream that separates our lands has some right *gut* trout in it."

"*Jah*," Samuel answered. "My fields are all planted. I might find an afternoon. You could show me where the fish hide?"

"If I were to do that, I'd need you to hold that between us only," Caleb joked. "I've trained them to wait for me, but I will try to talk them into jumping onto your hook as well."

The two shook hands, parting, Samuel back to his wife and Caleb back to his chores. The farm always had something that needed doing.

Meanwhile, inside, Ruby sat down with the twins. They were pumping her for information while explaining the pattern they were working on. It was one the market had requested over and over. They had already cut the fabric and were pleased to see that Ruby was not lost with a needle in her hand.

"So, Ruby," Emma began.

Before she got another word out, Ruby looked at Emma, then at Lizzie, and then back to her and said, "Yes, Emma?"

The twins looked at her, then at each other. The three of them started laughing and the conversation had to wait until the merriment subsided.

"Ruby," Emma started again. "You have agreed to let *donderkopf* drive you then?"

"*Jah*," replied Ruby with a small smile. "I guess now he is my *donderkopf.*"

The girls looked at each other and squealed, the sewing momentarily forgotten in their hands.

"Is it so bad then that I am falling for your *bruder?*" questioned Ruby with a tinge of fear in her voice.

"Oh no! It is *wunderbar*," came their reply in one voice.

Emma paused to jump up and hug Ruby. They talked and talked and hugged some more and somehow, during all of this, they managed to sew squares for the quilt.

Ruby was a good addition to the team. While she had not done much quilting, she was an adept seamstress and a quick learner. Time flew by, all the while the girls continued to press Ruby for more details.

Each listened to Ruby talk and thought back to their own first rides, feeling much the same. It was different for them though, for they would have to ride back with another next week. The both kept on a happy face and decided their twin was worth it.

The next Sunday morning, they gathered and went to Community services at the King farm. Samuel and Rebecca had offered their great room for services that day and Bishop Yoder had agreed. It would be good for the district to welcome them into the fold properly.

The only two not happy were Caleb and Ruby. There would be no drive home for them this day. They would speak at the afternoon meeting, but not have the drive to spend together. The twins, though, could not be happier. They would only be with the wrong man briefly, and could avoid a long unpleasant ride home with a disappointed suitor.

Service that day was exceptional. The singing rang out for the first time in years at the King farm. Each voice seemed to be looking to fill the surrounding land with a sense of community and belonging.

The sermon convicted the twins. Sitting together, they squirmed as the Bishop read from Galatians 6. *Do not be deceived: God is not mocked, for whatever one sows, that will he also reap.*

The girls had sown nothing but deception. Not only with the poor men, but with themselves and each other. This was the day that neither looked forward to, and now that it was here, it grew longer by the moment.

Service finished and while most of the community departed to their own farms, the Fishers lingered a bit longer to talk and marvel at all the work Samuel had been doing around the place.

He invited the family to stay for lunch, and Caleb jumped at the opportunity. Not wanting to disappoint him, Jacob and Ana agreed.

"Caleb, help Samuel set up for the youth this afternoon. We can at least be helpful to our fine hosts," Ana instructed her son.

Jacob smiled and said to his bride softly, "And the work will get done quickly with his desire to speak with Ruby."

Ana nodded her agreement and went inside to offer help to Rebecca. As she entered the *kich*, the smell of that wonderful bread that they had taught her daughters to make wafted on the air. She thanked Rebecca aloud for being so gracious to share it with them.

The kitchen was warm. The three women worked well together getting things organized, but Ana finally took pity on Ruby who kept peering out the window, and offered, "I am sure that Rebecca and I can finish in here. Why don't you check on the men's progress?"

Rebecca turned towards Ana and the two shared a knowing smile. Ruby tipped her head in thanks, fairly skipping out the door towards Caleb.

"It appears you and I may have some planning ahead of us, Rebecca," Ana said. "I've never seen Caleb as happy as this past week. Unless he manages to make a fool of himself again, I see this as a strong pairing."

"I was not sure I'd ever see her find a man. She is rather particular, that one," Rebecca laughed. "She remembers the way our *mutti und vater* were before the accident and will settle for nothing less. I was fortunate to find Samuel. He treats me the way my *vater* treated *mutti*, but to find two such men was not expected." She paused to look out the window towards her sister mooning over the man in question. "I see much *gut* in Caleb. I hope they can keep out of their own way to find happiness together."

"It sounds like your *eldere* did well by you two," reassured Ana. "You are both strong, God-abiding women. If you don't mind me prying, you mentioned an accident?"

Rebecca drew in a breath. "My *eldere* were driving home from market on a Saturday. The drunk *Englishe* did not see the wagon and it was several long weeks in the hospital until *mutti* passed over to *Gott's* hands. My *daed* spent all of his savings and still had debt on the medical bills. Partly from his refusal to take the charity of the *Englishe* hospital, he ended up having to sell off the land to a neighbor to pay the costs."

Rebecca sat, sadness taking over her countenance. Ana came to sit beside her, reaching out to hold her hand. She continued, "The neighbor allowed him to lease it back for as long as he lived so that he might live out his days on his farm. *Vater* passed within a year of *mutti*. He could not bear living without her."

She sighed, shaking her head to clear it and smiled tentatively, "By then, I had agreed to marry Samuel and he volunteered to bring Ruby with us until such a time as she married or chose otherwise."

Ana looked at this woman, barely older than her Caleb, and realized how strong she truly was.

"What a rough road, Rebecca. I am glad *Gott* has brought you here. Samuel is a blessed man to have such a strong woman by his side. Know that we are here for you both. If you should ever find yourselves in need, we would be honored to lend our hands to you."

The women shared a hug, then bustled back towards the counter, placing the last of the food on the lunch trays. It was too fine a day to spend indoors, so they called the others to the outside table to eat.

Everyone eagerly enjoyed the sliced meats and cheeses along with the homemade bread. There was fruit and fresh lemonade made from lemons ripe with summer goodness, which were stocked by the green grocer.

The seating outside fell out of traditional order. Samuel as head of the house should be at the head of the table. Instead, he sat between Jacob and Caleb and the three of them talked fishing and hunting. Ruby sat next to Caleb and the rest of the women sat opposite. No one seemed to mind the lack of decorum, if any noticed at all.

"Samuel," started Jacob, "I hope you do not mind me saying this, but the shed housing your forge is in rough shape."

"You are saying nothing I have not thought myself," replied Samuel. "I have started to cut some timbers to replace it. There is quite a decent bit of woodland behind the fields that is yet uncut."

"Right *gut* hunting land that is too," added Caleb.

"Jah, the deer here knock down my stone walls, they are so brazen. I think none have chased them in a while. We will eat venison this year aplenty. Rebecca makes a fine jerky."

"When you have the timbers ready, Caleb and I will help you put up the shed proper," offered Jacob.

"That would be *gut,*" smiled Samuel. "Perhaps if Caleb has spare time this coming week, he could come and cut nails with me. I should think the women would be willing to feed him for such work." Samuel joked with Jacob as he drew the interest of Caleb quickly.

"*Jah,* you tell me the day, I will be here to help. We will make fast work of it and make plenty of spares for you. A farm is always needing nails," he laughed.

Ruby smiled at her *schwager,* knowing he could make those nails himself. He was helping Caleb and Ruby spend time together. It was *gut* that her family liked her Caleb. They prayed, and they ate and they prayed again. It seemed everyone was enjoying themselves. Everyone, that was, except Lizzie and Emma.

5

How strange this is to finally get asked by John Beiler for a ride home and be dreading it so. At least it will be a short ride, Emma ruminated. Her sister, unbeknownst to Emma, was having the same thoughts about her upcoming ride with Peter.

It was shortly after cleaning up that the first of the youths showed up and the rest followed. They played volleyball and talked among themselves like every other meeting. After the service, which was held outdoors, the deacon began the ending prayer and the ritual of courting began again.

John walked over to where Lizzie stood, bending his head to speak to her without being overheard. She gave a faint laugh, side-stepping, and said that her sister was on the opposite side of the yard waiting for him. He frowned and walked off towards Emma.

At that same time, Peter approached Emma who was near the side of the house. He was sent off to Lizzie.

"Your sister sent me to you?" Peter asked Lizzie, appearing confused.

"It seems none can tell us apart. Do not worry I shall not hold it against you," replied Lizzie.

Peter looked strangely at her, but then led the way to his buggy, even as Emma and John did the same. The short rides home were punctuated mostly by the clack of the horses' hooves on the roadway beneath. Neither couple had much to say. Without really realizing it, both young men set their horses to walk faster and pulled into the Fisher farm at nearly the same time.

99

When they got them home, the girls alighted, then the strangest thing happened. John walked over to Lizzie who had walked close to the front door, and Peter walked over to Emma, still beside John's buggy.

Each man out of the earshot of the other said much the same thing.

"Emma," said Peter. "If you did not wish to ride home with me, why did you not say so?"

"Lizzie," said John. "I thought that you enjoyed our ride. I don't begin to understand, but I will abide your decision."

Both men turned, got into their respective buggies and left. The twins stood watching them go.

"Lizzie," Emma called, rooted to the spot in the front yard, "What have we done? Did you like John and he you?"

"I could not bear to tell you." Lizzie came to her side. "You have pined for him for the last year at least. I did not mean to ride with him. I thought you were with *daed* and we would all have a *gut* laugh. I see what you saw in him, Emma. He is much more than the boy I had seen him to be. Do you hate me for liking him?"

Emma's head spun as she heard this. It made sense that Lizzie would play that trick on her and John. She hadn't told Lizzie she'd left with Peter that day.

"Can you forgive me?" Emma hesitated, "I feel that I have stolen the affections of your Peter. Can you forgive me?"

"Wait, so you actually like Peter?" Lizzie said in disbelief. "I was glad he stopped bothering me. I have no affection for him. John, on the other hand, is another wonder all together," she said wistfully. Then she quickly added, "So long as you don't mind, that is."

The twins began to giggle, as they often did, and then stopped as one and turned to each other.

Emma grabbed her sister's arm. "But we have ruined it with them both, haven't we?" The question came softly from her lips.

Lizzie tried to deny it, but they had deceived both of these good men. They had sowed lies and this was their crop, disappointment.

"I do not think they would forgive us, do you?" sighed Lizzie.

"I am not sure I would if the table were turned," came the sullen reply.

Jacob and Ana had watched the whole proceeding from the window. Even without the words, it was clear their daughters had pulled their switch trick one time too many.

"Keep them busy, Ana," said Jacob. "Busy hands will keep them from brooding on this too much."

"*Jah*, Jacob, you are a *gut vater*, but I think I will give them the rest of this day to be miserable. Perhaps, they will learn from it. I will keep them busy tomorrow then they won't have time for self-pity," replied Ana.

Jacob turned to his wife and smiled, "You are right as usual. They need to learn their lesson from this before they forget the pain. No one tells you that having children makes you hurt inside for them. I would think fewer would be born if the young knew how much their child's pain becomes their own."

He held out a hand to his wife and she pushed hers into his, both of them staring a moment longer at their now almost fully-grown twins.

The week was flying by in a blur for the girls. Before they knew, it was Wednesday, and Ruby had come to quilt with them again. The three sat and began as if they had been doing this their whole lives together. Ruby could not help but feel the twins were strangely subdued. They were not laughing at all.

"Is this a bad day for the two of you? As much as I am enjoying learning how to do this with you, I do not wish to be a burden," Ruby offered.

And with that the twins began to cry and tell Ruby the story of their misfortune. They confided their disappointment in themselves and the feeling they had lost a true chance at happiness.

Ruby soaked this all in with appropriate nods and an understanding ear. As they finished, she offered, "So, it seems no one in this family is capable of simple courting. Is that what you two are telling me?"

The two looked at her with jaws open, then suddenly the three burst out in laughter.

"We are all *dunderkopf,* apparently," agreed Emma. "I wonder if there is hope for any of us."

Catching their breath and with the release of tension, the girls went back to their task, enjoying each other's company. They managed to get a decent amount of progress made before Caleb came in to drive Ruby home.

He saved Samuel the embarrassment and volunteered as soon as they had arrived, telling Samuel he would be willing to come get her next week as well.

Ruby told Caleb the basics of the twins' plight on the ride home. He could feel the hurt she felt for his *schwestere*. It filled his heart even as it tugged on hers.

"Perhaps," Caleb offered, "I could find a reason to speak to the two men in question. I make no promises."

Ruby turned to Caleb and startled him by giving him a big hug. Upon realizing what she had done, she blushed and moved away only to have him return with a hug of his own, before putting a much smaller space back between them. They both smiled and enjoyed the fifteen-minute ride that seemed to always take them about a half hour to travel.

Upon arriving at the King farm, Caleb went in and spoke with Samuel before saying his good-bye and heading back home. Tomorrow he had to go to the market. It seemed an item had been added to his list.

6

"Guten morgen. You must be Peter." Caleb said reaching out to shake the young man's hand. He noticed that this was the hand of a working man, calloused and firm.

"You have me at a disadvantage, friend," replied Peter.

"I am Caleb Fisher," he started. "I hear that you have met my twin sisters. I bring apologies for their behavior. They have been pulling that switch trick for years. Many times, we have told them it would eventually bite them back."

Peter looked at him oddly. "They think none could tell them apart? They are night and day." He continued, leaning against a pillar between two open air shops at the market. "I spoke briefly with Lizzie and saw there was no spark to be had. But with Emma, my breath was taken. I believed she felt the same, but it appears I was fooled."

Caleb nodded, wondering if it was so. Soon the conversation turned to the furniture that was around them.

"Whomever you have making this for you is a true craftsman," Caleb remarked, running a hand along the back of a finely made chair.

"This is my work," Peter waved an arm encompassing all the carved tables, shelves, and chairs.

"Truly?" Caleb's eyes widened. "This is amazing. Could I get you to make something for me?"

He described what he wanted, and Peter agreed that while it was not something he usually did, it was something he could do. They agreed on a price and a deadline and shook hands.

Caleb went about the market and finished his tasks. It was easier and faster without Naomi, but he knew that she had wanted to come. He got her a honey stick to make it up to her. They were her favorite.

He returned to the farm and offloaded his purchases, some to the barn, some to the *haus*. Once that was all done, he went in just in time for dinner. *Mutti* was a fine cook and none left her table hungry. It was good to have his family surrounding him for such a fine meal.

Shortly after dinner, Caleb approached Naomi and gave her the treat. Her eyes lit up and she hugged her *bruder*.

"I had thought that you had forgotten me completely since Ruby became your favorite," she teased him.

"I have more than enough room in my heart for you as well. It is important to me that you always know that," Caleb said in a most serious tone.

"I know, Caleb. I know," she replied, fearing she had hurt his feelings.

"Now, where were we?" Caleb asked, picking up the Bible to read with her.

The two fell into their routine and read for a good hour, praying before reading and praying after, both times asking for understanding of the words they read and heard.

Shortly after they finished while they were talking, Ana called out to all, "It is time for bed. Tomorrow will come soon enough."

Friday found Caleb rushing through his chores. Jacob wondered about it, but as everything was being done well, he could find no fault in the speed. At lunchtime, with all but the chores that had to wait to be done, Caleb asked his *vater* for permission to visit the Beiler farm. Jacob raised an eye but said nothing. He nodded his head yes and wondered what would come of this.

The ride was pleasant. The early summer heat was dampened by the breeze. Caleb loved the smells of this season. The honeysuckle so sweet it overwhelmed in places, the sage growing as weeds added a savory smell when passed by. At last, he came to the Beiler farm.

He had been here for meeting before, but had not looked at much of it. He stopped at the *haus* asking for John and was told he was tending the cows in the small barn. Caleb looked around, spying two barns. One was perhaps the largest in the county. The other was ever so much smaller.

He looked about for a third, one he would call the "small" one. Seeing no others, Caleb headed towards the second of the two. As his eyes grew accustomed to the lower light inside, he saw a group of men standing and talking. He walked towards them, stopping before he would be considered eavesdropping.

"Can I help you," came a voice from within the group of men.

Caleb stepped forward. "I am looking for John Beiler."

Two men separated themselves, one saying, "Which of us?"

Caleb smiled and said, "Ahh, John Junior. Do you have a moment that I might speak to you?"

"I do not wish to seem rude, but I am working with the veterinarian here, we have an embarrassment of good fortune this year as we have ten cows that have calved. He is here to check on them."

"Go, John. I can work with Doctor Schweitzer here," replied John Senior.

The junior stepped forward, "How can I help you?"

Caleb walked away from the others, putting a good distance between what he was about to say and the other men. He began to explain.

"I am not sure I can help you after all, Caleb." John said, interrupting. "I have waited for Lizzie to mature for years. I also saw Emma's interest in me, so I did nothing to harm her. She is a decent girl in her own right. When she left to take a ride with that new man, I thought my time had finally come." He continued, clearly uncomfortable. "Then, after what I felt was a connection, she offers up her sister the next week. Did she think me a fool that I would not know them apart? They are night and day."

Caleb smiled hearing the same phrase from each of these men. They knew the twins apart.

"John," Caleb began. "I think I see a way clear through this. If you are willing to hear me out."

John answered, "I have waited years to win a smile from Lizzie, I would let her explain herself if she is able to. Now, I should get back to my work."

Caleb's mind formed a plan. He thanked *Gott* for the revelation. "Do you plan to keep all the calves or sell them?"

"We will keep about half," John replied.

"I have a neighbor that was talking of adding to his herd this year. When they are ready he may be willing to save you the auction fees."

"I am sure we could work that out. Have him come see me soon."

Caleb smiled to himself as he drove home. Now he just had to talk to his *schwestere*.

"You did what?" they screamed at him in unison.

"But I thought you liked them?" he shakily replied.

"That is not the point, Caleb," Emma said, getting angrier as she went. "We made our mistakes and will live with the consequences. But now you want to parade us as fools before them?"

This was not the chorus of praise Caleb had expected at all.

"You two are impossible." Caleb threw his hands up while leaving the girls fuming at him for all his efforts.

He left the house and headed to the barn. Jacob found him there some time later, coming up behind him to put his arm on Caleb's shoulder. "You are a *gut* son and a *gut bruder*. Give those two some time to swallow their pride. They may come around yet."

Caleb nodded in response, putting down the pitchfork and shaking his head.

"Now, since we have a bit of time yet and the day's chores are about done, come with me," his *daed* said.

Caleb followed him out and across the field. He realized the destination was the *grosshaus.*

"We will need to get a fresh coat of paint on this, I think. Inside and out, *jah?*" asked Jacob.

The house was one story and much smaller than the main home. It had served his grandparents well in their declining years, but had been vacant for some time.

Caleb looked at him then the house, confusion clear on his face. *"Daed,"* he replied, "that is a hefty cost, *jah?*"

"Do you think I would have my daughter-in-law live in a run-down *haus?*" he replied, not looking for an answer.

Caleb looked at his *vater* and shook his head. "I cannot ever hide anything from you, can I? I have just come to this myself, and you knew it before me?"

Jacob smiled at his son and said, "She is a right *gut* match for you. You know this farm will be yours. Once Naomi has gone off, we will swap *hause* and you can paint it fresh again for *my* bride."

"I am honored to be your son. You *und mutti* have shown me what to look for in life and I believe I have found it. I would be happy to live in the *grosshaus* for however long you wish to stay in your home. Thank you. I was not sure how to speak to you of this. I am glad, *vater.*"

"I can see the happiness clear on your face. Let us decide how much paint we must have to clean this up." Jacob put an arm around his son and led the way into the home.

"You know, I have not spoken to Ruby about this," Caleb said. "She may be unwilling."

"*Jah, und* tomorrow might not come, but we make plans for it do we not?" replied Jacob, smiling.

7

Sunday Meeting was at the Fisher home this week. Samuel, Rebecca, and Ruby arrived early, offering help to get the great room ready, if need be. As the preparations were nearly complete, Caleb stole Ruby away for a private walk around the yard.

"Ruby," Caleb started. "How do you see your life?"

Ruby stopped in her tracks. "Caleb –," Ruby said softly. "What is it you are asking me?"

"I wonder how you see your future. Do you think you might like to be a market *frau* selling jams and jellies, or that lovely honey bread of yours?" Caleb teased. "Or do you see yourself a farm wife with *kinder* running about?"

Ruby was not going to make it that easy for him.

"Yes, I could see those things." She laughed in reply. "I have been to market often enough to know how it is done. I was always *gut* with my numbers in school. As for a farm wife, I would rather marry a man than a farm. So long as it was the right man." With this she dropped her eyes from Caleb's, fearing that she was being too bold.

Caleb reached out and with a finger lifted her chin until her eyes met his again. "What I am asking, Ruby is … do you think I might be that farmer?" Caleb held his breath, awaiting her reply.

Ruby shook her head. "It is so early in the season for this. I would not want to be a summer bride. I know it is done, but I always saw myself following the traditions and waiting for after harvest."

"I would see you as an October bride as well, Ruby. Yes, it is early, but I know my heart and think that I know yours. There are plans to be made." Caleb scuffed a shoe against the dry earth. "We need speak of this to no one else and I shall wait to ask you properly until harvest's end, if that is your wish."

"Oh, no you don't," Ruby replied, looking up into his face. "You have done so much as ask me already and I am giving you my answer today. I'll not let this go by unresolved."

Then she became silent, her face unreadable for what seemed an eternity to Caleb. She then took Caleb's hands in hers. "I could see no other than you as that farmer. Yes, I would gladly be your wife and if that makes me a wife to this farm, so be it. If it means that we farm *und* market as well, I will be there by your side throughout."

With that, Caleb surprised them both by giving her both a hug and a peck on the cheek. They both blushed crimson, but their hands met and they held on.

"I think that we should let immediate family know perhaps today at lunch, if you will stay," Caleb suggested.

"*Jah*, I would not be able to hide this from Rebecca and Samuel if I tried," Ruby said. "But I would not want this made known until the end of harvest, as is proper."

"It will be hard to wait. But I would not trade a month less waiting on your happiness. But you will be my intended the first day of the wedding season. I'll wait not a moment longer than that," Caleb teased.

"No, my Caleb. I'd not be willing to wait longer either," she agreed.

And they walked back into the home completely unaware of the glow of happiness all about them.

The Bishop arrived as did the rest of the community. They read *Gott*'s Good Word and they prayed. For Caleb, three hours of service never went by so quickly. His voice rang out with joy as he sang and, to him, the words of the Bishop seemed especially full of the spirit today.

Before he knew it, the service was over, and people were taking their leave. He asked Samuel to stay for lunch and to help set up the youth meeting with him. Samuel was happy to oblige.

"You and Ruby look exceedingly happy this day," Samuel teased his friend.

"I cannot lie. She makes me that way," Caleb replied. "I have business to speak with you, but this is not the day for it. Might I stop by tomorrow after lunch then?"

Samuel knew not to push thoughts of work on the Lord's day and agreed. He was, however, intrigued by the conversation. If it were about Ruby, there would be no business in that. This must be something else entirely. A day was not a long wait for a patient man and Samuel was a patient man. He would wait.

"Let us set up the net, then see what might be for our luncheon," Caleb replied.

The net was in the barn and the area for it, close by. It took only minutes to get the net up and square enough to play. They looked at their work, nodded to each other and went in.

Inside, Ana had organized the women and had plates with cut meats, cheese and fruit waiting. The three men were served, then the women, and the conversation ranged from the service to the weather. Jacob agreed to show Samuel where to fish and Caleb offered up use of his rod for the day. He was glad his *vater* was a friend to his friend Samuel as well.

The women, seeing the men were going to stay the day, decided to make a dinner for all to enjoy together, and their discussion went to planning what to make and who would help with what.

It was not long after lunch that the youth of the community filtered back into the farm. Caleb saw neither John nor Peter come this day. He was somewhat glad for that as he had more work to do on his end of things. He did notice that the twins spent much of the first half hour with their necks on swivels, looking all about for someone that was not there.

As was the custom, they prayed and played and spoke with their peers. After a time, they prayed again with the crowd thinning discreetly while prayer wound down.

Caleb, at the end of the service, walked over to Ruby and asked in a rather non-discreet voice for permission to drive her home. She blushed her acceptance.

"That was not subtle, Mr. Fisher," Ruby whispered in mock horror.

"I'll not let another waste his time thinking of asking my Ruby to court," Caleb replied in turn with mock seriousness.

They held hands and laughed their way to the buggy.

"Where are you taking me? Our families have agreed to eat together this evening."

"I thought we might go gather up our fishermen and give them a ride back," Caleb offered up.

"You mean to lay claim to me, Caleb Fisher. I see through you like a clean window," laughed Ruby.

"You know me already," Caleb said wistfully. "Now let us see how long we can make this ten-minute ride take, shall we?"

They talked and laughed to the stream, then teased and laughed with Jacob and Samuel all the way back, and their hands never parted for a moment of it.

Dinner in the Fisher's large dining room was a rousing success with the families sharing stories. Samuel talked of how he saw his farm growing in the future to be more like the Fisher's, and Jacob offered advice on how to bring the King farm back to its former size and stature in the community.

After the meal, Caleb looked at Ruby for her nod of approval and upon seeing it, stood.

"Family, I am right honored to have you all here. I hope you noticed I did not say families." At this the room became even more silent. "While we do not intend to be public about it until the fall, Ruby has agreed to become my wife. I am blessed beyond my dreams not only with my future bride, but with my family ... both those I have grown up with and more recently, the new family I have grown to care for."

The table exploded with congratulations and Lizzie and Emma squealed with joy as they were oft to do, exclaiming in unison to Ruby, "You are marrying the *dunderkopf?!*"

The gathering went quiet again until Ruby answered, *"Jah,* I am marrying the *dunderkopf."*

At that, everyone broke into fits of laughter, even Caleb. The women agreed to keep this quiet and make what preparations were needed. The rest of the night went by too quickly for all.

As darkness neared, the Kings said goodbye to the Fishers and made their way home with much animated discussion and laughter.

8

Monday morning saw the dairy man at the house just after midnight to pick up Sunday's milk, then again a few hours later to pick up Monday's offerings. It was more work for them, but Jacob was of the old way. He'd do no business on a Sunday. The cows needed milking, but he'd not allow that milk to be sold on Sunday.

Chores went by quickly for Caleb and before he knew it, it was time to go see Samuel. He let his *vater* know that he would be going to market after to order and pick up the paints and whatever else they might need for the week. His *mutti* gave him her list and off Caleb went.

Samuel met Caleb by the barn with a handshake and a greeting of *"bruder"*. It made Caleb happy inside knowing that he and Ruby would always have family this close by.

"Samuel, I was out at the Beiler farm. It seems the Lord has blessed them with more calves than they can keep. They will have at least six head available for the auction."

"I might get two or three to start building up my herd," Samuel began hesitantly.

Caleb broke in and added, "Yes and I might want two and, if we could save the Beiler family from paying the auction fee and we avoided the auction fee, we might save enough to make it more affordable for both of us."

Samuel was grateful that Caleb seemed to understand that the finances of growing a farm were delicate and that every penny was important to them.

"So, you think we might get the six for the price of five then?" Samuel asked.

"I think we can make a fair price with this man," Caleb replied. "Perhaps a better one if we can get that old cattle wagon out back there in working order to pick them up when they are ready."

"Then I will make time to get it rolling. Yes, let us do this. It will be a fair deal for all three involved. I would like to go with you when you strike this bargain. I need to know and be known to my community better."

"I'd have it no other way, *bruder.*" Caleb replied warmly. "Speaking of which, I would be remiss if I did not speak to Ruby before I depart. She might come to her senses and find a better man than I." Caleb laughed as they walked together to the *haus.*

Ruby, having overheard the end of the conversation, met the two with cups of coffee at the kitchen entrance and then turned to Caleb.

"I'd not be reminding me what a poor catch you are," she teased. "The way you describe yourself makes being an old maid sound better and better."

Behind her, she heard Rebecca stifle a laugh.

He shrugged even as he reached out to hold her hand, "I am nothing more than you see before you. But I offer it to you with all of my heart."

"You are shameless." She blushed and laughed with him. "You already have my yes and you still plead at me so. I will give you no more than thirty years to stop that."

"I fear we may have scheduled our first argument then. For in a mere thirty years I will clearly need more time," Caleb replied.

Samuel and Rebecca could take no more. Rebecca broke into a fit of laughing first. Samuel did his best, but followed a few moments later.

In their levity, Rebecca looked to Samuel. "It was only a while ago when you had such stars in your eyes for me."

"My dear Rebecca," Samuel tried to sound offended, "I never sounded quite so sappy. I do recall I could barely speak a sentence without stuttering near you for almost the first month we courted."

"Yes, that is true enough, but your heart spoke to mine around those twisted phrases. did it not?" She then added in a louder voice, "I had planned to mention this later, but this is as opportune a time as any. I wish to go on record as being very happy for *all* the additions to our family."

Caleb and Ruby looked to each other and smiled. Then as one, they got a confused look and turned to Samuel and Rebecca who had silly smiles plastered on their faces. It came to each as one and a chorus of joy went up.

Samuel stood by his bride and his hand went to Rebecca's belly as if it would magically rise like bread dough.

"We had planned to tell you last night, Ruby, but the night was full of your joy," Samuel said, then teased, "And once we are rid of all your belongings, we might even have room for another couple *kinder* in the years to come."

"It is great news you share! Samuel, I would speak more with you, but I am in need of supplies from town. Perhaps you might come with me and let the women talk *bobblin* for a bit?"

"Yes, go on. I have made up a list for later this week. Go! Talk your man talk while we discuss the important things," teased Rebecca.

So the men went to town and the women went back to the endless work in the *haus*, though they did more talking and laughing than real labor. The men, likewise, felt the blessings of the Lord upon them as they went about the afternoon's errands.

It was not until Wednesday when Samuel brought Ruby to quilt that the men got to speak again.

"I got the old wagon out and it was in better shape than it looked. I replaced a few planks and greased up the wheels. I think we should be in fine shape," Samuel advised.

"*Gut*. I am thinking of going to see John this Friday morning. Let's bring the wagon to him and see about making this deal."

Samuel couldn't understand why they would bring the wagon, but he trusted his friend and thought no more of it. There was much to do with the early hay harvesting and replanting, so they parted with a handshake and went back to their respective farms.

Caleb had most of his early crop cut and raked into rows drying. He would finish cutting today and perhaps start making his piles. Some farms used mechanical bailers, but Samuel did not sell theirs, it was all for their own use as feed.

He preferred to make the old-style piles with what did not fit in the loft. Leaving the *haus*, Caleb saw his *mutti* and Naomi picking the crop of peas in big baskets. They would sit later and all help with the cleaning and canning of them. Caleb also knew that meant fresh sweet peas for dinner tonight. It was a simple pleasure, but wasn't that the best part of farm living?

Off he went to do what needed doing. There was an order to successful farming which involved much work and little play. Caleb was born to this life and embraced it.

The day ended with him driving his Ruby back home, managing again to spend twice the time it takes to make the trip. They talked nothing and everything as all new couples do, and said their goodbyes too soon it seemed.

"I am coming on Friday to get Samuel to look at some calves," Caleb said. "I get to see you again this week, much to my good fortune."

Ruby smiled down at him as he helped her from the carriage. It was as if the world had warmed and given him a hug all at once. His heart squeezed suddenly at the joy of it all.

She entered her *haus* and Caleb did not turn to leave until she was safely inside, then he started the ride back home. He had extra work to do this evening.

Arriving back home, he lit the kerosene lamps inside the *grosshaus* and began to paint the inside.

He had found that Ruby was not partial to bold colors, but did like pastel blue more than any other. That was the color he was painting now in their bedroom. He blushed at the thought of it being their bedroom, then went back to the work of painting. No time for wandering thoughts.

He got two rooms finished that night and another two on Thursday after the sun went down. By Friday, he was looking a bit haggard, but was nearly finished with the interior.

Ruby commented on his looks when he arrived to get Samuel late Friday morning. "Are you well, Caleb? Have you taken cold?" The worry was clear in her voice.

"No, my Ruby. I am well. More so for being here with you and hearing your loving voice," he whispered to her.

She got him coffee which brought an even larger smile to his face.

After niceties were exchanged, Samuel and Caleb left, taking Caleb's wagon and Samuel's cart as well. They drove side by side as much as they could, both to speak and avoid one riding in the dust of the other. They approached the Beiler farm right on time to meet John Beiler coming back from the small barn.

"Ah, Caleb!" John Junior called. "I was coming to see you tomorrow. Six are available, but one of them is a bull. We were blessed with two bulls … we will keep one, but the other must go."

"John, this is my *gut* friend, Samuel King. He now owns the old Lapp farm near mine."

"Pleased to meet you, Samuel." John offered his hand. "That is a right *gut* farm you have. *Herr* Lapp had quite a herd on it. Some of these," he said waving his hand at some of the herd behind him beyond the fence, "came from that land when he sold off. So, you are the friend Caleb mentioned? It would be right for some of these to find their way back to the place they came from. Let us figure a price." The man paused to remove his hat and wipe his brow. "How many did you want, and do you want the bull as well?"

Bulls were a blessing and a curse. They were vital to being able to increase your herd without having to pay a stud fee to another, but they did not tend to get along well with other bulls. John, having no use for the bull calf, could always sell it at auction for a good price.

"I had not thought to be buying a bull this year," started Samuel. "But let us see what we come up with and make our decision on the facts, shall we?"

The three men did their business, doing some haggling that while serious was always cordial. In the end, Samuel and Caleb bought all six, getting a fair price and the bull, which Samuel needed but had not planned for. Then Caleb did an odd thing.

"We have a deal then, John. But, I will need you to deliver them to my farm for me in two weeks. Would that Saturday work for you? We will leave the cart to load them in here for you."

Both Samuel and John looked at him oddly. Then, shrugging, John simply agreed.

Samuel unhooked his wagon and tied his horse behind Caleb's rig. They shook hands with John and let him know they would pay him on the day of delivery, as was usual. Then the two friends got into the wagon and began the trip back to Samuel's farm.

"I am pleased we got the cattle from him, Caleb. He seems a fair man. He is old for his years, *jah?*" said Samuel.

"It is funny, when you meet him away from his farm, he is a boy, but he is all man on that farm for certain. He was kinder than he needed to be, Samuel. He could have gotten more for that bull at auction, even after paying the fees. It is important that you know that he did this as your neighbor, wishing you good fortune on your farm," Caleb advised.

"*Jah,* when you and I spoke, I expected to add two cows. Now I have a cow and a bull! I may be able to avoid auction and grow my own herd now," Samuel said enthusiastically, praising both his friend and the Lord.

"About that," Caleb started. "I have a stud bull already that I would lend you this fall. I would ask that when your bull gets of age that we might swap them back and forth to make the herds' blood lines stronger. We can avoid having to bring in studs to sire their calves this way."

Samuel immediately saw the good that both farms would get from this and agreed to Caleb's plan. In his head, he could see his farm coming to life.

9

The next two weeks flew by much the same. The women were busy canning the garden crops and making cheeses as needed. Wedding and baby talk took up most of their free time.

The men worked the fields, worked the herds, and Caleb worked on the *grosshaus* including cleaning the chimney, repointing the stone where the mortar was weak, and making it ready for his future bride.

Many newly married went back to live with their separate families until they could have a home of their own. Caleb and Ruby would start their married lives in their own home. Caleb felt the days were flying past, yet the fall was taking forever to get here.

On Friday of the second week, he told his *schwestere* there would be company coming on Saturday. John would be delivering the cattle to them. Lizzie went as white as a sheet. She had not seen him since that horrible day.

"Why is he coming here?" Lizzie asked, her voice tight. "Couldn't he take them to Samuel's farm?"

"You cannot hide from him forever, nor he from you," Caleb said flatly. "It is done, he is coming."

He couldn't tell if it was eagerness or fear he saw on Lizzie's face. Had he been able to read her mind, he'd have no better idea which it was.

Sure enough, John pulled up mid-Saturday morning with the six young cattle in the cart. Caleb made him welcome and they went inside to speak.

A few minutes later, Samuel came in and the men took care of their business. John went out to unhitch his horse from the rigging and Caleb joined him.

"John," Caleb began. "Do you recall our conversation a while back?"

"*Jah,* about the cattle," John offered, hoping to avoid the other topic.

"No, John. The one before that." Caleb tried not to laugh at the near-panic on John's face. "Please wait here a moment. Let us get past this. No matter what, you should not miss meetings for avoiding each other."

"Lizzie has not gone either?" John asked, surprise in his voice.

"No, and my *mutti* has made it my job to remedy that," Caleb replied with clearly mock fear in his voice.

"Well, then," John nodded, agreeing hesitantly. "We should not get you into trouble."

John sat on a stump under the shade of a tree in the side yard while Caleb retrieved his equally unsettled *schwester.* He brought her over to where John was waiting and tried not to laugh as they could not actually look at each other. They stayed silent for a minute, then three, and at five Caleb had had quite enough.

"Lizzie!" he said loudly, startling them both out of their silence. "I believe you owe this man an apology, *jah?*"

"Jah," she said holding back tears. "Not that I deserve to be forgiven, but he deserves to hear it." The rest came out in a rush. "I am a foolish child. I thought to play a prank upon you and thought that you had eyes for Emma."

She continued, taking a deep breath. "When Emma was not there, I pretended to be her. I thought you did not know. I was wrong for deceiving you."

"Why did you say nothing if you did not wish to ride with me, Lizzie?" John pleaded.

"She always had eyes for you. I could not think of you that way. As we drove, I found that I finally understood what she saw in you, but I could never steal Emma's dream. Little did I know that she had a different dream in mind." Lizzie was valiantly holding her tears in, the truth clear in her voice.

"Lizzie, I knew that Emma looked at me that way. It is why I never spoke to you before. When I saw her with Peter, I saw my chance. When you switched back, I felt that I had been played a fool. Why did you two do that to Peter and I?"

"Each of us thought that each of you was attracted to the other of us," Lizzie said.

"That is as tangled a statement as it was a thought," John said flatly. "How could any mistake you?"

It was at that point that Caleb came to Lizzie's aid.

"Um, John," Caleb said sheepishly. "They fooled me earlier that week, and until Ruby, and now you, no one could be certain which was which when they were around."

"I have always seen the difference. Your eyes have more sparkle to them. Your face blushes from the tops of your cheeks down, and you always put your hands together when nervous," John said, surprising her. Then he surprised her again. "Lizzie, if you promise me no more games, I would like to have a chance to know you better. I'd be honored to drive you home after meeting tomorrow."

Silent tears fell against her cheeks. She finally blurted out a "yes," then an, "I'd like that very much," before running into the *haus*.

Caleb turned to John and smiled. "*Viel gluck* with that one."

John smiled, and as he was walking to his horse, he stopped and turned, "This is why you had me deliver the cattle, isn't it?"

Caleb just nodded and asked if he might be available for a bit of *spiel* on Tuesday. He needed a few helpers to paint the outside of the *grosshaus*. John's head turned at that and looked Caleb over quickly, then agreed to come help.

"We don't need to speak to too many about this. I think you, Samuel, *vater*, myself and perhaps one more should be plenty. *Jah?*" Caleb remarked.

John understood what he meant. He felt honored that Caleb would trust him with this confidence. "I will look forward to it," he said before leaving.

Too quiet to be heard, Caleb said to only himself, "That went well, now only one more."

An hour or so later, another wagon came up the path. Emma and Lizzie had gotten over the giggles and grins of one of them being happy again, and paid the wagon no notice. They continued helping their mother with the last of their evening meal preparations.

Jacob came into the room and looked out the window, not recognizing the rig, then looked to Caleb who was clearly hiding a huge grin.

The wagon came to a stop and Caleb said, "Emma, I have gotten you an early birthday present. It appears to be here now. Come, let's get it together."

Emma jumped for joy. Her birthday was two weeks away, and she loved presents. She flew out through the house and out the front door with Caleb trailing behind, almost knocking the delivery man down. As she went to say her apology, she saw that it was Peter.

"What? Why are you here?" she said, most likely unaware of the accusatory tone of her voice.

"Well, hello to you too, Emma. It is Emma you are going by today, *jah?*" Peter replied.

Her eyes dropped to her feet and Peter immediately felt horrible for his words.

"I am sorry," they both said together, and a nervous laugh later … each said their sorry separately.

"Peter," Emma started. "I am sorry. I had a wonderful time with you until I heard Lizzie say that you had us mistaken. I thought she liked you, so I tried to not like you and let her be happy."

"And you thought none could tell you apart?" Caleb heard for the second time today.

Caleb replayed aloud the earlier conversation he'd had with John, and Peter shook his head, unconvinced.

"Caleb, I have finished what you asked of me. I have it here." He walked to the wagon and pulled out the replica Amish doll house. From the front, it was a classic farmer's home, while the back was open for dolls to be added.

"I do not make these normally, but I was willing to try. I am in your debt. While building this one at the market, I had six more ordered for Christmas presents. They take no longer to make than a decent chair, and the price they offered was equal to a table with four chairs!"

"I am glad some good came to each of us then," Caleb replied. "Here is the money we agreed upon." Turning to Emma, he continued, "I know you are old to be playing with dolls, but I hope you like this."

Emma, in tears, replied, "I will treasure it always."

She turned swiftly to go back into the house.

"I am sorry for upsetting her, Caleb. I do like her, but she still acts as a child. I thought her more a woman when I offered to drive her home." Peter then got back in his wagon, pulling away slowly.

Caleb stood with the dollhouse in his hands, saying again to himself, "Well, that might have gone better."

10

Sunday came and the services were all the way at the other end of the district. Everyone got up and going early, then made their way to the Yoder's farm. Because of the distance, they packed a basket lunch and planned a picnic between the service and the meeting after for the young adults.

The ride there was relatively uneventful, which was to Caleb's liking. The sun shone brightly down on Caleb who was accompanied by Naomi in the open buggy. The rest of the family traveled in the closed carriage.

Naomi looked up to him, asking, "Why is Emma so sad?"

He wondered how much a thirteen-year-old would understand about dating and decided to go with, "I am not sure, maybe she just needs more hugs."

The look he got in return let him know that she thought less of his opinion than before he answered.

"Perhaps that is a better question for Emma?"

"I think you must be right," came the response.

They both chuckled and kept the small talk going all the way there.

Bishop Yoder was his usual, charismatic self as he led the prayers and the hymns, choosing to read from Proverbs and spending a while on the importance of Proverbs 3:5, *"Trust in the Lord with all your heart, and lean not on your own understanding; in all your ways acknowledge Him, and He shall direct your paths."*

After the service had ended some three or so hours later, Samuel, Rebecca, and Ruby came over to where the Fishers had set up under a tree and joined them. Not long after, came a blushing Lizzie and a smiling John. They all sat and began to pray before the meal, heads bowed. After the prayer, Emma was surprised to look up and see Peter standing there before her.

"Do you have a moment, Emma?" he asked.

"Yes, of course," she said, worry clear in her voice.

"This will take but a moment, then you can get back to your lunch," he apologized.

They walked far enough away to be private, then Peter began to speak. "I was listening to the sermon today." He hesitated, trying to find his words. "I am compelled to come speak with you, Emma. I felt from the first time I saw you that I was drawn to you. I feel that was the Lord's hand. I do not understand why what happened did, but today's service is a reminder that I am but a man. It is not for me to understand. I would like to get to know you, but must be clear. I do not seek a girl. I seek the woman I met that first day, and fear if that is not you, we will not have much to say to each other."

"Peter," Emma said as she smiled, now feeling hope. "Would it be too forward of me to invite you to join our lunch? We brought enough to feed a barn raising. So, there is plenty."

"Give me a moment to tell my uncle, then I will return," he said, and sure enough a few minutes later, he came to the tree and was introduced to all, then sat with the group. They all ate quietly, enjoying each other's fellowship.

"We should offer to help set up," Peter remarked after the meal was finished.

Emma jumped up and agreed. John and Lizzie followed close behind them.

"This is your doing, Caleb, isn't it?" said Ruby, wide-eyed.

"I prefer to think of this as the Lord's work. I was just the hammer He used to move them out of their own way," he replied, not wanting to take credit.

"Ruby," Caleb began, his thoughts turning to the fall. "Would you have a white house, or one that has a color to it?"

"Caleb," she replied. "I'd have any house so long as it had you. But yes, I am a bit old fashioned. I am not taken with bright colors. A nice white or grey would be fine when we can afford one of our own. Why do you ask?"

"It is proper to get to know each other, is it not?" Caleb replied, not answering her question at all.

"It is," she agreed. "What color would you have then?"

"I was thinking the yellow of the school bus for the *Englishe*," he said as seriously as he could.

It took about a second for Ruby to know she had been had, then the whole group laughed again.

She teased him back, "I take it back, Caleb. I would not live in a school bus with you."

Rebecca and Samuel stood to say their good byes. "We need to speak to the bishop after lunch to volunteer our home in the rotation for services." Was their excuse for parting.

Before they went off, Caleb caught Samuel.

"Would you be able to help paint our *grosshaus* on Tuesday?" asked Caleb.

Samuel agreed with a smile and a nod of his head. "I will work with Rebecca to keep Ruby too busy to figure anything out."

Later, Caleb caught Peter alone and asked him for help as well.

"I have a stall I usually manage on Tuesday," started Peter. "But I think I can find someone to watch it for me."

Caleb thanked him and went to find his Ruby.

While their plan may have been to keep their blossoming romance a secret, no one could look at them without knowing. They sat next to each other so tight that light could not find a gap between them. Without trying, they finished each other's sentences when they spoke, and held hands nonstop.

They had but a few more weeks before they would speak to the bishop and have their engagement announced. They spent the meeting talking alone with each other, sharing dreams and tomorrows. They sang together, prayed together, then they left the meeting together.

Caleb smiled as he saw Emma leaving with Peter and Lizzie with John. He gave his intended a quick chaste hug, then stretched his arms before climbing into the buggy for the long ride home. Any who saw him stretching so would think he was trying to hug the entire world at once. If they saw in his head, they would see that was near the truth of it.

A Harvest of Brides

The Fishers

(An Amish Life 3)

1

Tuesday morning and the sun had not yet gotten a chance to kiss the dew on the blackberries along the path leading to the Fisher farm. Caleb was awake. This was his way. A farmer's life, like his father and the men in the Fisher family for generations past.

While most days found Caleb doing the very same things as they did all their lives, this day was to be special. There was a minor *spiel* at his farm this day.

Caleb, his father Jacob, his new friend Samuel King, John Beiler, and Peter Miller were all due after breakfast to help paint the *grosshaus*. This would be all the indication the area would have that a wedding was coming.

His *mutti* always planted an abundance of celery, a staple of every Amish wedding, so the rows and rows of it in the garden would not have told a passerby who knew them. But to put fresh paint on an empty house was as much a wedding announcement in an Amish village as a photo in the newspaper was to the *Englishe*.

Truth be told, Caleb did not mind the world knowing that Ruby had agreed to be his bride. She was a *godly* woman with the skills of a farm wife. He did not mind the way her smile warmed him either.

He got dressed and began getting the cows set for milking. It was a bit early for them and more than one let him know of the displeasure of slumber interrupted. He would normally leave this for the twins, but since their gentlemen callers would be here today, it was important to them that they assist with the meals and refreshments.

It was going to take a bit for Caleb to get used to his little sisters having gentlemen callers. These two seemed right *gut*. He had known John Beiler his whole life and had never been given cause to dislike him.

Emma's Peter was a visitor to the area, but had proven himself to Caleb both with his carpentry skills and with his ability to forgive. *Gott's own hand was upon this man,* Caleb thought, and not for the first time.

Milking went by so quickly that Caleb had to make sure he'd not missed any. He set the milk into the coolers the state had mandated they have. They used to be able to sell this as a class B milk for cheese, but now the state demanded these cooling tanks.

It was *gut* to get the better price for the milk and cream, but it required a diesel generator to supply power. They might have to have the coolers, but they would not be beholden to the outside world to provide the power for it.

The Fishers were more traditional than most, yet they were also a very practical people. They had put a kerosene refrigerator in their *kich* a few years back. Thinking of the *kich* got Caleb's stomach set to rumbling. It would take a big breakfast to keep that particular part of him quiet until lunch time.

As he entered the mud room, the smells called out to him … aromas of coffee, bacon or ham, eggs, and something sweet. He quickly cleaned up and went to join his family. A pan of potatoes sizzled on the stove next to the rest of the feast.

"*Gut,*" he announced. "I feared I would have to eat the new cow I was so hungry."

"You can have beef once or milk for all her days, Caleb." Came his mother's voice, using the same words probably used by every dairy farmer ever. "Which would you rather?"

"*Mutti,*" Caleb replied. "With the way you cook, I can do no wrong either way."

"Save that flattery for Ruby, young man," Ana replied, trying to hide her amusement. "She is young enough and so enchanted with you to think it true."

A good laugh was had all around at that, and Jacob led them in prayer before their meal. Caleb dug in to his meal with gusto. Fresh air and the sweet smell of honey bread in the form of rolls were his sustenance.

The family ate and talked, talked and ate, and as the meal wound down, they prayed again for *Gott's* blessing upon the day.

A knock fell on the front door as prayers finished. Caleb excused himself to answer it and was not surprised to see Samuel there. Living closest out of the invited friends for the *spiel*, he had by far the shortest ride.

"I thought you could use a hand helping set up the ladders and tarps," he said, explaining his early arrival.

"I set most of them out last night," Caleb replied. "But join me for a cup of coffee and catch me up on your farm."

"Not much to catch up on." Samuel followed him into the *kich*. "I sent the women to the big town to buy leather for me today. I knew you'd not want Ruby to see this work in progress."

"She will see it finished tomorrow when she comes to sew with Emma and Lizzie," replied Caleb. "It is why I chose this day. I am glad for the clear weather."

The two friends had just finished their coffee when a wagon pulled up. Peter and John had traveled together and now the painting crew was complete.

Hands were shaken, thanks and greetings were exchanged, then they set out to have their "fun". Caleb led the way to the *grosshaus* with a spring in his step.

Days like this were called *spiel* because they were a welcome diversion from the daily chores, and a chance to have fellowship outside the confines of church services.

Upon arriving, he knelt near the paint cans, then quickly stood again.

"I want to thank all that are here," he began. "As some of you know, and many might guess, this is to be my home with my intended, Ruby. We've let our families know, but until such time as we see the bishop, I trust all to keep this private. I know each of you to be of good character and look forward to having you there with us on the day of our union."

A small cheer went up and Caleb's back was slapped a few times as the men did what Amish men do, they divided up the materials and set to work. They split into two groups of two painting the long sides while Jacob painted the peaks of the short sides from the top of the ladder. In this way, any spilled paint would drop on the ground as opposed to a head.

Caleb spent the morning with Peter. He admired the ease with which he painted. Slow strokes, but they covered completely. He was truly a craftsman.

"So," Caleb began, "your craftsmanship on that dollhouse was inspired. It reminded me of my own home."

"It is funny you say that," Peter chuckled. "I'd no idea what to make it look like so I drove past and looked your home over a few times to try to match it as best I could."

Shifting the topic from himself, he remarked. "Say, did you see the Lapp farm is now occupied?"

"The young lady that has agreed to marry me is from that family. That is her *schwager*, Samuel, here to help us paint," Caleb said, pointing towards the man. "I will introduce you proper at lunch."

"Thank you. I'd like that very much," came the eager reply.

The rest of the morning was spent getting to know each other better. Caleb tried hard not to be the big brother, but there were things he wanted to know about this man.

What he did learn pleased him. And at about the time he came to that conclusion, the women came out with lunch in baskets for them. Not surprisingly, John's basket was made and carried to him by Lizzie and Peter's by Emma.

They all sat at a nearby picnic table, prayed together, then dug in with both hunger and the desire to show appreciation to the respective cooks. Both suitors had the good sense to say wonderful things about the baskets they were brought. Caleb knew that there was little need to fake delight when either of them cooked for you. He was glad John and Peter were honest in their words.

"Samuel, before we get back to it, I have been errant in my duties as host. Have you met Peter Miller?" Caleb asked, drawing the two closer after the meal.

"I think I have seen him, but his attention was directed elsewhere," Samuel teased, glancing quickly toward Emma and Lizzie who were now cleaning up after the meal.

"I'm glad to make your acquaintance," Peter began. "I was telling Caleb here that I drove by this way a while back and I saw that you had taken up at the old Lapp farm."

"*Jah, Herr* Lapp came and offered it up after meeting me several times. I was blessed with the opportunity," Samuel responded.

"Would you know who owns the wooded area just past your place?" Peter asked. "I noticed it has poplar, oak, maples and unless I am wrong, a good stand of ash trees on it." His excitement was tangible.

"I am sorry. I don't." Samuel said, shaking his head, the desire to be more helpful clear in his voice. "I think I know the place you mean, though I can't tell an ash from an oak myself."

"I think I know the land you speak of," came Jacob's voice from behind them. "Are you sure you went past the Lapp ... I mean, King farm before seeing those ash trees?"

"I cannot be for certain, but thought so," Peter said.

"I helped John Lapp plant a field of ash trees on the far side of his farm in payment for him teaching a young lad here to "bend hot metal", as he liked to call it. Perhaps that is *your* land, Samuel."

"It appears we will not need the whole day for painting. We could take a ride out that way?" offered Caleb, who then added, "Perhaps the ladies could come with us for the ride?"

With satisfaction, he saw his *schwestere's* unhappy looks change to smiles once they were included in the plan.

"*Jah, gut,*" replied Peter. "I'd have an interest in those trees if you've a mind to sell them to me, Samuel."

"Let us see if they are mine to sell," he replied. "But first, let us finish this painting so that I might be one step closer to having quiet in my home."

Samuel laughed with the others at his own comment, knowing that while the *haus* would be quieter, he and Rebecca would be glad to have Ruby so close by with the baby coming.

By early afternoon, the painting was done, and everything was cleaned and stored away. Lizzie and Emma returned from the *haus* with a basket containing a pie.

"We can have a bit of a picnic as we look at your trees, Peter," said a blushing Emma. "I made blueberry pie."

"What are we waiting for then, let's get there quickly that I might have a slice of my favorite pie," Peter said, winking at Caleb.

Off they went, loading into the Fishers' wagon, except for Samuel, who drove his own home. They stopped at Samuel's drive and then he joined them, heading to the opposite side of the property.

"Here," said Samuel. "This is where my land ends."

Caleb saw the look of disappointment on Peter's face. He did not, however, notice the look of surprise on his *daed's*.

"Are you certain, Samuel?" came Jacob's question.

"See, there is the stake to mark it," Samuel replied, pointing.

"The trees are just up ahead," Peter said.

"On land that used to belong to *Herr* Lapp," stated Jacob, the puzzle clear in his voice. "*Herr* Lapp's lands went on for another quarter mile or so, as I recall. I wonder if he sold this to another, or if the stake was set wrong?"

This news had dampened the mood noticeably, but the twins got it back on track by reminding them they had pie to eat. They found a flat clear spot beneath the cool shade of the trees and served everyone a slice, while both Peter and John each got two.

Having eaten, they then rested and talked, enjoying the soft sway of the breeze-swept trees. A short time later, dropping Samuel at his door, they made their way back to the Fisher farm. All were talking in turns except for Jacob, who was deep in thought.

Goodbyes were said, and hands shaken. The twins ran inside and returned with a pie apiece for John and Peter to take with them. This had been a *gut* day, Caleb thought. Well, except for the part about the trees for Peter.

2

"Caleb Fisher!" yelled an excited Ruby, entering the Fisher farm the next day. "What have you done? I know we spoke of marriage, but I will not put your parents and sisters out of their home!" Her face was red and her chin tight as she looked upon him with resolve.

"Well then," Caleb replied, holding back his laughter. "It is a right *gut* thing that it is to be our home until my *schwestere* are all married off. Well, assuming they don't become angry old maids and frighten off their suitors."

At this, Caleb lost his resolve and began to laugh. The rest of the family, touched by Ruby's concern for them, tried as long as they could not to join in, but once Ruby began, they were all done for.

"I am sorry, Caleb. I should have known that you had a better idea and would not be so with your family. I would rather us wait than to put them out." Turning to Jacob and Ana, she continued, "You have made me feel a part of this family, each of you. I could not think of doing anything that would bring any sorrow or pain to you. Along with Rebecca and her Samuel, you are all my family."

"It warms my heart," Ana began, "that Caleb has found his match. Not only do you care for my son, you are filled with love for each of us. Please know that love is returned in full, Ruby. You are a Fisher in all but name, and Caleb will tend to that part in time. I would call you *dochter*, if you would allow it."

Ruby fought back tears. Not in her warmest dreams or her deepest prayers had she dared hope for anything so great as this. She cleared her throat to speak clearly, "No, Ana. You shall not call me *dochter.*" The family hushed. "Unless I might call you *mutti*, as Caleb does."

At that Ruby ran to Ana and held her. She would never get her *mutter* back, but it was good to have *mutti* Fisher to hug.

"We have sewing to do, Ruby," called out Emma, who began setting up for sewing in the front room. Upon Ruby's entrance, she continued, "Do you know the name of this pattern we are working?"

"My *mutti* always called it wedding rings. I'm not sure if that is the right name but that is how I know it." Ruby explained. "it has always been one of my favorite patterns. Rebecca has one that belonged to *mutti.*"

"Yes, it is the wedding ring design," explained Lizzie. "This will be our gift to you once finished."

"But we started this long before Caleb ever spoke to me," stated a shocked Ruby. "I could not. There is so much of your time and energy in this."

"We make a few of these a year. *Vater* has an *Englishe* that buys them and sells them to others," explained Emma. "Once we knew that it would be yours, we added the roses and vines in between the rings to make it yours and Caleb's"

"So, come now," chided Lizzie. "I'll not be the reason my friend Ruby has to postpone her wedding."

"That," agreed Ruby, "would simply not do."

She thanked them both, a warm feeling spreading outward from her heart. They sat side by side now, getting back to work, the three feeling a kinship deeper than before knowing what they were creating.

Weeks flew by with the summer making its closing obvious to those who knew the signs. The twins' courting continued, and it looked favorable for them both with their men. In but a couple of more weeks, Caleb and Ruby would be betrothed officially. It had been a quiet, happy summer for all.

Then came the Sunday that Emma came running into the *haus* crying. Peter had just dropped her at home and was quietly leaving in his courting buggy. Caleb looked out the window and saw that Peter's face looked down at his feet instead of at the path before him.

Caleb turned and called out to her. She was half-way up the stairs. "Emma, what is it? Did you and Peter have a falling out?"

"No," Emma sobbed, coming into the sitting room. "Yes, I mean, I just don't know."

Caleb was many things. He did not consider foolish to be one of them. He knew this was a job for either Lizzie, who was not yet home, or for his *mutter*.

"Hold tight, Emma," Caleb reassured. "I'll run for *mutti.*"

And run he did, up the stairs, down the stairs, and out into the garden before he found her.

"*Mutti*," Caleb gasped. "Emma needs you. She is crying."

"Finish weeding, Caleb," Ana told him as she stood to leave. "Take your time at it. We will not need you in the *haus* for a bit."

Caleb nodded his understanding. He finished up the few minutes of weeding that was left and walked out to the barn, feeling somehow inadequate and needing to regain his footing.

"Emma," Ana called. "Are you hurt, dear?"

"No, *mutti,*" she sobbed then. "Yes, *mutti*, but it is my heart that pains me."

"So, Peter is leaving, is he?" Ana asked with a knowing look.

"He is going to … Ohio," spat out Emma between sobs.

"But he is not from there, is he?" Ana questioned her *dochter*.

"He wants to have a furniture stall of his own. We have discussed this much over the summer. He wants to have a plot of land where he can cut trees to supply his own lumber."

"That sounds a right *gut* plan," Ana said, sure they had not yet come to the cause of all these tears. She asked cautiously, "And so, he means to leave without you then?"

"No, *mutti*. He wanted me to leave here to go with him," Emma cried and was then lost to her tears for a spell.

"Come, let's go in the *kich* and start the morning bread and discuss it more. It will not help you to lie here with your tears."

Emma's sadness did not leave, but the flow of tears reduced to a trickle and then stopped as she began doing the routine of her life, glad to have her *mutti* here with her. How would she ever leave her *mutti und schwestere?* How could Peter think it possible?

"Jacob," Ana said as they lay for the night. "Peter has asked Emma to marry."

"Are we to be happy about this, wife of mine?" Jacob teased.

"*Jah,* we are happy for the pairing. But Peter seems determined to take our Emma to Ohio," Ana said to the darkness, tension clear in her voice.

"Does he have family there?" wondered Jacob aloud.

"None," Ana said. "They will be alone there."

"Now, Ana," Jacob said, kissing his wife's forehead. "Samuel and Rebecca came here with no family, and it has worked out for them."

"It is bad enough to have Sarah and my *enkelkinder* a two-hour buggy ride away. To have my Emma gone away farther is too much."

"The choice will be hers to make, Ana," Jacob began. "We will support her however she decides. Now, why is it that Peter wants to go to a new place and start over?"

The two talked for another half hour, then they prayed for guidance, kissed, and went to sleep.

3

"Caleb," Jacob said to his son the next day. "I will need you to tend the farm these next three days. I have business that will require me to be away."

"*Daed,*" Caleb held onto Jacob's shoulder as he spoke. "If this concerns the farm, should I not come as well?"

Jacob replied, "This is not so much a farm matter as a family one. I will say no more of it other than I expect you to see to the land and family while I am gone and not worry any with my purpose."

"*Jah, Vater,*" Caleb replied. There were few things his father did not share with him. He could not fathom what this might be about.

As was usual on the rare times his *vater* had to travel, Caleb kept the farm running smoothly. If either Caleb or Jacob wanted to be truthful with themselves, Caleb was now running it with Jacob there to offer a lifetime of experience when needed. Neither man would give this thought life though. It was not in their manner.

Caleb was glad to see Ruby on Wednesday as the three women got ever closer to finishing the quilt. He hoped they would continue to quilt together even as they married off and had homes of their own. There was a peacefulness to the gathering that he knew he would miss if it ended.

That thought was interrupted by the sound of Jacob returning. Caleb hoped there would be more answers than before he left.

"*Vater*, it is *gut* to see you," Caleb said with a loud happy voice. "I trust your trip went well?"

"Not as well as I had hoped, but I am glad it is over with," was all that Jacob would say.

Caleb knew not to pry. Jacob went around him, greeting Ruby and the twins, then found Naomi and hugged her before turning and leading Ana out to the porch for some privacy.

Caleb did not consider himself a curious man. When he wanted to know something, he learned it and the concern was done. The rest of the week, not knowing what was going on, rubbed him like a burr under a horse blanket.

He went about his work expecting at each moment his *vater* would come and tell him what this was about, but it never occurred.

Sunday morning found him at services, this week at the Beiler farm. Caleb sought out Ruby to ask her opinion before the Bishop was to speak.

"Caleb," Ruby said, trying not to smile over what seemed a small thing. "It is most likely to do with our impending wedding. I think we need fret no more of this nor speak of it to others. Allow your *vater* privacy in this, *jah?*"

"This is one of the reasons we are so suited to each other. You find the easy answer while I try to find them all." Caleb gave her a quick hug then continued, "I shall be glad when I can call you wife."

"As will I. Now come let us pray for patience, I can hear people settling in," Ruby said, leading him into the room with her.

After services, Caleb and Ruby sought the picnic basket from Samuel's wagon, Ruby having prepared it beforehand since the drive back was too far to go and return for the youth meeting. They saw others doing the same around the yard, pulling blankets and baskets from their buggies.

While seeking out shade, Caleb saw John and Lizzie talking excitedly as they went inside to have lunch with his family. He smiled for them, then turned his head to seek Emma. What he saw was more curious, as Jacob was standing with Peter, not Emma. He wondered what passed between them.

"Ruby, do they look angry to you?" Caleb asked, drawing her attention to the pair across the yard.

"No, they look more determined than anything else. It is clear there is weight in their words, but no anger," Ruby answered, agreeing to what Caleb had only thought. "We will know in *Gott's* own time."

She continued, "Let us enjoy our lunch. We have few of these left before you make me an old married woman."

"It suits you better than being an old maid," Caleb said and received a playful slap for his humor.

Caleb was sad to see that Emma did not ride home with Peter. She had arranged with V*ater* for him to return for her. It was clear from both her and Peter's faces that neither much cared for this choice.

Caleb, as always, took his time driving Ruby home. They talked of furnishings for the home and what they already owned between them. She went on about the curtains she was sewing, and Caleb added an acceptable number of nods and sounds of agreement. Too soon they came to the King farm and said their goodbyes.

They were more fortunate than most as they got to see each other midweek when Ruby came to sew. Most young couples had but the time at meetings and the drive home together. Caleb realized again on the ride back to his home that they were surely blessed, as that was not their fate.

Arriving at the *haus*, he passed John's buggy still parked outside. A commotion could be heard from where he paused on the porch. Caleb stepped up his pace and went inside. Scanning the sitting room, he noted everyone was in a circle around Lizzie and John.

"Caleb," John walked towards him. "Lizzie has agreed to become my wife. It may be next spring before I will have a *haus* for us to live in, but neither of us wish to wait for next season, and Lizzie refuses to be a spring bride."

"I know it is done, but it will not be me doing it," Lizzie said, leaving no room for question.

"It is best not to argue with her when she takes that tone, John," Caleb advised shaking John's hand, then pulling him in for a hug.

"*Ach*, now you tell me this," John whispered back to him, and they both laughed.

"*Mutti*," Caleb joked, "it appears you will feed everyone twice this season. It is good that you grow so much celery each year to can creamed celery for the winter."

"Caleb, it is good you have taken a liking to creamed celery so that all I have grown these past years for your wedding has not gone to waste," Ana joked back, and everyone laughed with her.

Emma smiled and laughed for her sister and Caleb felt for her. This could not be an easy time.

After more fellowship, John begged his leave. "I must go let my *familye* know that I was blessed with a yes."

Lizzie blushed and replied, "It is I that am blessed, John Beiler. It is I."

John left to begin his drive home. While they were still gathered together as a family, Jacob cleared his throat to speak. "I have a request. I would ask you to do your sewing at Ruby's this week and if possible, to do it in the morning tomorrow. I have business here that I would like not disturbed."

He faced Caleb, "Drive your sisters and try not to be too much a bother to Ruby as she sews. Perhaps you could find something to help Samuel with on his farm."

4

Monday morning, the three were greeted warmly, albeit unexpectedly, and plans were altered to make Jacob's request work. Samuel had some items he had put off forging for the heat, and while not cool, this was not a bad day to get going on them.

Back at the Fisher farm, Peter arrived, tying his horse outside by the front porch. It was an odd thing. Jacob had spoken with him briefly yesterday about Emma, but demanded Peter come to see him today. He had been curious since.

"Peter," Jacob greeted him from the now open front door. "Come let us have coffee and discuss business."

Now it made sense. None would discuss business on a Sunday. "How may I be of service to you, *Herr* Fisher?"

"Firstly, you might call me Jacob. Having won my *dochter's* heart entitles you to that at least," Jacob said, removing any fear of ugliness from the conversation.

He poured coffee for the two of them and gestured towards the small kitchen work table. They both sat facing each other.

"My son is getting married, as you know. I would like to have a couple items either made or from your stock. They will need a bigger bed. The one in the *grosshaus* is small and pine, and was not built for long use."

"I have a very nice oak one all finished," Peter said, glad that he would not have to rush a piece like that, especially for a friend. He took his time on his furniture and it showed. "The *Englishe* that asked me to make it tried to lower the price when it was finished. I can have it here whenever you would like."

Jacob nodded his agreement on the piece when the cost was stated.

"What else is needed?" Peter asked.

"This, I fear, you will have to make for me. Ruby sold her linen chest well before moving here. I should like her to have one, but with four *dochtere*, I have no family pieces left to give her. I would want this to be a fine piece. Not all gaudy and gilt, but one that speaks of the love that we have for her."

"Jacob, I am honored to do this for you," Peter replied. "Let me draw you a sketch of what I had hoped to make for Emma."

"I do not mean to pry, but it is decided then? She has told you she will not go?"

"Her tone was clear enough. She intends to live out her days here. I cannot blame her. It is a wonderful area," Peter replied, shaking his head sadly.

"Yet you are determined to leave," prodded Jacob.

"No, sir. I am rather desiring to stay. I have looked for a wooded lot all this summer hoping that I might be able to, but I can find no land for sale here that fits my needs and budget. John Beiler's father even offered to cut off a dozen acres of farmland for me, but he has already cleared it. For most, that is a dream. Rich farmland indeed, but I am a carpenter. To support a family, I would need lumber of my own to harvest."

"I see that you have given this much thought and I can hear the truth in your telling of it as well. When did you plan to pack up and head west, then?" Jacob asked quietly.

"It was my thought to begin packing this week and leave next, but now will hold off a week that I might make this box for you, Jacob. I've come to know Ruby through Emma's eyes, and I'd have no other make this for her," Peter said with resolve.

"You are a *gut mann*, Peter Miller. A right *gut mann*," Jack said, shaking his hand and thanking him for coming out of his way.

Later that day, Jacob got a letter, an uncommon thing for him as he lived most of his life within buggy distance of those who would speak to him. Making the day that much more uncommon was the speed in which Jacob wrote the reply and made off to mail it from town. Afterwards, he came home to find all had returned.

"Lizzie and Emma, I would like to speak with you privately for a moment if I might," he announced.

Caleb took Naomi upstairs to read with her, leaving Jacob and Ana with the twins.

"*Dochtere,* for the last five, almost six years you have been making quilts for the family to sell at market," he began.

The twins sat nodding at him, then turned to each other, asking silently what this might be about. Neither saw an idea in the other's eyes and looked back at their *vater*.

"I have never told you of how I came to find the buyer for them, have I?" he asked, knowing the answer. "I have reason to share this with you now."

He settled in to a chair and the girls took a seat on the small couch. Ana left the room, leaving them to their discussion. He drew in a deep breath before beginning his story.

"The two of you had just finished a nice quilt and your mother asked me to take it to market with me when I went to buy goods for the home. I had it in a sack and after loading the wagon with our supplies, I took it to an *Englishe* sitting near a truck he was filling with items purchased at the market that day. I thought this might be a man interested in buying a quilt, so I asked him. Girls, he looked over the quilt front and back, not showing interest nor disapproval, then he said that he would be willing to buy it for two hundred dollars."

At this the girls looked at each other, then their *vater* again. "So much as that *daed?*" asked Emma.

Jacob nodded, then continued, "I was about to shake his hand when a woman started yelling at the man, called him a thief. I was not sure what was going on, but was certain I'd not have that two hundred dollars. That is when she grabbed my arm and spun me about. I did not know who this woman thought she was, but was certain that I did not like her."

"What happened then, *daed?*" both girls asked as one voice.

"What happened next was that this woman let go of me and apologized. She said that she knew once I had agreed to that deal I'd never take it back. She asked to see the quilt and looked at it with wide eyes. She spent about two minutes examining it, then eyed the man in the truck. The woman then told the man, 'I will tell them all what you tried here. I doubt you will be sold to if you are fool enough to return.' I asked her what was going on and she explained it to me. The quilt I was glad to have two hundred dollars for would have been sold again for close to a thousand dollars."

"What?!" both girls let out at once. "No one would pay that for a quilt," Emma said.

"I have seen yarn-tied quilts at markets for much less than that," remarked Lizzie.

"But the two of you do not do simple yarn ties, do you? You sew patterns onto the quilt and that takes even more time. The *Englishe* fill their time working for machines and have none to make something like this. They do, however, value the work of others."

Jacob paused, adding weight to his next words. "She made me an offer that day to sell them for you and pay me as they sold. She would keep twenty percent as she had no additional overhead and the only thing she would have to do was price them and haggle if needed. I have come to respect her ability to do so over the years."

"That is amazing, *daed,*" gushed Emma.

"So, she has sold all those that we have made these years," wondered Lizzie aloud.

"*Jah,* and that brings me to why we are speaking. Since that first, she has sold twenty-four of your quilts, totaling a bit over twenty thousand dollars after she took her part," Jacob said. "I had planned to save it for you to give you upon your wedding days, but I find the family has need of this money. I am asking your permission to use it."

The girls' eyes widened at the number. Emma turned to Lizzie and Lizzie to Emma and they squealed, hugging. This went on for nearly a minute before Lizzie looked back to Jacob.

"*Daed,* I will let Emma speak for herself, but I thought that whatever you got for them was long since spent on the farm. I felt glad to be helping. I will not let you take that from me by offering the money to me when the family has a need."

"You have not heard the need, *dochter,*" Jacob began to argue.

"And I never need to. If you say it is important to this family, I have all the information I need," Emma said, perhaps as curtly as she had ever spoken to her *vater.*

"I will not need the reason either, *daed.* We kept making the quilts because we enjoy it. We thought that some small help being given was a bonus. I have no need for that much money and even if I did, my *familye* comes first," Emma added.

Jacob hugged his girls and they hugged him back. This is how Ana found them as she rounded up help for the dinner meal.

"You can hug him later," Ana said. "Come set the table for dinner now." Her false harshness fooled no one.

To Jacob, she quietly asked, "What are you up to, husband?"

Jacob only smiled back at her.

Wednesday came and having already done their quilting for the week, the twins had time on their hands. They decided to help teach Naomi how to make different quilt squares and the patterns they knew.

"Naomi," Emma said, surprise in her voice. "You are a natural. We will have to include you in our bee next week."

"I have been watching you both for years and practicing with scraps. I'd be glad to join you," Naomi declared.

The three of them spent several hours talking and sewing, pleased to be together as only *schwestere* understood. They were so intent on their business that they missed the car pulling up to their *haus*.

A crisp knock on the door was answered by Ana. She saw an *Englishe* with papers in his hand.

"I am here to speak to *Herr* Fisher," the man began, but before more could be said, Jacob appeared as if from nowhere.

"I have this, Ana," he said, dismissing her.

Once she closed the door to the *haus*, leaving them on the porch, Jacob asked, "Are you from the bank?"

"*Jah, Herr* Fisher. I am John Lapp," the banker said. "No relation to your former neighbors. It seems you cannot toss a rock in this area and not strike a Lapp," he joked. "I was raised on a farm such as this. I think that is why the bank has me take care of cases like this. Shall we go somewhere private, so we can discuss our business?"

Jacob led the way to the *grosshaus* where they talked for a short time then, breathing a deep sigh, Jacob signed the papers he had been brought. With his copies in hand, the two men walked back towards the main house.

"I oft-times think I should never have left the community, *Herr* Fisher. It tugs at me every time I come close." Mr. Lapp walked to his car. "Good day to you, then."

Jacob Fisher took the papers quietly to his room and stored them away. When asked, he would say nothing of his guest nor their business, but frowned and remained quiet.

5

"I do not think *Frau* Beiler cares for me, Emma," Lizzie said in near whisper. "I do not think she approves of our plans to marry."

"What? Who could not like you, Lizzie," replied a surprised Emma.

"I've not wanted to burden you with this, but it is eating at me so. She is polite, but distant. I am sure she does not approve." Lizzie continued, "She wanted us to wait for next season to decide marriage. But John has already asked me."

"He is the last of her sons. Perhaps she is as worried for herself as for him," Emma said.

"What would she worry about?" asked Lizzie her face scrunched in confusion. "I love John and he me. I am certain of this."

"Maybe she thinks you chase him for his farm," laughed Emma. "Or perhaps she thinks you will have a tiny room made and force her to live out her days in it."

"Do not make me wish for something so mean-spirited, Emma," Lizzie laughed with her.

"When the Lord takes pleasure in anyone's way, he causes their enemies to make peace with them," Emma quoted from Proverbs. "Perhaps we should pray for the Lord's own guidance in this?"

"*Jah.* I would not want to call John's *mutti* enemy," Lizzie said, then began to pray on it deeply.

The following Monday found Peter at the King family farm. Samuel had asked him to stop while at services on Sunday. Since Samuel did not mention the cause, he came to think that it was business. He parked the wagon by the *haus*.

Samuel and Rebecca were expecting their first child and perhaps needed a crib or a bassinette. It was just as well to do today. He had the chest made for *Herr* Fisher and could deliver it while he was this way. As Peter contemplated this, Samuel rushed out of the *haus*.

"Come, Peter," he exclaimed, jumping aboard Peter's wagon. "Let us see those trees you wanted."

Peter was not sure where this was going, but he had come this far. "Alright, then. You will explain when we get there?" asked Peter.

"It will take no explaining at all, I am sure of it." Samuel said, eagerness clear in his voice.

A few minutes later, the men came to Samuel's property stake. Neither looked at it though. Neither did they look at the trees. Both stared at a bright yellow sign that clearly stated, "FOR SALE 30+ Acres," below which was a phone number.

Samuel had brought a pencil and paper, handing it to Peter. "I am not sure when the sign went up. I noticed it Saturday afternoon," Samuel advised. "It could have been there a while before I saw it, though."

"Thank you, Samuel," Peter spoke, with great interest. "I will drop you off, then go to a phone to speak with them about the land."

"I'd gladly call you neighbor if this works out, Peter," replied Samuel, clearly excited for the young man.

Peter dropped Samuel back at his *haus* and went straight to town for a phone. He knew some kept phones for emergencies, but he was not familiar with enough of the families to know who might have one.

"Hello," said the woman's voice at the other end of the line. "Country Real Estate, can I help you?"

"*Jah,* I saw a sign on a wooded lot with this number on it," Peter said, rushing his words in excitement.

"What address was the sign at?" the woman asked.

"It is near the King farm by the stream," Peter replied, unsure.

"Hold, please." The woman said, sounding much less interested in the call now.

"Hello?" came a man's voice now. "Did you mean to ask about the parcel next to the Lapp Farm?"

"*Jah,* it used to be the Lapp farm. Now it is the King farm," Peter replied.

"I was afraid of that," the man continued. "That land belonged to Mr. Lapp's daughter. She had no use for it and sold it."

"It is my *gut* fortune she had no use for it then. How much is she asking for the land?" replied Peter.

"I am afraid you misunderstand me," the man replied. "That land is already sold."

It was as if all the vitality drained from Peter, his hopes crushed. He would go deliver the box to *Herr* Fisher, then begin packing up his wares.

"Peter," exclaimed Caleb. "It is *gut* to see you. Are you here for Emma?"

"I am here for Jacob, but then, yes, I should also speak to Emma," replied Peter, the words falling like heavy stones.

Caleb patted him on the back and helped him carry a large box covered with a twine-tied tarp into the house. He then left Peter with his *vater* in the *kich*.

"Jacob, I have brought you the linen chest," said Peter.

"Let us see it then," remarked an excited Jacob.

Peter lifted the chest upon the table and unwrapped it. It was solidly built and sized to sit at the end of a decent sized bed.

"This is what you had envisioned to give to Emma, you said?" asked Jacob.

Peter then opened it and Jacob held his breath. He had lined the inside with cedar, but had spent time to fashion a heart along the back wall of the case with the deep red heartwood of the cedars.

"I've never seen that done, Peter," Jacob said with awe in his voice.

"It was my desire to protect her heart as it protected her belongings," came Peter's only reply.

"I'm not sure I can take this from you," Jacob said. "You have put much of yourself into this, *jah?*"

"I am going to begin packing today. I'll not see it damaged by a long move," Peter replied flatly. "I had thought I had wonderful news, but I was too late."

"What news would that be?" Jacob asked, shutting the chest and facing the clearly defeated man.

"Do you recall the wooded lot?" Peter started, then explained how his morning had gone for the next five minutes.

"It was bought by an Amish spinster," Jacob replied, nodding. "I heard that *Herr* Lapp's *dochter* sold it for less to keep it in Amish hands. She married and had moved a few counties away. It seems *Herr* Lapp wanted her to have some piece of the land she grew up on."

"A spinster you say," asked Peter, his chin lifting. "Do you think she would part with it?"

"I would not think so. I believe she intends to catch a husband with it," laughed Jacob.

While Peter might have found this amusing under ordinary circumstances, he saw no humor in it now.

"Perhaps though, you might ask her. She is here today. Let me go and get her," Jacob said, turning to leave the room.

In a few minutes, Jacob came back, Emma with him. Peter gave her a small smile, waiting for the owner to follow them into the room.

"She is coming?" asked Peter.

"She is here," Jacob replied.

"*Vater* said you had some business to discuss with me, Peter." Emma glanced at the large chest on the table, her eyes widening. "I hope you will not try again to get me to leave with you. I could not bear to go through that again," Emma said, her voice cracking as she did.

"But, Jacob. Where is the spinster you described to me?" remarked a bewildered Peter.

Emma's eyes grew wider and her face reddened. "Spinster!" she spat out.

"Not you, my Emma," Peter said.

With that, Emma's heart broke again, and all the rage fell from her.

"Your *vater* said that a spinster had bought up that piece of the Lapp farm and was here to speak with me of it."

"*Und* here she is, Peter," Jacob said, pointing at Emma.

"*Vater*, what is the meaning of this?" Emma said, her voice equal parts anger and confusion.

"What? I have heard Caleb call you spinster, have I not," Jacob teased Emma.

"*Jah, und* I think I like it even less in your voice than his," she huffed. "What is this about land?"

"It seems you now own the tract of land next to the Kings, *dochter,*" Jacob said, as if it were nothing unusual. "And this young man wants to buy it from you. I tried to explain that you were probably trying to get a husband for the land, but he still felt the need to speak with you of it."

"I am no spinster that needs trade land I do not own for a man to care for me," Emma stormed. She paced away then back toward the two men.

"Oh, but these documents say that you do own it, *dochter,*" Jacob said with a huge smile. He pulled a folded paper from his shirt pocket.

The truth hit her. Her *daed* had bought the land and meant to give it to her. "*Vater*, I cannot take this from you. You yourself said the family had needs." She dared not speak more of it, not wanting to embarrass her *daed*.

"The land belonged to *Frau* Mueller. She lives on a large farm in a different county. She was *Herr* Lapp's *dochter*. When I spoke with her, she said this was an answer to her prayers. Her *vater* wanted her to have a piece of her homestead, but she could not tend to it nor bear to sell to the *Englishe*. She agreed to sell it for the money you had from your quilts, as well as a quilt a year for the next three years for her *dochtere*. I felt you would not mind me committing you to such labors." Jacob finally explained it, so all would be clear.

"I would buy this land from you, Emma. It would let me stay here and be a part of this community," Peter said, turning to her.

"No, I think my *vater*, as usual, is right. I think the spinster who owns this will want a husband as part of the bargain. Do you stand by your previous offer, Peter? Even if a move is not a part of it?" asked Emma, her face serious.

"You are my reason for wishing to stay. I have never taken back my offer. I would gladly still accept your answer." Peter smiled, but his face suddenly fell. "I would feel better if I might buy the land from you. It would not do to have debt to my wife's family."

"It is not my family's money. Apparently, it is mine. I suggest you take the money you had saved for that land and begin to build us a home to live in."

"If you start now, you could be ready to move in by spring, Son," Jacob remarked.

"I will not be a spring bride!" Emma snapped out, sounding even more like her sister Lizzie.

"Then we will marry this fall," Peter offered. "And move in when the *haus* is ready in spring. Would that suit you better?"

"I find that offer acceptable. But," she then turned to her *vater*. "You will have to explain this to *mutti*. I will not tell her she is to feed the community three times. This will be on you, *daed*."

Emma hugged Peter and the two laughed as the look on Jacob's face changed from happiness to something akin to fear then back to happiness, repeating this pattern several times.

"Peter, I trust you understand that I will not have a use for this which you have made for me," Jacob said, after a bit. "I trust that you can find a use for it?"

"*Jah, vater* Fisher. I know just the use for it. Did you need another made?" Peter smiled as he realized that Emma was to get the chest he intended to build her after all.

"No, it seems I have one that none will need. I will use that," Jacob said.

Peter had never been so happy for a canceled order in all his life.

6

"That woman!" Lizzie fumed. "If she continues, I fear it will be the end of us, John."

"I am sure that *mutti* did not mean to insult you," John replied, even as he wondered to himself if he believed that. "She simply pointed out that we are young, and the responsibilities on a farm are many."

"Do you forget as well now that I have spent my whole life on a farm?" she replied, her irritation now aimed at her betrothed. "I know well the work of a farm. The cooking, the cleaning, the milking, and the making a *haus* into a home."

"But, like she said, Lizzie, your farm is smaller. This farm entails more than even you know," John offered, trying to appease, and instantly regretted it.

"Yes, so your *mutter und* now you remind me." She bristled. "Yes, our farm is smaller, but we do not hire help to tend it. We do not need to. We are all hard workers, and our farm does not suffer for our lack of numbers."

"So now you think your farm is better than ours?" John asked, the heated argument getting the better of his wisdom.

"No, I am not saying better. I am saying it is no worse for being smaller. If you think that more of something is always better, you are like the *Englishe*," Lizzie said, throwing down an insult she had never thought to say. "Take me home. I have no desire for this ride to last a moment longer. We both need to pray for guidance from *Gott.*"

Lizzie arrived home in tears, meeting both her *mutti und* her twin, who now seemed happier than she remembered her for ages. Each twin looked at the other and said, "What happened to you?"

"You first, Emma. I could use some good news this day," Lizzie sniffled.

"Peter and I are to be married!" Emma squealed.

"So, you are going to Ohio with him then?" The horror of losing her twin clear on her face.

"No, *daed* has worked a miracle! Our quilt money has bought the land next to Rebecca and Samuel. We will build our home there, near *familye*. Isn't that wonderful?" she gushed.

"I've heard nothing so wonderful in ages, Emma," Lizzie spoke in truth.

"Enough of me. What has you down, Lizzie?" Emma said to her twin. "You can always tell me anything."

"Yes, you may say anything to us," agreed Ana as well.

"John's *mutter* does not want me for her family, and it appears she will have her way." The words exploded from Lizzie. "She speaks ill of me and of our farm. I now hear that in his voice as well. I have prayed for patience, but she manages to know just how to get to me each time we speak."

"Have you offended her? Lizzie, think hard," pursued Emma. "I cannot think of a person our whole lives that has not liked you. Well, except for me a few times," she added trying to lighten the mood.

"I have been extra nice to her. I compliment her home, her family, her cooking, and it seems the nicer I am, the less she likes me. I am at a loss. John and I argue more than speak lately from it," she replied.

"Perhaps the two of you need to speak privately of it?" Ana advised. "I will have them here for a meal. You can show her around and speak to her while you do. Caleb will run the invite over to them today for tomorrow."

With that the conversation ended. *Mutter* had spoken. None but *vater* would say no to her and even he did that only when needed.

Lizzie had been nervous all day. Truth be told, she'd been a wreck since Caleb returned with the news that the Beiler family had accepted and would be by for dinner tonight. She tried to keep busy by baking fresh bread, cleaning, and helping with meal preparation, but at no point did she find herself thinking the night would end well for her. As the dinner hour neared, her guests arrived.

I'll not let that woman get to me tonight, Lizzie promised herself. Thinking but a moment, she prayed for *Gott's* own patience that she could keep the promise.

"Good evening, *Herr und Frau* Beiler," Lizzie greeted them at the doorstep. "We have looked forward to your visit all day."

"I'll bet you have," *Frau* Beiler said loud enough for only Lizzie to hear.

"Come in, dinner is almost ready. I've made John's favorite. Fried steaks with potato." Lizzie tried again, leading them into the sitting room.

"Thank you," said an otherwise timid John from behind his *eldere*.

"Welcome to our home," boomed Jacob, coming up behind them. "It is *gut* to see you again John *und* Sarah. It seems but a few days ago we were celebrating their births, and now look at them, they have grown up and grown together."

"We are getting old," replied John Beiler. "But it is *gut* to do that surrounded by *familye* and friends, is it not?"

"It has always been so, friend," came Jacob's answer. "Come, let us share a meal."

The two families entered the dining room, then were seated and prayed. The meal was served and all, well almost all, spoke kindly of it.

Frau Beiler's face grew longer as the night went on. Shortly after the post-meal prayer, Lizzie steeled her courage.

"*Frau* Beiler, come let us take a short walk before dessert," she suggested.

Surprisingly, Frau Beiler agreed and got up to walk with her. "Yes," she said. "Let us do just that."

All eyes at the table followed the women out the door.

"Should I go with them, *vater?*" asked a conflicted John.

"No, but be ready to go and rescue her," said John Senior in a grave tone.

"Emma or *mutti, daed?*" John asked, confused.

"That," Senior said, "is yet to be seen." He began a soft chuckle. "This is long overdue, son."

Outside, the women walked towards the barn.

"This is the only barn, then?" asked *Frau* Beiler. "It seems small for the task, *jah?*"

"No, we have plenty of space in it," Lizzie replied, trying to keep a smile on her face.

The rest of their walk went similarly. Lizzie would point something out and *Frau* Beiler would say something less than nice about it. Lizzie doubled down on her determination to be nice. Praying hard for patience and then near wit's end, she prayed for *Gott's* help with her struggle.

"Well," remarked *Frau* Beiler, looking at the family garden. "I can see your *mutter* has her heart set on this match, now doesn't she. Look at all that celery."

Lizzie heard scorn, disgust, and spite in the voice, and could take no more of it.

"No!" Lizzie said aloud.

"Excuse me?" *Frau* Beiler replied. "No to what exactly?"

"No to you speaking of my *mutti* that way. No to you speaking of me in that way," she said, without a moment of hesitation. "No to your attitude towards my home and my family. No to all of it!"

"All of it? Even my John, then?" *Frau* Beiler asked as if testing Lizzie's limits.

"Even him! You may well want him to stay a mama's boy, but I will have a man for a husband!" Lizzie spat out.

"So, the little mouse has a spine after all, it seems." A slow smiled spread across *Frau* Beiler's face. "I had begun to wonder. You cannot expect to run a farm on kindness alone, Lizzie. Some days you will need to be tough."

Lizzie no longer heard malice in the woman's voice. "I am well aware of that," she said defiantly.

"I am certain that you are. Now I know you have it in you to stand up for yourself, for your *familye*." *Frau* Beiler then added, "Perhaps you should get used to calling me Sarah, it seems rather formal to call me by my last name. We are soon to be related, no?"

"But," Lizzie started. "But …" She tried again, but still could not form a sentence.

"I wonder which of us disliked this more? You or me when my mother-in-law did this to me. I have come to understand the need to be strong to run a big farm. She and I became friends once we got past her little test. I hope you and I might do the same."

"But, I tried so hard to be nice to you all this time," Lizzie said softly.

"*Jah*, and did a fine job of it. I, however, needed to be sure of the woman that marries my John. Clearly your love for him is as real as his is for you. You have shown yourself to be a *godly* woman, a kind woman, one who can even cook his favorite dish better than his *mutti*. But, I wanted to make sure he was partnered with a *strong* woman. I do believe you are that woman." Sarah looked at her kindly, a chuckle slowly forming, "So long as you would have my 'momma's boy' for the rest of his life."

She continued, "Just so you know. I know why your *mutti* grows so much celery. She does it for women like myself. When my last *dochter* married, I had little growing in my garden. Your *mutti* is known as a woman who always has extra for friends in need. You remind me very much of her." She gave an appreciative smile. "We should be getting back. I believe you promised me some dessert, *jah?*"

"That I did, *Frau*," Lizzie started, only to be interrupted.

"Sarah," replied Sarah Beiler, reminding Lizzie.

"That I did then, Sarah," Lizzie replied, opening the door to the *haus* and silencing the conversation going on within.

The two women entered the dining area to encounter a table full of worried eyes. The two women looked at each other and laughed out loud.

"It went well then?" John asked meekly.

"How would it not, John? Do you lack faith in your future bride? I will tell you she has no such lack of faith in you! I am not sure you deserve such a woman as Lizzie Fisher, young man," she chided John, tongue-in-cheek.

Sarah turned to Jacob and to Ana at this point and continued, "You have raised a fine *dochter*. Please know that even as we make her one of us, we will never take her from you. John is lucky to draw her eye and we could not be happier for the two."

Everyone at the table tried their best to hide the surprise of these words and went with the moment.

"Lizzie, could I help you serve the pie? It would do us both *gut* to get used to cooking and serving together," Sarah offered.

"I would like that. I'd like that very much, Sarah." Lizzie smiled as the two went into the *kich*.

"What just happened?" asked a puzzled John Junior to the table.

"You will learn, son. Never question *Gott's* will, nor your mother's opinions," laughed John Beiler and all laughed with him.

7

This would be the eighth Sunday of preparation for baptism for Emma, Lizzie, and John. Caleb had done it last year and both Peter and Ruby had been baptized in their own churches previously. It was a requirement for any who desired to be married in the church to first be baptized into it.

After services, the bishop asked the existing members to vote on accepting the new members. Once accepted, next week would be their baptismal Sunday. To Lizzie, service seemed to take longer than the usual three hours, but it was just that she was anxious.

There was nothing to do but wait now. Members had stayed after and were voting.

Lizzie turned to John. "How long does this take, again?"

"It takes as long as it takes. Just like the last time you asked me," John laughed at his nervous bride-to-be. "You have nothing to fear, my Lizzie, nothing at all."

It was about that time that the members emerged from the church. Ana and Jacob came and hugged Lizzie. She was to be baptized next Sunday and become an adult in their world. John's *mutti* came over shortly after and made a point to congratulate Lizzie even before her son.

"Now, there is nothing further to get in the way of this," said Sarah Beiler to her husband. "You should go to see the bishop after next Sunday's services."

"It seems we will both be speaking to him then," added Jacob. "Let us make that journey together, old friend."

"*Jah*, we will go get old together as friends should," laughed John Senior.

"Ana, since you have two weddings to cook for, let us hold the baptism celebration for them both, *jah?*" offered Sarah.

"That is *gut* of you," came the reply. "I will have Caleb slaughter a hog and come by before church to get it roasting."

"We will surely eat well then," Sarah smiled. "If he learned at Jacob's side, it is sure to be popular."

"What can we bring?" asked Rebecca.

"Do the apple trees still grow behind the main field like when *Herr* Lapp lived there, or have they all fallen?" Sarah replied.

"No, many are still there. We just picked a few bushels of them this week," Rebecca responded. "I'd planned to can applesauce with much of the harvest."

"*Jah*, that is what I would do as well," Sarah began. "But I was hoping you could fry us up some apple rings for the baptism party. They are a favorite in our home."

"Certainly. I have never had much luck canning those. By mid-winter, they are applesauce," Rebecca said, laughing. "Do you have a way of canning them and keeping them from going soft?"

"We will discuss the secrets of our *kiche* at the party, *jah?*" Sarah replied. "I hear that you and Ruby have a bread I might want to know of."

"That sounds like a right *gut* trade," Rebecca said, smiling.

Emma, Lizzie, and John each went to see the bishop on Thursday. They committed themselves to their baptisms and prayed with the bishop for *Gott's* blessing upon them all. The bishop had been doing this long enough to know that he would be seeing these youths soon enough to arrange wedding dates for them. He smiled as he let them go.

Sunday finally arrived. Caleb woke up, got the pig and the roaster loaded into the wagon, and went to the Beiler Farm early. He had done this often enough to know how long he needed so as not to be late to meeting.

After lighting the fire and setting the spit roaster in place, he was introduced to an *Englishe* that had been hired to help set up while the *familye* was in church. He explained to the man when to turn the spit, when to add wood to the fire, and was confident all would be well until he could return.

He then knocked on the Beiler's door afterwards and was let in to wash up and drink a cup of coffee with the family.

Baptism service is different than other services. The teachings focus around the verses and importance of baptism in the Bible. It is a life-long commitment of the church to its people and of its people to the church.

Today, as in all baptisms, each candidate was asked to answer four important questions. Lizzie, Emma, and John were asked individually, "Do you confess and believe that Jesus Christ is the Son of God?"

The ceremony continued with the bishops questioning, "Do you also confess this to be a Christian doctrine, church, and brotherhood you are about to submit to?"

"Do you now denounce the world, the devil, and all his doings, as well as your own flesh and blood and desire to serve Jesus Christ, who died on the cross for you?"

"Do you also promise in the presence of God and His church, with the Lord's help, to support these doctrines and regulations, to earnestly fill your place in the church, to help counsel and labor, and not to depart from the same, come what may, be it life or death?"

After a yes from each of the young candidates, they kneeled. Emma and Lizzie removed their head coverings and the bishop cupped his hands over each of them, while the deacon poured water over them, three times each as the bishop spoke the words to confirm their baptism and their rebirth in Christ.

Now it was John's turn. He also was baptized with water. The bishop then offered him his hand and a kiss of peace. For the women, the bishop's wife offered them a kiss.

Standing tall before the congregation, Bishop Yoder turned to announce, "You are now no longer guests and strangers, but fellow citizens with the saints and of the household of God."

As services closed and prayers given, friends and family began heading over to the Beiler farm to celebrate.

Caleb grabbed Ruby's hand to help her into his buggy. They started off while others were still shaking hands and having fellowship.

"Caleb Fisher!" said a mockingly distraught Ruby. "I do believe I have been fooled by you."

Caleb turned to her with his face showing no clue as to where she was going with the conversation.

"As many times as you have driven me in this buggy, I have never known it could travel so fast." She was now laughing at him. "If I didn't know better, I'd think you were going slow all those times on purpose."

Caleb joined in her laughter and came back with the only reply he could, "There might be something to that way of thinking, Ruby. But, it seems to be working for me, so I will most likely go back to it when we are not racing to a pig over a hot fire, *jah?*"

"I will leave that to you, my strong husband-to-be," she replied, still laughing, enjoying the sunshine on her face as they drove.

"Now, you mock me," Caleb grinned, happy to arrive so quickly at the Beiler farm.

Much to his relief, the hog was almost done and the *Englishe* had not burned it nor let the fire grow too cold. Caleb walked over to him, then patted his back and complimented him for doing so well with it.

As the rest of their Community arrived, the men set tables up, the women prepped the rest of the food, and the newest members of their order were celebrated by all.

Before long, the food began to stream out of the *haus* with bowls and plates of fresh fruit, vegetables, potato salad and more piling up on tables.

Seeing this, Caleb used his fork to make sure the pig was cooked and began slicing plates of meat for the tables. Ruby and Rebecca came over to help get the plates passed out quickly.

At last, all the tables had food and drink. Next, the children and elderly were helped with their plates, and then the group turned to a standing John Beiler, Senior.

"Friends," he began. "I am most pleased with my son today. He has become a man of the church and has pledged himself to Christ."

A small cheer went up at this, then John continued.

"I am grateful to our old friends, the Fishers, for allowing us to host this today. We also celebrate their twins joining the church and professing their love for *Gott* and Christ. It is customary for a church member to pray before each meal. It is my privilege to ask my son, John, to lead us in that prayer today."

John was surprised. This was no small thing for his *vater*. It was customary for the man of the *familye* to do the prayers. This was John Beiler acknowledging his son's manhood as well as his baptism.

"Let us pray," started John. He thanked *Gott* for his family, for his church, for his district, for his friends and, turning a few heads, for his Lizzie as well. He thanked Him for the provision of each day and this day in particular. He closed the prayer with Mark 16:16, *Whoever believes and is baptized will be saved, but whoever does not believe will be condemned.*

The crowd replied with a solemn, "Amen."

John then said to those gathered, "I am glad to be a baptized believer among you now." Then in a louder voice, "Who then is hungry?"

The rest of the day was full of food, fellowship, and congratulations. As the day began to dim, the process of cleaning up finished up as well. The women had everything orderly and the men began breaking down tables as they emptied.

"Sarah, Rebecca," called Ana. "I think we should talk with our husbands and children while we are all in one place together."

The two agreed and set out to gather them. They congregated inside at the dining room table away from the busy *kich*.

"As we all know, it is customary for the bride's family to host the wedding feast," Ana said to the gathered group. "As Ruby's mother has passed, I would like to ask Rebecca if I might hold hers as well. I would, of course, need as much help as you can give me," she added quickly.

"With this bump in front of me growing larger by the day, I would welcome that offer," said a rather tired looking Rebecca.

"When do you plan to publish?" Ana asked the young betrothed before her.

The three couples looked at each other, then at the other couples, then back to their own fiancé again.

"*Mutti*, Lizzie and I have shared everything all our lives," replied Emma. "We have discussed sharing a wedding day as well."

A bit of a rumble went around the room at this, but their grooms had been prepared and had already agreed so long as the bishop would do it.

"Well, I see I will not talk you two out of this. That leaves you, Ruby. When do you want your wedding?" asked a rather surprised Ana.

"Would it be horrible?" Ruby looked to the twins.

"To go first? No, we would not take that from you, Ruby. Especially after *dunderkopf* called you an old maid. You can certainly get married before us," said Lizzie with a grin.

"Well that is very kind of you, but I was going to ask if I might share your wedding day. You are the best friends I have, and to be able to share this with you would mean so very much to me," Ruby suggested, tentatively.

At this, the twins squealed, stood, and ran to her side.

"We had hoped you would ask," Emma said hugging her.

"But we did not want to put any pressure on you if you wanted a day of your own," added Lizzie.

"It is settled then, *mutti* Fisher. I think that not only do we agree to be brides together, but we all want it as soon as possible."

"Not that any asked my opinion," Caleb interjected, "but I am all for any plan that gives me a bride and creamed celery all winter."

At this, Ana Fisher shook her head and turned to the men. "Bishop Yoder is still here. Run and fetch him, please."

Minutes later the bishop came up on a table of intent faces. "Well, this promises to be interesting. I can tell that already," he joked. "What service can I be to you?"

"Bishop Yoder," started Jacob. "We felt it would be easier for all to ask you as a group instead of one at a time."

The bishop's eyebrows raised at this and he bade them continue.

"My two girls and their brother are all desiring to be wed this season," Jacob added.

"So, Caleb. You are the husband after all then?" chuckled the bishop, watching Caleb turned beet red.

"*Jah*, Bishop Yoder. It would seem I am," he replied.

"So, do you want these spaced out or near each other on the calendar?" Bishop Yoder asked. "I know of at least three other couples planning to wed this season. There always seem to be one or two that I am not aware of also."

"Well," said Jacob, extending the word to easily three times its usual length.

"Ah, we have come to the crux, then?" the bishop asked.

"Yes. They would all like to be married the same day." At this point, Jacob was half-stating the desire and half-asking if it could be done.

"I'm certain I have never married off three siblings in a single day," Bishop Yoder replied, his face deep in thought. "Are you so eager to be rid of them all then?"

Poor Jacob was so concerned with the reply that he failed to see the spark in the bishop's eye nor the smile creeping upon his face.

"No, bishop. It is their desire not ours. I'd keep the lot of them forever if I could." The truth of it clear in Jacob's voice.

"It is not something often done, but I can think of no reason it cannot be." Bishop Yoder said. Then he turned to the prospective couples. "We will have to meet separately still. I will not have any enter marriage lightly and without counsel."

Relieved, the three brides hugged and kissed and hugged some more, the twins giggling and Ruby joining in with even that.

"Caleb and Ruby, I will see you Thursday then. John the week after, and Peter, you and your bride last." It was stated, not asked. The three couples nodded an obedient yes to the bishop and promised to be there.

8

The mothers and Rebecca got together, picked a date, and decided the arrangements for after the ceremony. It was customary for the couples to spend their wedding night at the bride's home. In Caleb and Ruby's case, they had a home of their own waiting, so they would go there and then perhaps join the family for breakfast.

Emma would keep her room, and Lizzie would use Caleb's old room.

Lizzie would stay with her family until John had a home ready for her. He was far too needed on his family farm to stay elsewhere. Peter would move in with the Fishers and stay there while he cleared their land for a home for he and Emma. The couples would be told of this when needed, but the women wanted it sorted ahead of time.

The women agreed to meet each Saturday afternoon, rotating *hause* until the plans were set and the weddings complete. They organized the menu and began asking for help from married siblings and neighbors. The food would be cooked at the Fisher's, the *grosshaus,* and the King's. All that could be made beforehand would be, such as pies and canned delights.

Once the date was confirmed, letters went out to family to let them know *quietly* to expect a wedding. This would allow any desiring to attend to make their plans.

In a whirlwind, the brides worked together sewing three near identical blue dresses. They also worked feverishly on the quilt, and because they only worked on it when all were together, it was going slower than the twins normal speed completing one. Everything was moving smoothly towards the day.

Each couple, in order, spent their time with Bishop Yoder. He prayed with them, questioned them, and questioned them more. Marriage was forever. This was the biggest decision of their lives after promising themselves to *Gott*.

Each couple in turn passed the test, and on the Thursday two weeks before the wedding, they went arm in arm to meet the bishop to get *published*. The whole church would know their plans in but three days from now.

Bishop Yoder welcomed the six in.

"And none of you have changed your mind about doing this the same day?" he asked, scanning faces for any doubts or uncertainty. Finding none, he continued and prayed with the three couples.

Afterwards, he explained how the ceremony would happen and where each needed to stand. "A week from today, I will pronounce you married. I will start with Caleb and Ruby, then Peter and Emma, then John and Lizzie. I have decided that by age of the husbands. I trust that will not be an issue."

"That is fine," they all agreed.

Sunday morning, three days later, the three couples met at the Fisher home. On this day, they would not be expected at services. As couples, they would eat breakfast and get a view of married life before the wedding day arrived.

Each of the brides cooked her future husband's breakfast in whole. They would not give up that tradition, even though it made the *kich* a tangle of bodies moving in every direction. They ate at separate tables, each set up in a different room. Each couple prayed for their marriage as well as for the two other couples'. They held hands as they ate and prayed after the meal was done.

"I've a fresh pot of coffee," came Ruby's voice, after each couple had had their fill. "Come let us rejoin and enjoy the fellowship."

The young people found their way to the big table where they prayed and took turns speaking. It was clear this was a lifetime bond they were signing up for and all were content with it. They eventually had to get back to their homes, and only Caleb had a shared buggy ride ahead of him, the twins were already home.

"Perhaps now, we could walk for a bit. I'd like a bit more time with you alone, Lizzie," suggested John to his beloved.

"And I with you, Emma," added Peter.

The girls were all content then. Caleb headed towards the King farm as slow as he could get the horse to walk. Ruby did not complain a bit about it, either.

The next week was a whirlwind of activity. Pies were baked, bread was made, canned goods gathered, and all was made as ready as could be.

"Are the invitations all sent then, Peter?" Emma asked.

"And you two as well?" quickly added Ruby to John and Caleb.

All three grooms-to-be answered a quick yes and promised to be on time. This was it. Wednesday. Tomorrow they would all be married. It was customary for each couple to have two male and two female "side sitters", *newehockers*, which is as close to a best man or maid-of-honor as the Amish got.

Each couple had the other two couples as their *newehockers*, keeping the wedding party to a reasonable size even as three weddings took place at once.

The three couples oversaw the planning of tables. Again here, tradition dictated the married couple take the corner and the *newehockers* sit at their sides. They had decided to take three small tables and set them as if diamonds, so that there were three corners side by side. Caleb would take the center with a *schwester* on either side.

With plans in place, the three said their good byes and would not see each other again until tomorrow.

9

In three separate places, three men woke at near identical times. For John and Caleb, there were farm chores that needed doing. For Peter, he needed to finish packing his belongings. He would live with the Fishers until he had a home built for his Emma.

Once the vital chores had been done, the men cleaned themselves up, ate their breakfasts, and then put on their black suits, black socks and shoes, with a crisp white shirt. Each had a bow tie for the day and a black hat with brim. It was about this time that the helpers began to show up at the Fisher farm. John and Peter began their trek to the farm as well.

Ruby and Rebecca had arrived at the Fisher farm in the early morning hours. They were squirreled up in the twin's bedroom for quite some time chatting and giggling. Before breakfast, the three donned their new blue dresses and lace caps.

Coming downstairs, Lizzie was the first to meet her groom. John smiled warmly and held out an arm to accompany her into the *kich,* which was a flurry of activity.

Caleb continued to pace, even as Emma made her way down the stairs and into Peter's waiting arms. Caleb saw the happiness on his two *schwestere's* faces and wondered if he had ever seen a woman as happy as either of them.

While contemplating this, he heard a light step behind him which set the hair on his neck standing. Spinning around slowly, he saw Ruby gliding down the stairs to him. As her foot landed on the bottom step, he met her there.

"You should probably breathe now, Caleb," Ruby said.

"Beloved, let us love one another. For love is from *Gott* and whoever loves has been born of *Gott* and knows *Gott*." His eyes held unshed tears as he looked at his Ruby. She brushed a finger down his cheek.

He offered his arm and they joined the others. By seven o'clock, the couples were found in the Fisher kitchen all smiles and laughter greeting their guests. By the time the last had arrived, it was coming close to the traditional start of services at eight-thirty.

Sure enough, as the sound of the congregation singing the first hymn came to them, the bishop came and grabbed each couple in turn to counsel them individually again as to the importance and permanence of marriage.

He then spoke to them as a group and they made their way to the Fisher's great room set up for the service. Bishop Yoder spoke to the congregation of the sanctity of marriage. When he quoted Ephesians 5:25, *For husbands, this means love your wives, just as Christ loved the church. He gave up his life for her,* the congregation knew he was wrapping up and he ended the sermon with Genesis 2:24, *Therefore a man shall leave his father and mother and hold fast to his wife, and they shall become one flesh.*

At this point, he brought each couple forward from the congregation, asked them a few questions, and blessed the couples, one after the other.

Being common for fathers or ordained men of the community to give testimony about marriage to the congregation, Jacob stood first, his voice strong as he began to give his testimony.

"Most of you know me," he said. "Some of you have known me as a child. For those that have not, I will tell you, I was a headstrong child. Willful and eager to make my way. I was raised in a good home, shown a love for *Gott*, but had never felt that connection to Him in my heart. Then one day, I met Ana. I was struck by her. She was so calming and *gut*. I knew I wanted to know her better. The more I got to know her, the more I saw *Gott* in her. She drew me to *Gott* even as I was drawn to her. To this day, I wonder if I would have found *Gott* without her." At this, Jacob turned first to Ana and saw a small tear in her eye, then to the three new grooms. He continued, "A bride is a gift from *Gott* Himself. She is equal parts tough and fragile. Treat her as the precious thing she is, and you will share happiness all your lives."

Jacob stopped then and sat. Ana gripped his hand and glowed at him.

John Beiler, Senior, and Samuel each spoke on the blessings of marriage as well, then Bishop Yoder gathered everyone in a final prayer. A loud "Amen" rose up and the celebration portion began.

The room was quickly set to the plan with tables. The brides and grooms were congratulated, hands shaken, backs slapped, and necks hugged by nearly everyone in the whole community. The three couples made their way to the corner tables. John and Lizzie to the right, Peter and Emma to the left, and Caleb with Ruby at the center.

There was a jar with fresh cut celery centerpieces on each table as well as roasted chicken with bread stuffing, bowls topped with mashed potatoes, ladles of gravy, coleslaw, fried apple rings, fruit salad and much to Caleb's delight, creamed celery.

As big as the great room was in the Fisher haus, they still needed to serve in two rounds to seat everyone. After eating, the brides and their grooms walked about chatting with friends and sharing their joy with others.

As the final guests finished up their meals, the helpers cleared the tables and began preparations for the evening meal. There was already a group playing volleyball out back and a table of girls doing what all young girls do, talking about boys. It took nearly all day for each couple to make their rounds of all the guests and make their plans to visit later in the fall and winter.

The sun was starting to droop in the sky when the helpers corralled the brides, the grooms, and the parents and got them seated again. This time the main table was with the parents of the brides and groom. Samuel and Rebecca were honored with seats here as Ruby's guardians.

The evening meal was chicken and dumplings, baked macaroni and cheese, canned peas from spring, and lemon sponge cake for dessert. No one walked away from the day hungry unless it was their intent.

Finally, the festivities drew to a close between ten and eleven. The farms would still need tending in the morning. Goodbyes were said and plans for the upcoming visits were finalized.

Each pair would visit six homes each weekend throughout the winter. This was as much to get accustomed to being a couple and being thought of as one, as well as receiving wedding gifts from family and friends. They would be celebrating this day for the rest of the winter.

Jacob turned to Ana and hugged her, "You have put on a wonderful wedding this day, my wife. I am blessed to have you by my side."

"You, my husband, have reminded me of our wedding day and how much purpose you have added to all of our lives," Ana replied softly. "May we always remember the love of our youth."

"Come, let us finish up the cleaning and leave the couples to some privacy. You spoke to your daughters?" Jacob asked quietly.

"*Jah,* and you spoke with Caleb?" replied Ana.

"*Jah,* Ana," came his soft reply. "*Gott* has added greatly to our family this day, even as he has taken from it."

Later that night, in three separate rooms, brides and husbands began their paths in marriage with tenderness and love.

In the morning, Caleb woke early, in his own bed, in his own home, on his own farm. He wandered to the window, staring out into the early morning darkness. Ruby rose and stood next to him.

He yawned then stretched his arms out. She quietly tucked herself into his arms as he stretched. To any who looked, it would appear that Caleb was trying to hug the whole world. In his mind, his world was hugging him back.

As one, Caleb and Ruby bent to their knees and prayed. Giving all thanks to *Gott* and asking guidance for this new part of their lives.

Forging Friendships

The Fishers

(An Amish Life 4)

While this is the fourth book about Barnville, it happens long before the others. We hope that it stands alone, but if you have read the first three, this may help to fill in some of what happened.

1

Otto Lapp looked across the peeling white paint on the rails of his porch at his farm. He would always think of it as his, even now as he was moving away from it. He had expected to die and be buried here. *Life does not always do what you expect*. How many times had his *vater* said that to him?

The crisp autumn air brought the smells of a dairy farm to him. The livestock had all been sold off, leaving the farm silent, but for the birds. He was happy that most of the animals would stay here in Barnville. He could have gotten more money from *Englishe*, but at this point in his life, he had less use for riches than even most Amish.

Starting today, he would live out his days with his *dochter* Sarah and her *familye*. He had finally given up trying to get them to run this farm and he was past the age to do it himself.

Everywhere he looked, he saw proof of that. The fields he had not planted were being claimed back by weeds and saplings near the tree lines. The fieldstone fences had not been repaired in several years now.

Last season, the deer ate nearly as much of his feed crop as his cows had.

"It has not always been so," he said aloud, as if justifying the disrepair that he saw around him.

This was once one of the strongest farms in the district and he was the reason.

Otto was by far the youngest child of John and Linda Lapp. He had two *brudere* and a *schwester*. He was several years younger than his youngest sibling. The Lapp farm had need for these strong youths with nearly one hundred head of dairy cows to feed and milk.

There was always hay to plant, cut, put away, or feed to the cows. This along with all the other things that had to happen on a self-sufficient farm.

Otto, like most Amish, grew up surrounded by hard work and took to it. When he was not working the fields, or praying with *familye*, he applied himself to his schooling. He liked his maths so much as to be a help to those ahead of him in class.

By the time he was able to help with planting a field, he was figuring out how to add a couple more rows here and a few more there. While it amused his father at first, when the fields were harvested, the yields were noticeably improved. They had more hay and straw than they needed for feed. They could increase the herd or sell off the extra.

The summer of his twelfth year would see a change for Otto. His oldest *bruder*, Jacob, moved to Lancaster to build sheds with the *familye* of his new bride. While Otto was happy for him, he missed Jacob's fellowship. The second thing that happened was a result of the first. Otto was introduced to the forge.

"Otto," John Lapp began. "It was always my plan to teach you the basics of the forge. Your *bruder* Jacob was a natural with bending hot metal. I had thought his heart would keep him here with us, but the heart goes where the Lord calls it. This means more of the forge will fall upon you if you have the desire and skill."

One thing Otto had plenty of was desire. He wore his *vater* out with questions of varying shades of why.

Within a short time, he could weld a broken panel. After a year, he replaced all the fence hinges and cut nails with his spare iron to trade in town for more coal for his fire. There always seemed to be a demand for handmade nails.

Not much more than a year afterward, Sarah met a farmer of her own and moved away. It was only two counties away, but to Otto it might as well have been another world.

Sarah was the one person other than his friend and neighbor, Jacob Fisher, that he had fun with. When she wasn't helping *mutti* with dinner or doing her chores, she spent her time with him, reading and listening to his ideas.

When she left, there was just him and his *bruder* Hans. Hans, as far as Otto knew, had never picked up a hammer in the forge. He had learned to work with wood. First carving, then joining. He went through his farm chores with no interest, but his eyes lit whenever he was making a table or even a simple box.

Hans spent much of his spare time at the local market, so it should come as no surprise that it was where he found his match.

Most Amish youth kept dating private so as not to scandalize should the pairing prove unfit. Hans and Amy kept theirs quiet for a totally different reason. Amy was Mennonite, not Amish.

Her family kept a stand at the market, they built dressers and cabinets. Like the Amish, Mennonite quality was much sought after by the *Englishe*. Unlike the Amish, they were able to use a wider range of power tools to accomplish their tasks. That was how they met, Hans admiring the work of Amy's *familye*.

"This is fine carving on these dowels. A man's leg must get right tired spinning a lathe to make this, *jah?*" Hans asked the man near the rocking chair he was admiring.

From the other side of the stall he heard a melodic laughter. In equal parts it called to him and mocked him. He kept his eyes on the man before him.

"The motor does not ever tire, friend," the owner of the stand said. "It does however take a steady hand and a keen eye." At this the man reached out to shake hands with Hans. "I am Franz Schoen. Pleased to meet you. You seem more to me a man who makes furniture rather than a man who buys it, *jah?*" He read him like a book at once.

"Hans Lapp *und jah*," Hans replied weakly. "I have made many such pieces. But, not so …" He hesitated, looking for a polite way to say gaudy, "decorated."

"Ha!" laughed Franz. "A smart tongue and strong hands as well!"

"I mean no offense," rebutted Hans, fearing he had insulted the man.

"None taken, young man. None taken," assured Franz. "I mean that you took a moment to find the right word instead of the obvious one. You would make a good merchant, if that were your calling."

This high praise inspired a young woman near Hans' age to turn her head and make her own opinion.

"Do you dislike my company so much as to give my job to the first man with callouses that comes to look?" Amy said, placing both hands on her hips. The smile on her lips belied her words.

"What good would it do me to give your job to another, Amy? You would come here to torment me even if I did," Franz teased.

"We both know that I am good at this. Getting to tease you all day is just a little extra reward for my efforts," she replied. She came alongside her father and patted his arm.

"I fear I could not take you up on the offer if you made it, sir," Hans said with mock seriousness.

"You have another job then?" Franz asked.

"Well that and fear of being cut up by her sharp tongue," replied Hans.

After about fifteen seconds of silence, Amy tilted her head back and brought back that melodic laugh Hans had heard earlier. First her father then Hans himself joined in.

"You had best watch out for this one, Amy," her father winked at her. "He is not so timid as most, nor fearful of your ways."

Amy had already decided she would be keeping an eye out for this Hans Lapp.

From that day, Hans found a reason to go to the market at least twice a week. He spent more and more time speaking with both Franz and Amy, then more of it with Amy as time went forward, until he merely waved to Franz as he went to sit speaking with her.

"*Vater*," Hans began one Monday afternoon in the fields. "I think we must talk."

"So, you have decided finally to tell me of this girl?" John Lapp said with humor in his voice. "You have been to market enough to supply ten farms as large as ours. Tell me about her then. Who are her parents?"

A brief silence followed. As the silence became uncomfortable, John tried to help his son continue.

"Come, tell me of her. Do not fear. We are *familye*. I am sure we will come to like her as much as you," he offered.

"Her *vater* has a furniture stall at market," Hans began, then hesitated again.

John's mind began to run down the names and faces he knew from market. There were the Broders, but their three *dochtere* were far too young to be courting. The Smythe's only *dochter* was already married.

"Her *familye* is Mennonite, *vater*," Hans finally blurted out.

"You are baptized in this church, son. Does she mean to join us?" came out of John's mouth immediately.

"We have talked much about what we might do," Hans quietly replied. "I have spoken to her *vater*. He would like me to come and build cabinets with him. He is starting to build them for the *Englishe* that live near."

"Is it so easy then for you to turn your back on your *familye und* your church, Hans?" John said, his voice growing in volume and disdain in equal measure.

"They are *Anabaptist,*" offered Hans.

"Those who play closest to fire are those that get burned by it," John replied. "I have seen those who leave the church for the world. It swallows them up and ruins them."

"You have raised me better than that, *vater.*" Hans replied, crossing his arms and kicking with his toe at the ground beneath him. He blinked rapidly under the harsh stare, but continued to meet his *vater's* eyes.

"You will speak to the bishop about this before you say a word to your *mutti,*" his *vater* said, ending the conversation.

Once he had been baptized into the church, Hans had become subject to *Ordnung,* the rules of the church. He was forbidden to marry outside of it.

To marry Amy, Hans would have to leave his church and face the *bann*. The bishop tried to talk him out of it and upon failing, offered him a way to leave without subjecting himself to the permanent stigma of the *bann*.

And, so it came to be that Hans left his church, his *familye,* and Barnville behind and made his way into the mechanized world.

2

There was still a stigma to have a *familye* member leave the church. Otto found himself with fewer and fewer friends at school. Eventually, there was just one, Jacob Fisher. Jacob's friendship had never wavered. He still sat with Otto, played with him, and went fishing with him when they had the free time. Jacob never understood how much value his friend Otto placed on that.

"Jacob," Otto said one late Saturday afternoon while fishing, "you never speak of my *bruder* leaving. Why is that?"

"Did you want to talk about it?" was Jacob's reply while casting a fresh worm into the water.

"No…" came Otto's quick answer. "But many ask anyway. I wonder why you do not."

He leaned against a tree trunk, holding his fishing pole tightly in his hands.

"I have been with you when others ask. You do not like to speak of it. It is plain on your face," came Jacob's unfiltered reply.

"I would like your help," Otto said, his voice full of resolve. "I am going to plant some ash trees. Hans always talked about ash trees being great for furniture. 'Strong, straight and clear,' he called them. I have made up a barrel of nails for trade, but will need help digging fifty holes and bringing them water."

Jacob thought a bit. Digging fifty holes would be a hard day's work. He would have to get permission to miss working on the farm to do this.

"Why do you want to do this, Otto?" queried Jacob, his eyes on the cloudless blue sky above them.

"I would like a place I can go and still be near something of him, Jacob." Otto said, the sorrow of his loss plain. "And, if he were to return to us one day, he would have a start."

"Well then, we will have to plant this grove of yours. But, my help will cost you," Jacob said, trying to hide his smile.

Otto was silent for a moment. Here was his last friend demanding payment for helping? *How bad has my life become?*

"What price would you have me pay, Jacob?" came the flat voice of Otto.

"I would have you teach my sons how to work the forge. Of course, you do realize that means you cannot leave and must remain forever my friend, don't you?" Jacob said, smiling, his eyes now meeting Otto's.

"I think that is a fair price to pay, my friend. I will gladly do this for you. So, have you a girl chosen already?" Otto asked, with laughter mixing back into his voice.

"I have a few years to make my choice. No sense rushing this," Jacob said defensively with cheeks blushing.

"I see how you look at Ana Yoder," Otto teased. "If you are not careful, she will make that decision for you."

They both had a good laugh at that and then continued fishing until the sun began to set on the slowly winding creek that divided their properties.

So, it was that Otto and Jacob remained friends even as Otto grew more and more unto himself. It was but a few years later that Ana did indeed make the decision for Jacob and they got married.

Otto, of course, was a *newehocker* for Jacob. Ana arranged to have her friend Else paired with Otto. Within a year, Jacob was a *newehocker* for Otto.

They still found time here and there to go fishing together even as each came to run his own farm.

Years later while working on his farm ...

"*Herr* Lapp?" came the hesitant voice of a twelve-year-old Caleb Fisher. "*Herr* Lapp?" he called out again, slightly louder. "My *vater* sent me to see you."

Otto had been kneeling behind a wagon, examining a wheel hub. He looked around, then his eyes stopped at Caleb. Not many came to see him since his Else passed in childbirth. *Who was this boy?*

"Who is your *vater* that he sends a child to do his business?" spat out Otto, full of the disdain he still harbored against those who had sneered at him his whole life.

"My *vater*," Caleb started in a voice sterner than the body that said it, "is Jacob Fisher. He sent me to you because, he said, you and I have business."

Otto smiled inside. *This is truly Jacob's son. He has a spine to him just like his vater.*

"Well, young Fisher, what business do we have, then?" Otto inquired flatly.

"My *vater* said that I am to collect a debt from you. He said to tell you," and at this point Caleb took a deep breath, "the payment is due for those ash trees. I am to receive payment for myself. So, this is now my business, *Herr* Lapp."

Ash trees? What debt was due from his bruder's grove? Then it struck him.

Otto Lapp spun at that point and took another look at Caleb. This time he judged his height, weight, and muscle. He saw before him a child barely tall enough to strike an anvil with the build of a farmer. *I can make this work.*

"What do you know of the payment you are to get?" Otto asked, his voice hardened more by practice than desire now.

"*Vater* said you are to teach me something of value," Caleb replied with no more knowledge than that.

"Well, it is like Jacob Fisher to send a child to learn a man's job," Otto chuckled as he said this. "I have a bit of time. This is not something you are to learn in a day, boy. This is something that may take your whole life to learn. Many give up before learning anything." At this he wiped the straw off his shirt and looked deep into Caleb's eyes. "Are you a quitter, boy?"

"I have always run the race in such a way as to receive the prize, *Herr* Lapp." Caleb said alluding to 1 Corinthians 9:24. "I do not always win, but I do not ever give up."

Otto smiled inside himself. Jacob and Ana had raised themselves a *godly* young man here. He let none of that smile see daylight.

"We shall put that to the test. Not every man is suited to bending hot iron. You must be as the metal you strike if we are to shape you into something more useful."

Caleb's eyes lit at this. He was to learn the forge from *Herr* Lapp.

"I will work hard, *Herr* Lapp," Caleb said, eagerness clear in his voice. "When do we start?"

"You have started already. 'Though your beginning was insignificant, yet your end will increase greatly'," Otto quoted 2 Corinthians to him. "Come show me that you can start a fire. That will be today's lesson."

So, began the education of Caleb in bending hot metal. True to his word, Caleb put his all into it. Otto was always pleased with his efforts, even if he never seemed quite satisfied in his results. There was always a slight change needed here or there.

After the first year, Otto began to call him Caleb instead of boy. After the second year, Caleb was told to stop calling him *Herr* Lap and to call him Otto. It surprised Otto as it was happening. He intended to help forge a man, he did not expect to forge a friendship as well.

Caleb ate many a meal with Otto Lapp and his *dochter*, Sarah. She was as animated as *Herr* Lapp was stoic. She was the woman of the house and bore that responsibility with apparent ease. She cooked, cleaned and acted like a woman many years older than she was. Little did Otto know how much Sarah came to enjoy Caleb's company. While he was much too young for her, she could let herself be her real age around him.

It was the summer of Caleb's fifteenth year that Otto came to him and gave him a new task.

"Caleb, my tools are all showing their age. I would have you make me a new hammer, tongs, poker, hot-cut, square punch and a nail header. Save the header for last, I will show you how to make that one. You must join steel to the iron or it will bend as easily as the nails it makes."

Caleb looked at Otto's tools. He saw little wear, but knew not to question his mentor. He set out to make a fine set of tools.

It was a few weeks later that he was ready to do the nail header.

"Grab that bar of square iron, Caleb. Cut off about a half-foot or a bit better of it," Otto said to his student.

Caleb heated the bar and used a hot-cut chisel to slice the piece of stock. He put the long piece back into storage to cool while the hot end of his working iron was in the coals keeping hot.

"Now, you will want to make the end a half-inch by inch flat square," instructed Otto, watching Caleb shape the metal with skill and ease.

Caleb's arms showed the effects of these two years farming and those same years swinging a hammer at this forge. They were now the arms of a man.

"Now, cut a piece of steel from this wagon spring. Make sure it is a proper fit or it will break quickly in use." Otto reminded his student, but as they had added steel to iron previously, Caleb knew how this was done.

He fluxed the steel, heated his iron, and welded them together. He heated it a couple of times to welding heat to make sure there were no gaps, and then set it on the anvil to punch the hole through the steel and iron for the nail to sit.

Otto watched silently as Caleb did this. He was, despite his best efforts, very proud of his young friend. He was a natural hot iron bender.

"Now, once it cools enough, decide if you want to put a loop on the other end to hang it or not," Otto instructed. "Then heat the piece and quench it to harden it up."

Caleb did this then set the piece to cool.

"You will want to run some nails through the head to break it in, Caleb," Otto said, more suggestion rather than demanding now in his tone.

"*Jah*, Otto," came the reply of a busy man with hot iron in his hands.

Later, as Caleb finished cleaning up his area, Otto spoke, "We are done then. My debt to your father is paid."

"You will teach me no more?" Caleb replied, with the disbelief hanging in the air.

"You have learned how to shoe a horse, how to make what you need around the farm. There is little else I might teach you," replied the flat voice of Otto Lapp. "There is one more matter of business, Caleb. I will need you to gather a wagon of flat stones on your farm. I will speak of this to your *vater*. In two weeks, I will visit your farm to see this pile of rocks."

Caleb looked at Otto Lapp. In the near years they had been doing this, he had given Caleb many strange requests. This was perhaps the oddest of all.

"*Jah, Herr* Lapp," came the safest answer to one of these tasks.

3

So, it came to be that two weeks later Caleb, Jacob, and Otto were standing looking at a large pile of flat stones that Caleb had assembled near the back of a shed on the Fisher farm.

"Tell the boy your plan, Otto," came Jacob's deep voice.

"Is this where it is to go, then?" Otto asked.

"Unless you see a better spot," was the reply.

"It will do." And with that, Otto turned and scratched off a large rectangle on the ground then pointed at Caleb. "Dig here, down maybe a foot. Be quick about it. I am going to have a coffee with your *vater* to catch up with him."

"What am I digging?" asked a befuddled Caleb.

With this, both older men spun around and said in unison. "A hole," then laughed as they walked to the *haus* for a cup of Ana's coffee.

It was a good hour before the men came back and checked on Caleb. They found him sitting on a barrel with his hat tipped over his eyes.

Otto was about to chastise him when he saw the hole was dug and dug well with the corners sharp.

"You could have come up for coffee, Caleb." Otto said, a touch of gentleness in his voice.

"And miss seeing that surprise in your eyes? That would seem a less than fair trade I think," laughed Caleb.

"Go to my wagon then and bring us the bags of mortar and the tools," Otto said, all business again.

When Caleb returned, he saw a smaller rectangle drawn on the ground near the other.

"I have your barrow and all the tools. We are building today?" Caleb asked, still not sure what they were building.

"Yes, your *vater* and I will be building," Otto said, pointing at the second rectangle. "You have another hole to dig."

The two older men sorted out a bit of the stone, setting corners into place and beginning to make a large base. As they worked, it dawned on Caleb that they were building a forge. A bigger one than even at the Lapp farm.

Over the next two days, the forge took its shape. The last day, *Herr* Lapp asked Caleb to give him a hand with the last of the materials in his wagon.

Caleb walked over and threw back a tarp. There on the back was a new anvil. It was a bit larger than he was used to, but should last generations. There was also a hand crank bellows to keep the fire hot.

He backed the horse and wagon as close to the work area as possible and rigged a rope to the anvil to move it. The three men made quick work of the anvil, getting it set on the new stone stand near the forge. They wrapped chains around the bottom to help deaden the high-pitched dings of the hammering that would be done here.

When all was complete, Otto reminded Caleb to let the cement cure before heating the forge. He then did something surprising. He grabbed Caleb and hugged him.

Then he stopped and held him at arm's length, saying, "There is one last thing in my wagon for you, boy."

Caleb went out and found nothing but an oak box with a handle. "I cannot see anything here, Otto."

"*Ach*," came the gruff reply. "It is there before your face."

Caleb pointed at the box, "This?"

"Yes, boy, that," barked Otto. "Bring it here."

Caleb lifted the heavy box and brought it to Otto.

"Set her down over there …" the older man dismissed him with the tone of his voice.

As Caleb set it down and began to step away, Otto frowned at him and pointed him back to it.

"Well, open it already," Otto said in his gruffest voice.

Caleb opened the box and saw the new set of tools he had fashioned for Otto. When he looked further, there were also a few newly forged items that he had not made himself. Caleb said nothing but looked at *Herr* Lapp, then at his father, then back to *Herr* Lapp.

"But these were for you…," he finally got out.

"Those were never for me, Caleb. A man who can bend iron needs tools from his own hand. These are proof of your skill. I have added a couple of pieces to remind you of your time with me and as payment for the many jobs you did while learning."

Shocked, Caleb stuttered, "This – this is all too much." Then after a moment, "It has been my privilege to learn at your forge. I should not get further reward than that."

"This debt I paid was to your *vater* who proved himself a friend when no others did. As often is the case when I have dealings with Jacob, I am coming away with more than I expected. I have seen the hot iron in you, Caleb. I have seen the fire in your eyes and the strength grow in your spirit. You are another Fisher man I am glad to call friend."

"I can but thank you, *Herr* Lapp," came Caleb's appreciative reply.

"Ha!" chuckled Otto. "If you were but a few years older, I'd be pushing you to court my Sarah. You are a good man, Caleb Fisher."

Caleb, knowing how Otto treasured his *dochter*, knew this was high praise indeed from the man. While he never thought of Sarah *that way*, he was touched by Otto's sentiment.

It was a mere month later that Caleb's older *schwester*, also named Sarah, came home from meeting with Mark Tanner. Not many weeks later, they were married and moving off to Lancaster to run the Tanner Farm.

Mark brought his friend Elmer Mueller who was paired with Sarah's friend Sarah Lapp. While Sarah Lapp never felt that she had time for a suitor, she made time for Elmer. The next season, they were wed with Mark and Sarah Tanner as side-sitters for them.

This left Otto Lapp alone on his farm. Jacob and Ana had him over for meals weekly and even Caleb tried to convince Otto that he was young enough to re-marry, going so far as to mention candidates by name.

Otto could not ever forget the way his family had been treated by the people here. It was different when his Else was alive. They treated her better, but he always felt them looking down upon him, even long after the town had forgotten.

Caleb helped on both farms for planting and for harvests. Otto came to think of him as part nephew, part son, and part farm hand. Their mutual respect grew as the seasons rolled past.

Just before Caleb's seventeenth birthday, he came across his *vater und* Otto finishing what seemed a heated discussion. As Caleb rounded the corner, he heard Jacob's voice, full of resolve saying "No, Otto. It would not do."

Both men quieted as Caleb came in to view. There was an awkward silence until Caleb made an excuse and left the men to speak.

"But Jacob, my Sarah will not take the farm from me," Otto argued. "She and Elmer have a farm in Lancaster County that has been in his *familye* for generations. Please. Your Caleb has been a son to us both, let me do this."

"You have seen for yourself it is too much for one fully grown man. He could never possibly farm both. It would mean hiring men to help and he is too young to manage that properly," came Jacob's repeated disapproval.

"I will not sell this land to any who scorned my family," Otto said, a plea in his voice.

"I wish you would re-think that. There are many good young men here that would love to farm that land," Jacob said, not for the first time.

Otto stood, his arms crossed, and his face set deep in a scowl. "If you will not let Caleb take this land from me, I will sell to *Englishe* before I sell to any in this community."

Jacob knew his friend still harbored ill-will against those who had judged him for his *bruder's* actions. He had not, however, thought it ran as deep as that.

"Otto, my old friend. When did you last see your lovely *dochter?* I confess that I ask for selfish reasons. My Sarah lives near your Sarah. I would have you deliver her a quilt the twins have made for her," Jacob said, changing the subject to something more pleasant.

"It will do no good to go there and speak with her," he replied.

"I did not say go and make trouble, you old goat," Jacob laughed. "I said go and enjoy your *familye*. You spend too much of your time alone. Get yourself surrounded by love and pray for guidance."

"I suppose, if you need me to deliver something to your Sarah, I might as well," Otto agreed, latching onto Jacob's quilt as his excuse to see his Sarah.

"Caleb and I will watch your farm while you are there. Spend the time you need," reassured Jacob.

4

Two days later, Otto set out for Lancaster county. He looked forward to seeing his *enkelkinder*. The two young girls each reminded him of his Else. It would be *gut* to see Elmer as well. He liked the young man who had married his only *dochter*.

As much as he disliked her being so far from him, he was glad she was not going to be a part of this place any further.

Thursday afternoon found him at Sarah Tanner's front door. She looked confused for a moment until he introduced himself, "Hello, Sarah. It has been a few years, *jah?* I came to visit my Sarah, and your *daed* asked me to bring this to you from your *schwestere.*"

"Oh, *Herr* Lapp," Sarah burst out. "It has been too long. Won't you come in for some lemonade?"

"I'll take you up on that another time, if I might. I have come straight here and am eager to see my own Sarah," Otto begged off.

"I am sure she will be thrilled to see you. And those girls of hers will be all over you," Sarah laughed as she spoke.

Otto nodded and handed off the parcel. He made his way to his wagon and then started his horse towards the Mueller farm. Behind him, he did not see the confused look on Sarah's face.

She had taught Emma and Lizzie how to quilt with their mother. Sarah had more quilts than she needed already. She decided that her *vater* was up to something and she was just a part of it. She examined the quilt and was impressed with how far her *schwestere* had progressed in skill.

The Mueller farm had a split oak tree at its entrance. The oak was the largest tree in the area, by far. Otto now saw the top branches in the distance. Despite himself, he set the horse to a faster gait and began to smile.

"*Vater* Lapp," exclaimed Elmer who was hitching up his own horse as Otto arrived. "It is *gut* to see you. Sarah and the girls are inside. I would lead you in, but I must get to the local smith for some repairs on my windmill. We have had to hand pump the water for the cattle these last two days, but it is hard to keep up with them."

Otto looked behind Elmer and saw the building that held a small forge. He knew Elmer had no skill with it, but was surprised to see he did not have anyone on the farm who did.

"Let me look at it, Elmer. Perhaps I might be of use to you," Otto said, taking a real interest. "Do you still have tools and coal for that forge?"

Elmer looked behind him at the shed with the forge. It was as his *grossvater* had left it. Neither he nor his father ever learned to smith.

"I am somewhat embarrassed to tell you that I do not know, *vater* Lapp," replied a sheepish Elmer.

"Let us go find out together then," came Otto's eager reply.

They swept back the webs that had served generations of spiders as home, and found a forge in generally good shape. Some of the mortar needed repointing from lack of use, but there was a full set of tools and a large bin of coal.

The roof over the coal was sound and it did not seem too damp. *I can make this work*, thought Otto. To the side was a wall of tools, no doubt made here on this very forge.

"We have all we need. Go get that part and show me ..."

"Otto," Elmer interrupted, "we will do this, but first, go see your *dochter und enkelkinder, jah?*"

Otto blushed. He was so eager to be of use to another that he had not even said hello to the whole *familye*.

"*Jah*, Elmer, that would be a much better place to start," he nodded.

He had brought several bushels of apples from his trees with him. Sarah used to love to bake apple pies with them. He set a basket of them down inside the Mueller *haus* and took Sarah into his arms.

She hugged her *daed* and reminded him of the names of her *dochtere*: Else was now almost three and Violet was two. She blushed then, and gave her *vater* the news that they were expecting a third child this spring. He congratulated her and Elmer, and heard Else squeal in delight at the thought of a new *bobble* in the *haus*. It was clear that Sarah and Elmer had saved telling the girls until he was here with them.

"She will sleep in my room," claimed Else.

"What if it is a boy?" asked Sarah.

"Then he can sleep with Violet," replied Else, done with the conversation and thinking of a *bruder*.

A round of muted laughter swept through the adults at this.

"Are you hungry, *daed?*" asked Sarah. "We haven't had our lunch yet."

"That would be right *gut*, Sarah," Otto replied. "Elmer and I have some work to do in the forge it seems. Come get us when it is ready."

Otto turned back towards the door. Sarah grabbed his arm and faced her husband.

"Elmer Mueller! You will not be putting my *daed* to work before he even has a chance to bring in his bag. I thought you were going to have the smith fix those vanes."

Before Elmer had a chance to defend himself, Otto stepped in. "Sarah, I'll not see you waste money on a smith while I am here. You can refuse my farm, but you will not refuse my help," Otto said, leaving no room for argument.

This was the first time her *vater* had accepted her refusal to take the farm from him. She knew that was not an easy thing for him.

"I am sorry, *daed*. I did not mean to offend you. We would be delighted if you could help us with the mill. The vanes needing repair are the very ones the smith repaired last for us. It would be good to have a new set of eyes on them."

Elmer kept silent during the exchange. His wife had just yesterday insisted he go back to the smith and demand the repair be made right. He was wise enough not to mention this to her now.

"Elmer," Sarah said, "please show *daed* to his room. After lunch you two can work on that wind mill."

Both men followed her directions and went for Otto's bags.

After lunch, Otto looked around the forge shed and found most everything he would need. The forge tools were all in good condition and there was a decent mix of implements. Not as many as he had at home, but clearly enough for this job.

He started a coal fire and set out the two blades that needed repair. It was clear they had been spot-welded before, but never finished. The steel had not been lined up properly so every time the blade spun it worked to free itself. The visible damage to the blade was from it falling to the ground ... the real problem was the old repair.

This would take a bit of work. He asked Elmer to get him a vane in good order down. They used that to make a template for the pair of new blades.

About the time they got done cutting the new blades, Else came out to get them for supper.

"C'mon, *Grossdaed*, you can sit next to me," Else said and that is how they sat.

"So, am I going to water by hand tomorrow or have you two strong men come to my rescue?" joked Sarah.

Both men looked down at their plates. Sarah started to laugh at this reaction and the girls followed, not really knowing why they were giggling so.

"We have the vanes ready, but we have not replaced them yet. Definitely, right after breakfast, *jah*, Elmer?" Otto questioned.

"Jah, Otto," Elmer agreed, "definitely before lunch."

"I'll pump the water in the morning for the cows. It will be good to be useful for a change," Otto said.

"*Daed*, you don't have to do that," Sarah said, reaching out a hand to cover his own atop the table.

"Working with Elmer today is about the best day I have had in years. I feel like what I did mattered and was appreciated," Otto held back tears as he said these words.

"If you've a mind to be useful, *vater* Lapp, I have a fairly long list of things I've not had a chance to get to," Elmer said, passing a knowing look over to his wife. "If it is not too much trouble, perhaps you could help me with a few?"

"Jacob Fisher has promised to tend my herd while I am here. I am sure we can get an item or two done," Otto said, the warmth of belonging somewhere re-igniting in his chest.

It came to pass that Otto was made irreplaceable at the Mueller farm. After two weeks, he spoke with his *dochter* and Elmer at the breakfast table after prayers.

"I will ask you both this question one last time," Otto began. "Are you both certain you do not want my farm?"

As they started into their oft repeated reasons, he stopped them.

"I understand," he said. "I have felt useful these past weeks and appreciate your efforts to make that happen. I must return to my own farm though. I've relied on my neighbors enough."

"*Vater* Lapp," began Elmer, "if we had said yes to your farm, would you have lived there with us?"

"Of course," answered Otto.

"And since we said 'no', you will sell the farm, or have it sold after you pass, *jah?*" Elmer led Otto.

"I'd sell it before I passed to make sure it was not sold to any that had looked down upon us," Otto said, still not sure where this conversation was leading.

"I would like to combine those then," Elmer said as if that made sense to everyone.

"I am sorry. I do not follow you," Otto replied after brief thought.

"We want you to come live with us, *daed,*" said Sarah. "You are as useful here as you are welcome. Your *enkelkinder* do not wish for you to leave, nor do we."

"But, my farm ..." started Otto.

"You have already said to us that you will sell your farm before you die, *jah?*" Elmer asked.

"Well, yes but ..." Otto sputtered.

"And you did say that you'd live with us on a farm, *jah?*" Elmer continued.

Otto tried to think of a reason, but now saw that Elmer had talked him into a corner as easily as a cow into a pen.

"I will give this some thought. I must get home and tend my farm for now," Otto said. "I cannot ask my neighbors to do that for me any longer."

"Please, *daed,*" Sarah asked him again. "Please come to live with us here. What you are calling your home is a place where you are surrounded by bad memories. Come and live with your *familye.*"

"Sarah, Elmer, I will give this much thought. I will stay for a while today and help with the girls, so that you might go and help at the Stoltzfus farm. With their *mutti* in the hospital, they may need some help."

"*Gut*, I want to get over to see how Rebecca and Ruby are doing. They are good girls," Sarah replied with concern in her voice.

So much like my Else, thought Otto, admiring her desire to be a part of this community.

Sarah did not make it back until an hour or so past the lunch hour. She worked to get dinner going and the children settled in.

"How are they?" Elmer asked.

"They are doing well and did not need much help. Their *vater* is not doing well at all. It does not look like their *mutti* will be coming home soon. We all need pray for her," Sarah answered.

Otto had waited for Sarah and the kids to return before leaving for Barnville. He was not a half hour into his trip when he realized there was much more behind him than he had waiting at home. It was then he realized that home was behind him with his *familye*, not back at his farm.

5

He stopped at Jacob's to let them know he was back, and had a long talk with his old friend.

"Otto, we will miss you. *I* will miss you, friend, but you look happier than I have seen you since Else passed. I think you have made the right decision," Jacob said after Otto told him about his plans. "What will you do with the farm?"

"I will go see the auctioneer tomorrow," replied Otto.

Jacob had a large frown on his face hearing this. It was likely the *Englishe* would buy up the land. But the frown disappeared as Otto continued.

"I will need him to sell off the livestock and remaining seed and feed," he said. "I cannot ask my friends to tend my farm as well as their own forever. It was a great gift that you did this for me, old friend."

Jacob pointed to Caleb. "That is the man you need to thank. He has run this farm nearly by himself while I have tended yours," Jacob replied, pleased with his son. "It was good practice. This is the life he has chosen. It did him *gut* to get a taste of doing it."

"A little more tired than normal, but no worse for the wear, *Herr* Lapp," Caleb said, smiling.

Otto thanked the men again and made his way to his farm. As he pulled into the path to the barn, he felt the emptiness of the old place.

There were no lights burning, no bread baking, no children laughing, crying, or napping. He no longer felt at home here. He prayed before entering the *haus*, thanking *Gott* for his safe passage and guidance with these decisions. He then did something he had not done since he was a much younger man, he prayed for his neighbors in Lancaster, the Stoltzfus family. He did not know them, yet he wanted to help them. He missed that feeling.

With an auction already scheduled, it took only about a week to get his animals included and sold off. The Beiler farm took a good number of his herd, most of the rest stayed in the community as well.

He had four cows delivered to the Fishers with orders not to return with them no matter how much they said "no". He could no more charge Jacob than he could charge his own *familye*.

He sold off many of his personal items and loaded his wagon. The next morning, he had his last cup of coffee on the front porch. He prayed for a safe trip, praised *Gott* for the abundance he had been given, and asked for guidance as to what he should do with the land. Finishing his prayer, he got up on the wagon, tucked his empty mug next to him, and left his farm for the last time.

He had sent a letter to Elmer to prepare him and Sarah. With the money from selling his herd, he would help them expand the farmhouse to include a bigger great room and add a small *grosshaus*.

Sarah had spent much of the last week running back and forth to the Stoltzfus farm. Their *mutti*, Mary, was in very bad condition and their *vater* was not handling it well at all. She remembered how her *vater* had grieved the

246

passing of her *mutti*. She was only five at the time, but could remember him crying. He cried for one day and never again in front of her.

Otto arrived at the farm and they unpacked his belongings into the *haus,* the barn, and some items went to the forge. Otto noted that Elmer was wasting no time, the stakes were already set for the *grosshaus.* It would be mere months before the *haus* was ready for him.

In that meantime, Otto went with Sarah several times to the Stoltzfus farm. He offered help with the planting, the harvesting of hay, and general repairs as they came up. He came to like the girls and spent time with their *vater,* Vernon, who seemed to have lost his way in the world.

It was on one of these visits he met up with Samuel, a gentleman caller for Rebecca. He reminded Otto of Caleb.

With Vernon away at the hospital from dawn to dusk most days, Otto and Samuel arranged to be on the farm together so that what needed doing could be done without causing a potential scandal of Samuel being alone with the sisters. Riding home from meeting was one thing, but spending most of the entire week at the farm would not look right for the girls.

One day, Otto answered a knock at the door of his *dochter's haus.* It was Samuel.

"I am glad it's you that answered. She has passed, *Herr* Lapp. I am here to let your family know. Will you help me deliver this news? I know this is going to be hard for Sarah. She and my Rebecca have become close."

"*Jah*, friend Samuel. I will help you," Otto replied, admiring this young man's strength, not only in what he was doing for the Stoltzfus *familye*, but for getting help when needed. That was a rare quality indeed.

The two men broke the news to Sarah and Elmer. Otto and Elmer consoled her as she cried for her friend. Samuel went back to the Stoltzfus *haus* before heading home.

A few days later, Samuel came by again with the details of the funeral. It was to be held that Saturday at the Stoltzfus *haus*. Sarah was asked if she could assist with the meal while they buried their *mutti*. The medical bills were so large from the hospital stay that their *vater* would not hire help or rent a *kich* to make it easier. This would be a traditional funeral, done in the old ways.

Sarah made breads, pies, and desserts leading up to the date, and Elmer slaughtered a number of chickens to help feed the crowds. One of the Stoltzfus' neighbors offered the use of a wagon-size grill used for occasions such as this throughout the community. Otto volunteered to help Samuel retrieve the grill.

"Otto," Samuel started as the men traveled the short distance between the Stoltzfus farm and the neighbor to get the grill. "Please speak with *Herr* Stoltzfus. He was offered help with the hospital bill by the *Englishe*. The man that drove into them had no insurance, but the hospital has offered to lower the bills. He refuses."

Otto was doubly troubled with this. He was conflicted by which disturbed him more: his new friend, Vernon Stoltzfus, was perhaps not making *gut* choices, or that his other new friend, Samuel, was speaking out of turn about another's finances.

The sneeze of the trailing horse behind the wagon broke the silence, then Otto spoke. "Samuel, I am not willing to be a part of gossip. The matter is not of my concern and I would think it would not be yours either, *jah,*" he said quietly.

"I intend to marry Rebecca. I do not mean to gossip. I am concerned for her *familye*. I am concerned for her," replied Samuel.

"I am reminded of Romans 5," Otto said, staring ahead at the bend ahead of them in the road. "Therefore, since we have been justified through faith, we have peace with *Gott* through our Lord Jesus Christ, through whom we have gained access by faith into this grace in which we now stand. And we boast in the hope of the glory of *Gott*. Not only so, but we also glory in our sufferings, because we know that suffering produces perseverance; perseverance, character; and character, hope."

"So, you think this suffering is *Gott's* work, then," asked a downhearted Samuel.

"I rather think that how we persevere is *Gott's* work in this and the test of our own character, Samuel. I will pray for help and guidance. I would ask you to do the same," Otto replied.

"I have done little else but pray. I would not have mentioned it, but the more I prayed, the more called I felt to ask your opinion. Perhaps *Gott* wants me to read Romans, *jah?*" Samuel said after some thought.

"Perhaps so, my young friend. Perhaps so." Otto said, nodding his head.

The two men made short work of hitching the second horse to the grill wagon and started the trek back to the Stoltzfus farm. Each man thought long and hard on their conversation.

According to custom, *Frau* Stoltzfus was embalmed, placed into a simple pine casket, and set for viewing in the great room. Throughout Saturday, friends came and paid their respects and reminisced about her life. The preacher's first sermon was centered around Psalm 133:1, "See, how good and how pleasing it is for brothers to live together as one."

The second sermon was centered around biblical passages pertaining to death and beyond. After an hour, he closed with Thessalonians 5:9-11, "For *Gott* has not destined us for wrath, but to obtain salvation through our Lord Jesus Christ, who died for us so that whether we are awake or asleep we might live with him. Therefore encourage one another and build one another up, just as you are doing."

After this, he spoke *Frau* Stoltzfus' name and prayed over her as the attendants filed past the body for a final look. The close family would attend the burial, the rest would eat the prepared meal and socialize.

Because he was not yet engaged to Rebecca, Samuel stayed and helped with the meal along with Otto and other community members. There were few tasks that the women did not have well in hand, but they helped where they could.

In between tasks, the two men stood close and spoke of the future. As in most cultures, the young man talked about his plans and the older man listened to him, reminiscing of his own youth.

"In a little over a year, I hope to have the money to get a farm near here," Samuel shared. "The *Englishe* are buying up so much of the land nearby, but I believe *Gott* will take care of the details."

"It is *gut* to have both faith in *Gott* and a plan, Samuel," Otto replied. "One without the other does not always work out as well as both together."

"*Herr* Stoltzfus talked about selling his farm to pay the hospital bills. I've not enough saved to stop that from happening," bemoaned Samuel.

"Have you spoken to a bank about this?" Otto inquired. Like most he did not like the thought of debt, but for something so large as this, perhaps it would be an answer.

"The farm is too big, they tell me, to loan me enough to buy it," Samuel shook his head. "I am hoping it does not end in the hands of *Englishe.*"

"That would not do at all." Otto looked around the great room at the dispersing crowd. *No, that would not do.* "I will speak with Vernon on this. We have become friends. I shall see what his mind is on this."

"Thank you, *Herr* Lapp," the younger man said with respect.

6

The following week, Otto sat with Vernon over coffee.

"Please, Vernon. Forgive my speaking of this," began Otto. "I was told that you are to be selling your farm. Is that true?"

"I'll pay them every cent," a clearly distraught Vernon Stoltzfus spat out. "I'll not have them treat me like I am not *gut* enough, that my Mary was not *gut* enough."

"I am not here to question your motives, friend," Otto reassured him. "I am curious if you had a plan or needed help is all. Do you know of any Amish in the area needing land for an elder son?"

"There are many in the area. I do not know any actively looking," Vernon said with a mix of anger and frustration in his voice. "I am sorry. I am not myself. I need to do this soon and have many plans to finalize between now and then. I need to find a new home for my girls."

"Give me a few days, Vernon. Let me do what I can for you. I would very much like to be helpful. I remember losing my Else. It was hard enough without also losing my farm," Otto said, sharing the man's grief as no other could.

Otto went to the bishop and spoke with him, looking for any that might have both desire and ability to purchase the farm. He got a couple of names to follow up on - the Yoder family, the eldest Weaver boy, and the Millers. He also was given a date to come back and join the district.

Despite his efforts, he found either desire and no ability, or no desire. Otto then did something he found distasteful. He went to see an *Englishe* developer.

He pulled his wagon in front of the office building. The noise of the cars and the people was near-deafening. He made his way inside the building and was glad the office was on the first floor. He had ridden an elevator once and did not much care for it.

McManus Builders the sign said. Otto opened the door and asked to speak with *Herr* McManus. The receptionist looked at this elderly Amish man in his blue shirt and straw hat and stifled a laugh. Mr. McManus only spoke to people who spoke to others to do his work.

"Do you have an appointment?" she asked him.

"No, but I have business to speak of with him," Otto said firmly.

A door opened behind the receptionist and a middle-aged man came out. He wore a suit without the jacket on and the sleeves rolled up. He looked around for someone then stopped, looking at Otto and the receptionist.

"You are *Herr* McManus, *jah*?" Otto asked.

"Well, who have we here, Donna?" the man replied to the receptionist instead of Otto.

"This man has no appointment, sir. I was about to tell him to call for one before coming in next time," Donna replied.

"That would be a problem for you, would it not?" This time he spoke to Otto.

"I have no phone, nor any desire for one, if that is what you mean," Otto said plainly.

"Well, it seems my three o'clock is not here yet. I do not abide by tardiness, Mr …"

"Otto Lapp, *Herr* McManus." With this the men shook hands.

"I have very little time. Come into my office and let me see what business we might have." Turning to his receptionist, he added, "Donna, when my three o'clock arrives, tell them they can wait until six or reschedule."

The two men went into the office and both sat down. Otto was offered and accepted a glass of water from the builder, then began to speak.

"I have a friend. He has had some things go badly in his life recently," Otto explained.

"I am a builder, *Herr* Lapp," said McManus, being as respectful as he could. "I am not sure how I might be of help to him or to you."

"You buy land to build your *hause* on, *jah?*" replied Otto.

Now he had Bob McManus' full attention. He built quality homes and land was at a premium. He had recently purchased a big tract, but any time Amish land became available, he wanted to at least see it.

"I am always interested in opportunities," McManus replied. "I am not in an immediate need, but tell me more about this land."

The two men discussed the land, the situation, and the reason that Otto was there and not the owner. Despite himself, Bob McManus respected both Otto and the man who had earned Otto's friendship. He agreed to go to the farm the next day and speak with the owner. The two men shook hands and Bob McManus led him to the door.

"Who was that?" asked Donna after Otto left.

"That, Donna, was opportunity," McManus replied to her, then added, "I will be leaving after lunch tomorrow. Clear my afternoon, please."

"Yes, sir," came the reply.

A bit after one in the afternoon the next day, a car pulled up to the Stoltzfus farm. Bob McManus got out and looked around. He had already pulled the county records. This was sixty acres of land with roads on each side of it. The road to the rear of the property had power, water, and telephone lines running past it. He would make the community entrance there if they could come to terms.

Vernon and Otto sat at the table sipping lemonade when a knock came at the door. Rebecca answered it and led the *Englishe* to her father.

"Vernon, this is Robert McManus, the man I spoke to you about," Otto said, introducing the two men. "*Herr* McManus, this is Vernon Stoltzfus. You have met one of his twin *dochtere*, Rebecca, at the door. Come, sit." With this Otto pointed to the wooden seat across the table from Vernon.

"Your friend speaks highly of you, Vernon. May I call you Vernon?" started McManus.

"*Jah,* I think it would be *gut* to dismiss with the formalities. I am a tired man and I think we both know this was not what I had hoped would happen with my farm," Vernon said, with sadness clear in his voice.

"I have taken the liberty of looking at the maps in the county building. I can minimize the disruption to the rest of the community by not making the entrance here amid the other farms. I will make some homes on this side for the Amish. I find it helps if we do not insult and ruin that which makes us what we are. Many wish to live peacefully near the Amish, Vernon. I would like to make that work for everyone," McManus finished, stating his case.

"My friend Otto, here," Vernon said waving his hand to Otto. "Has he explained why I am selling?"

"Yes, my condolences to you. I would hope you do not judge us all by the actions of one," Bob McManus said with conviction. "I would very much like to buy this land from you. I would be willing to pay a fair price for it." With this, he wrote a number on a piece of paper and folded it. He then handed the paper to Vernon. Vernon looked at the number. It was enough to pay off his debts. Before he could accept, Otto broke in.

"*Herr* McManus."

"Please, call me Bob," he replied.

"Bob, then. You mentioned that you had no real need for this land, but you did have desire, j*ah?*" Otto asked.

"Yes." McManus looked at the man before him, seeing shrewdness about his eyes. "I have a pair of communities in development now. We should be building in them for years before they are full. This land will be developed after those."

"Would you be willing to let my friend live out his days on the land, rent back the part you intend to make Amish *hause* on?" Otto asked.

"Well, so long as I could start development on the backside of the property when I am ready, I think we might be able to work something out. It is called lifetime tenancy. You would live out your days here and I would offer a bit less for the land," Bob said, explaining to Vernon. "Say ten percent less?"

Otto interrupted again, "With so much of the money going to the hospital in this case, would you consider waiving that reduction? You would still be able to build all but the Amish *hause,*" Otto spoke up for his friend.

Bob McManus looked at both men. He knew his numbers, knew that with the market and the way it was growing, the houses would be worth more a few years down the road.

"I will drop it to a five percent reduction," offered Bob.

"Make it two and then shake this man's hand, *jah* Vernon?"

Vernon nodded his head and then after a few moments, Bob reached across the table and shook his hand. He then shook Otto's hand.

"You are a good friend, Otto Lapp. I wish I had friends as protective of me as you are of yours," Bob said with much respect.

"You have made a fair deal here, Mister McManus," Otto used the *Englishe* word out of respect. "When the time comes for you to need labor to build these homes, please remember the Amish here. They will work hard for a fair man."

Bob McManus, like most, tried hard to recruit Amish workers. He had had limited success. It would be beneficial to him to have the good will of the workers nearby.

"I would be willing to employ those who desire it and would go so far as to make an Amish-only crew if enough have experience building. I know that working with us is not always easy for you," Bob said.

"I will speak to many on your behalf. This deal you have made will also speak for itself," Otto finished, standing.

The two men bade Bob McManus farewell with the assurance that the paperwork would be forthcoming.

Otto and Vernon stood side by side in the kitchen alone.

"So, I will live out my days here," Vernon said somewhat flatly. "That is a *gut* thing. I must thank you, Otto. This McManus seems decent enough for an *Englishe.*"

"I am sorry that I could not find an Amish boy to become a man here, Vernon," Otto said to his friend.

"You have kept some of the land Amish. That is more than I had hoped for."

A few weeks later, the deal closed. Bob McManus gave Vernon two checks. One to pay the hospital with and another much smaller one for himself. Otto had driven his friend to the bank for the closing and then drove him to the hospital to pay the balance.

"I am tired, friend. Please take me home." Vernon said, melancholy in his voice.

"I would think you would be pleased to no longer have that debt," Otto tried to cheer his friend.

"I would rather still have my Mary and my farm, Otto, but yes. It is a relief not to have such a large debt." Vernon tried and failed to sound cheerful.

They rode home in silence. Otto was glad to have been helpful to both his friend and his new community, while Vernon was deep in his own thoughts.

Otto bade his friend farewell at his doorstep and returned to Elmer and Sarah's *haus*. His home was to be ready soon, as much as he would enjoy some quiet, he was glad to be as close to the happy noises of life.

7

Summer came and went, the crops neared ready for harvest, and Otto helped on Elmer's and Vernon's farms.

Increasingly, he was concerned for his friend. Vernon had yet to shake the melancholy that was now overtaking him as an afternoon shadow overtakes the dirt near the barn.

Otto's skill with the forge became well-known and he came to know many of his neighbors by providing quality repairs and quality iron works for those in need. Many days, he looked out from his forge and thought, *This is the life Gott meant for me.*

As fall approached, Samuel asked Rebecca to marry. As he had predicted, she agreed. They would live with Vernon until Samuel could afford a farm of their own. Otto was happy for the pair. They were always happier when he saw them together than when they were alone. He was also pleased for his friend to have another man there to help with the now smaller farm.

Samuel came personally to invite the family, making sure to specifically include Otto, to their wedding. It still delighted Otto to be accepted and wanted in a community.

At the wedding, Otto was surprised that Vernon did not smile much at all. He looked like he had lost weight and the spark of life was weak within him.

Otto tried to get his friend to eat the fine spread that was before them, but Vernon claimed he was not hungry.

Otto found the groom and his bride a short-time later, congratulating Samuel and the now Rebecca King. He made them promise to visit him when they did their rounds this winter. He would feed them a dinner, then Elmer and Sarah could feed them breakfast. It would make for a weekend with less traveling for them. They accepted his hospitality and it was settled for late February.

It was customary to give a wedding gift to the couple when they visited. Usually the items were utilitarian: pots, pans, glassware. Otto wanted to make something for them.

Both Rebecca and her sister were *gut* bakers. When Rebecca left, they would have to divide their mother's tin bread pans. Otto decided to make up a bunch in different sizes and let the twins decide who got what when Samuel had his farm ready to go. Otto began work crafting the pans. It would have been easier to buy them, but these would last forever if taken care of.

Thanksgiving came, and Otto spent it with his *familye*. His granddaughter, Else, sat on his lap for an hour listening to him read to her. They read of Jonah and of Samson. She loved these stories. Little Violet sat at his feet listening to his voice as he told the stories with inflection and much interest. They prayed, and Otto found that what he was most thankful for was in this room.

He also said a prayer for his friend, Vernon. He was getting thinner by the day and had lost much of the spark that used to fill him.

Christmas arrived, then New Years. Otto's worry for his friend grew stronger as the days grew shorter and colder. Otto found excuses to visit the man at least twice most weeks. While Vernon appeared pleased to see him, he was not his old self. Otto redoubled his efforts to help his friend.

In February, Samuel and Rebecca came calling. Otto welcomed them and they all sat for coffee. Samuel and Rebecca spoke of all the places they had visited and the wonderful people they had met. When Otto gave them the tin bread and baking pans, Rebecca's face lit up.

"*Herr* Lapp," she said almost in tears. "You made these?"

"*Jah*, it seemed to me that the ones you can buy are not so sturdy," he answered back.

"These are like my *mutti's*. She told me that she had gotten hers as a wedding gift. I had feared that either my *schwester* or I would have to cook without them. I do not think you could know how much this present pleases me," she replied between silent tears of joy.

"I am pleased that you like them. I hope you can pass them down to your own *dochtere* many years from now," Otto replied.

They prayed together and ate a fine meal that Otto had cooked himself. He had saved some of the applesauce from the trees on his farm for just this day. After eating, they made the walk to Elmer and Sarah's home and prepared to bed down for the night. This was the last weekend of their travels and they would be home tomorrow for good.

When March arrived, it did so as no one's friend. First was a late snowstorm putting nearly a foot of snow upon the ground. A few days later came the news that Otto had dreaded. Vernon had passed. He had truly lost his will to live and given up. Otto prayed for understanding and helped the newlyweds prepare for the second funeral in too short of a time.

"Samuel," Otto said to his young friend while they moved chairs into the *haus* for the funeral. "What are your plans now?"

"I have been giving it much thought. I was thinking I would go speak to the *Englishe* to see if he will rent us the land for another year. I think by then I will be ready to find a smaller farm for us," Samuel said without conviction.

"I would go with you, if you would like," Otto replied.

"*Jah*, that would be *gut*. We are praying for *Gott* to show us our path," Samuel replied.

"I will join you in that prayer, friend," Otto agreed.

Two days later they went to Bob McManus' office. When they entered, Donna looked up and smiled at them.

"*Herr* Lapp, isn't it?" the receptionist asked.

"Yes, ma'am," he replied. "I was hoping to see *Herr* McManus if it is not too much trouble."

"I will let him know you are here," Donna replied and went into the office behind her.

A few minutes later, three men came out the same door. They did not seem terribly happy. Whatever business they had did not appear to have gone well for them.

Donna returned and ushered them into the developer's office. "Otto, my friend!" boomed Bob's voice.

Otto saw the evidence of much work going on. There were rolled up blueprints stacked on a long table, framed pictures of *Englishe hause* leaning against a wall, and an inch of paperwork spread across the desk. The two were offered water by Donna. Both men politely accepted.

"I got word of Vernon Stoltzfus' passing. My condolences to you. I know he was a friend of yours," Bob began. "What brings you back to my doorstep? Do you have more land for me? I'm about finished with the permits and planning for that farm. This will be a community that benefits everyone."

"Well, no," began Otto in a much more serious tone than Bob McManus'. "I came to introduce a friend. This is Samuel King. He has married Vernon Stoltzfus' *dochter*, Rebecca."

"Glad to meet you, son. Any friend of Otto's is welcome here. My condolences to you as well. I did not know him well, but my dealings with your father-in-law led me to believe him a man of much integrity." Bob said, then shifted the conversation "Were you looking for work? I will tell you, Otto, we have had many new workers come to us from that community. We will be able to have two Amish-only building crews. I am going to have them build the Amish homes first as a gesture of goodwill to the community."

"You are a right *gut* man, Bob McManus," Otto said, the conviction of it strong in his voice.

"Mr. McManus," started Samuel, taking the hat from his head.

"Please, call me Bob," came the reply.

"Bob," restarted Samuel. "I have not come for work. I am glad to hear that there will be work for some from our community and thank you for that. I have come to see if you would be willing to lease me the land you allowed my father-in-law to retain for a year."

Bob McManus' face fell at this request. He leaned back in his chair and it was clear to all he was thinking hard about his reply.

"Samuel, Otto," started a clearly troubled Bob McManus. "I am sorry. When I got word of Mr. Stoltzfus' passing, I made arrangements with my bank to start development of the property. I cannot go back on my word to them. The men you just saw leave wanted to build some of the lots there, but I am told the community is selling out so quickly that we will be building them all ourselves. The estate should have gotten a letter requesting the property be vacant within a month. I can give you two, if that would help."

"That would be very kind of you, *Herr* McManus."

"I know this was not the answer you had hoped for. I trust you will not hold this against me, Otto," Bob said, the sincerity clear in his voice.

"No, my *Englishe* friend, you made a fair deal and have lived by its terms. I can hold no fault there. I also appreciate the extra month you have offered. It will give time to sell off the things they can and pack up the rest," Otto said.

With that, Otto stood, followed by Samuel and then Bob, walking them to the door, shaking each of their hands as they left.

"Samuel, if you are interested, I would make you a fair deal on the first of the Amish homes we are building there," Bob offered.

"I appreciate that offer, *Herr McManus*. Can I have some time to discuss it with my wife?" replied Samuel.

"Of course, take the time you need," Bob replied, feeling better for having been able to offer the clearly disappointed young man any path forward.

They took their leave and walked to the wagon. On the otherwise quiet ride home, Otto suggested they visit the auctioneer to reserve a date. Samuel reluctantly agreed.

The auction was scheduled for three weeks. That would give them enough time to decide what would stay and what would go.

Samuel and Rebecca sat alone in the *kich*. Ruby had gone upstairs to bed early, leaving them their privacy. They sat silent, each deep in thought. Finally, Samuel spoke.

"Rebecca, I fear we will have to find a home to rent. It will make it more difficult for us to have our own farm as soon as we had planned," he said. "We will need to sell everything not vital to help with expenses. With the little the hospital didn't take from the sale of the farm, we might still get land in a few years."

"But what of Ruby?" Rebecca asked, the love for her *schwester* clear in her voice. "Where will she go?"

"I assumed she would come with us until a husband comes looking for her. She is my *familye* now too, you know," Samuel said to his wife.

"You are a *gut* man, Samuel King. I should marry you again if you asked," she said to him.

"Then I will ask again and again, my Rebecca. All the days of my life," Samuel replied, the truth of his love plain in his voice.

So, the next morning they told Ruby of their plan. She was grateful and let them both know. She promised to work hard with them wherever they went to help them get their farm sooner instead of later. The dedication she had to that was evident when they were sorting items for sale. Many of Ruby's personal items were added over the objections of both Samuel and Rebecca.

"We will need to find a small place to rent. We will not have room for all of this," was Ruby's only reply.

On the day prior to the sale, Elmer and Sarah came to help their friends set up and prepare. The auctioneer was there as well to make sure his people knew what was being sold and what was staying.

"We will keep the wagon and two horses. The rest must go," Samuel told them when they toured the barn area.

They kept some furnishings, clothing, and a few small items; the rest would be sold. And sold it all was.

There was a big turnout of both Amish and *Englishe*. Much of the farm equipment stayed in the district. Much of the furnishings and personal items went to the *Englishe*. The auction took most of the day and when night fell, there was an echo inside the *haus* in all but the bedrooms.

The sale, even after the auctioneer's cut, brought more than they expected, but nowhere near enough to purchase even a small farm. Samuel hugged his wife, then she hugged her twin. They would have to find a home in the next few weeks and leave this place for the last time.

8

"Elmer," started Sarah to her husband across their dinner table. "I do hope they can find a place near here."

"*Jah,* we will pray for them to find their home," Elmer agreed.

"They have yet to find a place to rent?" asked Otto, who had gotten accustomed to eating dinner with his *familye* most evenings.

"Yes, *daed.* Samuel wanted to see how much the auction brought in before committing. He had hoped to maybe have enough to lease a farm or to buy a small one." The tone in Sarah's voice made it clear that was a hope that had not come to fruition.

"I will pray with you then for all of them," Otto said, and they bowed their heads and asked for *Gott's* wisdom and help.

Otto rose early the next day, did the chores he took upon himself, and made his way to see his friend, Samuel. He had much on his mind and was surprised when he looked up and found he had already arrived.

"Otto," Samuel's voice rang out in greeting him. "What brings you here so early this morning?"

"I hope I do not intrude. I would speak to you privately, if you have some time," Otto asked.

Samuel nodded his head and then Rebecca and Ruby left them the room.

"Samuel, I hope that you are not offended, but I would like to speak with you about your situation," Otto began.

"We are friends. Speak freely." Samuel replied wondering where this might lead.

"When I helped make the deal with *Herr* McManus, I thought that we had bought you enough time to save for your farm, and maybe even for Ruby to find her own husband. I did not expect Vernon to pass so soon," Otto said.

"You made a very fair deal for Vernon and for all of us and cannot hold yourself to blame for the results," Samuel replied, trying to absolve Otto of any guilt he might be feeling.

"How close are you to having the money for your farm? Perhaps I could loan you the difference?" Otto asked.

Samuel told him what he had saved. Otto did not have the money to make up the difference between that and what even a small farm in the area would cost.

"I am sorry, Samuel. I am not able to make up the difference," Otto said to his young friend.

"I would not ask that of you. You have been a blessing to my *familye* already. I'd ask no more of you."

"Perhaps ..." Otto began then stopped. "I must speak with Elmer and Sarah," he said, then stood suddenly, excusing himself.

Otto drove himself to the bank and spoke with the branch manager. After a brief conversation, they shook hands and Otto left for home. Upon making the turn at the large oak, he saw Elmer working on a pull-behind rake near the barn. He drove to him.

"Elmer, I would speak to you and Sarah together, please," Otto said to his son-in-law.

"Can I finish this up or is this an emergency?" Elmer asked, in part due to the speed Otto had come toward him with the wagon.

"Let me give you a hand moving that," Otto replied, showing some urgency.

The two men made quick work finishing the greasing and maintenance of the tool that made rows of hay in the fields to help it dry and make it easier to gather after it was cut. They then pushed it into the cover and protection of the barn.

"Let us go find Sarah," Otto remarked when finished.

The three sat at the table with the afternoon setting sun lighting the room. Otto explained his plan and they agreed. He had not expected much disagreement from these two. They were full of the grace and charity of *Gott's* own heart.

"It is done then," Otto said smiling. "I will speak to him tomorrow."

Otto drove out to the Stoltzfus farm the next day and asked to speak to the whole *familye*. It took a few minutes to get all three to the table.

"Samuel, since this concerns all three of you, I hope you do not mind having Ruby at the table with us," Otto said, looking at Samuel for his approval to continue.

"She is *familye*, Otto," Samuel replied.

"If this is business, do we need to be here?" asked Rebecca.

"I think it best, Rebecca. The business is simple enough. I have found a farm for Samuel. It is a bit smaller than this farm was, but it is not in this county. I know the owner well enough and can get it for a reasonable price, if you would have it," Otto said to the three.

Samuel's face lit up. "You know what I have to work with. Surely that cannot buy a farm near this size," he said, the confusion and disbelief clear in his voice.

"No, it would not. I think what you have is enough not only for the farm, but enough for a few cows, hens, and some feed and seed to get you to your first harvest if you were willing to make the move," Otto said to them. "It is a couple-hour drive from here. You would have to start new in a strange place. Would you find that acceptable?"

Samuel turned to his wife who shared his smile. The two then turned to Ruby. Her face was blank, deep in thought. As the silence ran deeper, she looked up seeing everyone looking at her.

"I am a guest in your home. If you would make room for me there, I would be happy to come," she said flatly.

"I have spent much time at this farm and can vouch for the fields and the condition," Otto offered, keeping his smile hidden. "Will you take my word, or would you need to see it?"

"Where is the farm, Otto?" Rebecca asked.

"Barnville," came the reply.

"Barnville? Didn't you say that you came from there?" started Samuel, then he stopped. "This is your farm, isn't it, Otto?"

"It has sat waiting for a farmer, Samuel. I will never return there. I am home here now. If you are all willing, then let you and I discuss the price, shall we?"

The women nodded agreement and left the men to speak. The two men took little time before they shook hands and agreed to meet at the bank in two days to finalize the paperwork.

"I fear I have forgotten to mention that the plow needs repair. Your neighbor there, Caleb Fisher, is a good man with the forge. He will be able to do the repair if you cannot," Otto said to him.

Rebecca stood with Ruby, packing their remaining belongings several days later. She could not help but see the hint of sadness in her twin's face.

"I will miss this home too, Ruby," she offered, trying to find what had her sister feeling blue.

"*Jah*, I will miss this farm. I am glad that we will not see it torn down though. I think that would be sadder than moving away," Ruby replied. "Perhaps there will be a farmer for me in this new town," she added, trying to sound hopeful.

"If not, you could always come back and marry the butcher's son" she teased Ruby, who had shied away from the advances of the young man at least three separate times.

"I trust it will not come to that. I would hope you would put up a shed and let me live out my days alone before you made me agree to that," Ruby laughed with her *schwester*.

The two men met, signed the papers and shook hands. Samuel and the twins would be ready to leave in two more days. They wanted to get there to prepare for the spring planting. On most farms, those preparations had started long ago.

That night, Otto ate dinner with his *familye*. He got hugs and special little girl kisses from both of his *enkelkinder* before he headed to his own bed. Sarah grasped his hand before he walked from the *haus*. "I love you, *daed*."

"And I love you. It has been one of the greatest joys of my life being here with you all," Otto hugged his daughter before heading out into the darkened sky towards his home.

He wiped a tear from his eye and thanked *Gott* for His good blessings upon his life. He fell into a contented, peaceful sleep in his warm bed in the *grosshaus*.

That night, for the first time since she passed, Otto dreamt of his wife Else. He could hear a chorus, like angels, singing off somewhere in the distance. Else grasped his hand, leading him through a wheat field. A sun he could not see warmed him like no other had before.

When he next looked up, Otto beheld the radiant figure of Christ. Otto knelt before him and cried out in joy. Jesus smiled and embraced them both.

"Welcome, my good and faithful servants," Jesus said.

At that moment, a sense of familiarity gripped him. He awoke in the darkness of night. The moon shined through the small window illuminating the room.

Humbled, Otto realized that what he'd been feeling these past weeks was him becoming closer to *Gott*. He hopped out of bed and knelt.

He prayed repentance for shutting out the people of Barnville and that Samuel and Rebecca would be better neighbors than he had been these past years. He also thanked *Gott* for the gift of whatever time he had left with his family.

Building a Future

The Fishers

(An Amish Life 5)

1

It was a mild February day in Barnville. The winter had been gentler than most. Snow had come as it always did there, but it came for brief visits, then leaving shortly after. Much like Caleb and his new bride Ruby had been doing for these last dozen weekends, visiting relatives both near and far.

This was the last weekend of it. They were headed home. Well, almost. They had agreed to save Samuel and Ruby's *schwester*, Rebecca, for the very last visit. They were nearly there. It was a Saturday morning. They would sleep in their own bed this evening and for the rest of their lives.

Caleb was glad to see so many of his *familye* and friends, but it would be *gut* for them to get into the rhythm of their own life.

"I do not wish to complain," Caleb said turning to his wife bundled in her warmest coat and snuggled next to him, "but I am glad to be done with these travels."

"Caleb," Ruby said sounding shocked. "Your *familye* has been so very kind and generous with us. I have been made welcome in a large and loving *familye*. It has been a wonderful experience for me."

"*Jah*, my Ruby. It has been great to see cousins and uncles and even cousins of uncles," Caleb said light-heartedly, "but I am glad that it has come to an end so that I might have you alone for myself a while."

"It is *gut* that you have yet to tire of this old maid," Ruby teased him.

"I wonder if I shall ever hear the end of that," Caleb replied with mock disappointment.

"Perhaps when we are old, and I get forgetful," came the reply from his bride.

"I know you too well for that, Ruby Fisher. You will have told our *kinder* to remind you," Caleb joked back with her.

This was one of the many things Caleb found captivating about his Ruby. They enjoyed talking with each other. They respected each other deeply, but still managed to tease each other playfully.

"We are nearly there. We are coming up on Peter and Emma's property around this next turn." Caleb let his new bride know so that she could do all those things she did before meeting with someone.

"Look, there is a path now back to a clearing. That must be where they plan their *haus*. Do we have a moment to drive up and see?" Ruby asked.

"*Jah*, we have the time," Caleb said, slowing the horse down to take the left turn into the new cut path.

"He has already not only cut the trees, but the stumps are all pulled too," he remarked. "That is much work done already! They will be living here in a couple more months, I would think."

"I will miss them being at *mutti's haus*. I am glad they will still be so close," Ruby said, looking over the land.

"*Jah,* I think that Peter will be a right *gut* neighbor." Caleb nodded his head in agreement.

With that, they left the empty lot and minutes later pulled into Samuel and Rebecca's drive. As they came slowly down the path, Caleb looked over to the forge wistfully. His bride caught the direction of his gaze.

"*Herr* Lapp was a *gut* man. I am glad he came into each of our lives," Ruby said to him, drawing him back into the present.

"I owe much to him that I will never be able to repay," Caleb sighed.

"Live a *godly* life, Caleb. Do your best to remind others of what he taught you. That is all that we can do for those who have left us." As she said this she nudged even closer and hugged him as he pulled the wagon to a stop near the front porch of the home.

"All these months married and still hugging like new?" came a laughing female voice from behind a screened door.

"We are twins after all. Would you expect different, *schwester?*" came Ruby's quick reply.

"Rebecca, so glad to see you. Thank you for your hospitality," Caleb said to the woman in the doorway.

"Come in, you two. It is warmer in here and we can talk of all your travels," Samuel said from somewhere behind Rebecca.

Caleb helped Ruby down and used it as an excuse to give his bride another long hug. They would not be staying here, so he did not bring any of their bags in with them.

"Samuel, Rebecca, it is so *gut* to see you both," Ruby remarked.

"Come, let us have a cup of coffee and catch up at the table," Rebecca said to them. "Ruby, I have tea as well if you prefer."

"Should you be drinking coffee or tea, *schwester?*" Ruby asked.

"The doctor said I could have a little caffeine, but this tea is without. I confess I do not like it so much as coffee, but it means I get kicked less," Rebecca said, laughing and rubbing her stomach.

"If she starts kicking, you will let me know, *jah?*" Ruby said to her twin. "I would like to feel, if it is alright with you."

"You two do know that it is equally likely to be a he rather than a she, right?" Samuel said and not for the first time to these two.

The conversation went on and Caleb looked to his Ruby. Her red hair was made even more fiery by the candles lit on the table. He was so captivated he missed a question put to him by Samuel.

"Caleb Fisher, if I did not love my *schwester* so much and were I not so happy for her, I would speak to your *mutti* regarding your manners," Rebecca remarked, her voice clearly giving away the teasing nature of her comment.

"If you have an issue with my husband, Rebecca, you will speak to me," said Ruby, drawing a puzzled look from Caleb as the man of their family. Then she continued, "You do not need to go to that *Frau* Fisher to be told 'mind your own business.' *This Frau* Fisher can do that for you well enough." Then she started laughing, followed by her twin, and the men joined in as well.

"Ooh," came out of Rebecca who immediately reached out to her now rather large belly. "I guess the *bobbel* agrees with you, Ruby. I have been kicked into silence."

At this, Ruby rushed over and put her hand on Rebecca's belly. After a short wait, she was rewarded by a kick and then, another. Ruby laughed at the strong kick and then Rebecca laughed at her twin laughing. Samuel stopped smiling at the two after a bit and looked over to Caleb.

"We saw how much Peter has gotten done so quickly," remarked Caleb.

"He had a crew of *Englishe* from the mill come out. They did the work in exchange for the trees. He told me he got them to take several extra trees to be milled for his own use as part of the deal," Samuel replied.

"My *schwester* seems to have married a right smart man," Caleb said, still smiling.

"And we seem to have a *gut* neighbor," Samuel added.

The twins and their husbands ate their lunch, and eventually said their goodbyes. Before leaving, Rebecca gave Ruby their mother's baking tins and an old cast iron covered pot that went back at least to their *grossmutti's grossmutti*.

"Are you sure?" Ruby said, looking at the old pot as if it were made of gold.

"It is important that each of us has our own connection to our past. Of course, with you being so close, I might wish to borrow it now and again," she teased her *schwester*.

"I should think that could be arranged but, you will have to teach me how you make your version of baked corn casserole in it," Ruby said, her eyes still wide in surprise.

"That is a fair deal, you have wanted me to teach that to you for almost a decade now," Rebecca said, walking them out to their wagon. She smiled within herself, watching Ruby who never handed the heavy pot over to Caleb, but rather chose to carry it herself.

2

Caleb backed the wagon down the path to the front of the home he and Ruby shared. There were a couple of gifts to be offloaded before he would put the wagon away and brushed the horse down.

As they went inside, it became clear that someone had prepared for their arrival. A fire was lit in the stove and the *haus* was comfortably warm. They had forgotten to ask Jacob and Ana that first weekend away, and it had taken nearly two days for their bed to warm up fully.

"Caleb, is this your doing?" came Ruby's voice from the bedroom.

He walked down to see what she was asking about and saw a sturdy new oak bed nearly half again the size of the old pine one they had been sleeping on.

"Not I," said Caleb. "I am grateful for it though. You, my dear wife, have very cold feet."

"It is your job to warm them, husband of mine. The size of the bed will not change that." They both laughed and finished unpacking the nightstands and the kerosene lamps they had been given as wedding presents.

"Let us run quickly to the big *haus* to thank the person who welcomed us with this gift of warmth," Caleb called out to Ruby who apparently had left his side and was now in another room.

"I am refilling the humidifier. It would not do to have dry air," she responded.

Caleb walked into the main room that served as dining room and family room. Ruby was using the hand pump to fill a rusty cast iron pot they left on the stove all winter. Without it, the air became dry, lips became chapped, and walking across the braided carpets became quite shocking.

"I am done here," Ruby said, placing the pot on the back of the stove. A light crackle and hiss came from under the pot as the spilled water immediately became steam and escaped.

She walked over and took Caleb's hand, and they exited their front door for the short walk to the main *haus*.

"Look. The daffodils are starting to come up. It will not be long before our first planting season together," Ruby remarked, pointing to the new growth of daffodils nearest the chimney where the soil was warmest. "Don't worry, *mutti* already told me to plant extra celery for you in the garden."

"It will not be long now. I will plow the gardens today. When the first daffodil rises it is near time to be planting peas. That bunch won't count, but the rest will not lag far behind. We will go Monday to the market for any seeds you wish that we do not already have."

And like that, they arrived at the front door of the big *haus*. Caleb was about to knock when Ruby chuckled at him, opened the door, and walked in.

"We are *familye*. We do not need to knock," Ruby said to him.

"Ruby, we do not lock our front door. Would you like others to knock before entering our home?" Caleb replied to her.

Ruby's face turned the color of her hair. "You know, knocking is probably a better idea from now on. We'd not want poor little Naomi to walk in and find your muddy self in a tub of hot water."

It was now Caleb's turn to turn red-faced. Then as if on cue, Naomi came down the stairs and said a quick hello before turning and going right back up.

"That is not like Naomi," Caleb noticed aloud. "She usually gives me a hug."

"She probably just ran to get your *mutti,*" Ruby offered.

Again, as if on cue, out of the kitchen came Ana and behind her Jacob, Caleb's parents. They settled to talk in the sitting room.

"Glad to have you back again, son." Jacob began. "You have fields to plan and plow. I will help you wherever you would like, but this year, it is your farm to run. We both know you are ready."

"Already, *daed?* You are far too young," Caleb said, surprise evident in his voice.

"You are old enough and I am eager to take your *mutti* to see her *enkelkinder,*" Jacob replied. "It is not as if I will be a retired *Englishe.* I will work hard for the farm every day."

"I will try never to disappoint you," came Caleb's serious reply.

"Well," interjected Ruby. "Who do I thank for warming the *haus* for us and for that lovely bed?"

"The bed is a gift from Jacob and I," Ana said, her face lighting up. "I did not think you back so early. I did not start the fire." At this, she looked to Jacob who shrugged.

"I did not light it and seeing as Emma and Peter are still out visiting, that only leaves Naomi. It appears she is the one to thank," Jacob answered.

"She welcomed us, then ran back up the stairs," Caleb said. "Does she have a project she is working on?"

"No, she has been keeping quiet and to herself lately," Ana responded to her son. "I never thought I would say this, but I miss her being underfoot more often than not."

"I will have to go read with her tonight. I miss my littlest *schwester* reading with me," Caleb said.

"Why don't the two of you plan to have dinner here with us tonight. You cannot have enough time to prepare a hot meal as late as you are getting in," Ana suggested to the young couple.

Caleb looked to Ruby. Ruby looked to Caleb then spoke.

"We would be happy to share your table tonight, *mutti* Fisher. I was going to throw together a quick dinner with the ham from Thursday. Whatever you are having will be a welcome change from that," laughed Ruby.

"We ate ham for lunch and dinner Thursday before leaving. Our hosts Friday for lunch and dinner both surprised us with ham instead of chicken. They figured we would be growing tired of chicken. Then we had ham and eggs for breakfast today," Caleb said, chuckling.

"What are you making, *mutti* Fisher?" Ruby asked. "How can I help?"

"Well, we are having ham with cheese potato," Ana said.

Silence filled the room and Caleb's face went red with embarrassment.

Caleb's words tumbled out, "*Mutti*, we are grateful for the meal. Please excuse my complaining. I did not mean to offend."

Jacob turned to Ana. Ana stood silent as stone for a good bit of time, then a smile broke her grave countenance and she gave in to laughter. "We are having chicken and dumplings, Caleb. Forgive your *mutti* for teasing you."

"From His abundance we have all received one gracious blessing after another," Caleb said, quoting John1:16. "I am twice today reminded that I am not sufficiently grateful for the abundance the Lord has given me."

Ruby gently held his arm, offering her solid support and love.

"Would you please go up and get Naomi? I'll need her hand in the *kich*," Ana asked Caleb. She turned to Ruby, explaining, "I am trying to teach her how to cook the meals she likes best. And of course, we could use extra hands."

Caleb, despite being the man of his household and now the person running the farm, was still his *mutter's* son. He walked out into the living area and up the stairs to retrieve Naomi. Coming to the top of the stairs, he was surprised to see her bedroom door closed.

He knocked at her door gently, not wishing to startle her.

"Naomi, *mutti* would like you downstairs in the *kich*. I would like to see my little *schwester* as well," he said in a soft voice.

A loud harrumph came from behind the door. After a moment, a rather unamused-looking Naomi stepped out and walked past her *bruder* wordlessly. To be more precise, Caleb took a step backwards to make room for her when she exited the door as she appeared intent on walking through him.

"Naomi?" Caleb called to her gently. Her reply was the sound of her feet heading down the stairs.

I wonder what that was all about. Caleb scratched the new beard coming in around his chin in thought. He looked into her now empty room and saw it was its usual slightly less than orderly fashion, but not any more so than he remembered it.

With a shrug, Caleb turned himself back towards the wooden stairs and walked quietly down to rejoin the *familye*. He smelled the familiar fragrances of his *mutti's* chicken and dumplings. History reminded him that the smell would taunt him for the next hour, but would be worth every minute of the waiting.

He walked into the *kich* and grabbed a carrot as a quick snack. His wife and *mutti* then chased him out. While the *kich* was not small, it did not have room for four if one was not helping or seated out of the way at the small work table. On his way out, he spoke quietly to his Ruby.

"Naomi seems angry with me. Perhaps you could listen and see if you can find the reason?"

Ruby cocked her head. This was not like Naomi to be angry with Caleb. She usually smiled at him and worked to be near him.

"*Jah,* I will speak with her." Ruby easily thought of the older twins as *schwestere*. While she did not spend as much time with Naomi as she had with Emma and Lizzie, they four had done some quilting together and she had begun to think of Naomi as her little *schwester* as well.

It was about ten minutes later with all the ingredients into the pot that Ruby finally got a chance to speak to Naomi alone.

"I understand it is you that we have to thank for our *haus* being warm when we got home today. Thank you," Ruby remarked, starting the conversation.

Naomi, drying off her hands at the sink, turned and said a quiet, "You're welcome. I did not want you to be cold. I kept it going all weekend."

"That was very thoughtful of you," Ruby said with genuine warmth.

There was a pause in the conversation. It went on a bit too long and Ruby took the lead, "Is there something that is bothering you, Naomi?"

"No, I am fine," came the forced reply, much too fast and too filled with angst.

"I thought since we are *schwestere* now, you could talk to me if there was something bothering you, even something silly," Ruby said quietly to her, resting her hand on the younger girl's shoulder and light blue dress.

With those words, Naomi's eyes blinked rapidly, meeting Ruby's own, then immediately she cast her look downward, hiding the fact that she became teary. "It is nothing. I am being a fool and I know it," replied the fifteen going on sixteen-year-old.

She bit her lip then spoke again. "Wayne Troyer has been picking on me at school. I thought he might like me, but now he is spending his time with Hannah Schrock." Naomi shrugged, sitting at the small table in the *kich*.

"Did you wish he was spending that time with you?" asked Ruby delicately, taking a seat next to her.

"No! I've no use for that boy. He spends his time with her and yet still goes out of his way to be mean to me," Naomi replied.

"How is he mean to you?" Ruby asked, wondering if she would need to have Caleb talk with this boy.

"He reminds me that in another year my opinion will have no value. He tells me I am good for nothing but cooking and having babies." With this, Naomi began crying.

Ruby scooted close and held the girl's head in the crook of her arm and let her cry herself out. It appeared that young *Herr* Troyer was one of those who thought of subservience as a power men held over women instead of the responsibility that it truly was for a man.

"Naomi," she started quietly, still running her hand through the girl's hair soothing her. "Do you think your *mutti* has no value?"

Naomi sprung up from her seat and spun, looking at Ruby as if she were holding a knife. "Why would you think such a thing? This *familye* is stronger for her holding us together and making it easier for *vater* to do the business of farming."

"Do you think your *daed* thinks of her as being without value other than breeding and cooking?" Ruby asked, knowing the answer.

"*Vater* loves *mutti*," came the reply.

"Are they happy together, or does he treat her poorly if he does not like dinner?" Ruby kept up.

"*Daed* is not that way. He even pretended to like what I cooked when I was learning not to burn things," Ruby replied, getting a bit of a blush in her cheeks remembering it.

"That is because your *vater* is all the best things of a farmer. It is in him to help things grow. Caleb is much the same way. That is the type of man you should want to spend time with. A man does not need to push others down to feel tall. A *gut* man helps you to your feet if you stumble." Ruby paused, looking into Naomi's eyes. "You are nearly old enough for men to come calling. It is important to make sure you choose the right man."

"Did you choose the right one, Ruby? Or does my *donderkopf bruder* make you subservient to him as well?" came Naomi's question.

"*Gott* made women to be a man's help meet," she answered. "Ephesians tells us we are to submit ourselves to each other. I serve Caleb because it fills my heart with joy to make our life together better. I know that he will make the decisions that are best for both of us. He will listen to me when I offer advice in private, not because I think he will make a bad choice, but rather to make sure he has all the information he needs to make the best choice."

"But what if he does not take your advice?" Naomi asked, clearly having trouble with this.

"In the end, the choice is his. That is his burden. He must choose for the two of us and later for his *familye* knowing that, if he chooses wrong, it will bring hardship to those he cares most about." Ruby saw Naomi gently nodding her understanding. "When I suggest something, and Caleb disagrees, he does not make my choice sound wrong, nor do I mention it when the choice he makes does not end how he thought. I would suggest you steer clear of boys who think like this Wayne Troyer. He is a long way from becoming a man."

"Thank you, Ruby. I guess I was a little disappointed that he did not act nice to me as he did to Hannah. If she is willing to put up with him, she is welcome to him," Naomi said as much to herself as she did to Ruby.

"Well, I am glad we settled that. There still is the question, what did *dunderkopf* do to earn your silence?" Ruby asked smiling.

"He is a boy, *jah?*" asked Naomi.

"No, Naomi. Caleb is a man. Caleb is a very *gut* man that loves you deeply and misses you much," Ruby replied taking a much sterner tone.

"I guess he is. It seems strange to think of him as such. Does this mean he is too old to read with me?" asked Naomi.

"I would think not. Perhaps that is a question better to ask him?" Ruby prodded.

With that, Naomi stood, brushed the wrinkles out of her dress, wiped the tears from her eyes and turned to go find Caleb. As she turned, she missed the smile that came across Ruby's face. It was a smile that Amish women use when they had made those they cared about feel better. Ruby wondered briefly if *Englishe* women had such a smile, then made her way back to the gathered *familye*.

3

Monday morning came, and after doing the chores he had to do himself and making sure the rest of the chores were divided among the family, Caleb hitched a horse to the wagon preparing to head to Peter's lot where he was working today. Before he left, Ruby came to him and asked to be dropped at her *schwester's haus* to check on her and to see if a very pregnant Rebecca needed a hand.

He agreed and soon the pair were sitting side by side in the wagon, heading down the muddy lane towards Samuel's *haus*.

Caleb turned to his bride with the reins in hand. "So, this is why you were up so early." He grinned.

"If she is up for the ride, offer to cook dinner for them tonight," Caleb said rather than asked, knowing that it would please her. "I will drop you there then pick you back up when Peter and I are done."

"Do you plan to be long? Your *mutti*, Emma, Lizzie, and I all have laundry to do. We have decided to help each other and make light work of it. I am also inviting Naomi. She is old enough to spend some time with us old married folks," joked Ruby.

"I am glad. She seems happier after you spoke with her. What was it troubling her?" Caleb asked.

"Girl problems," Ruby said as if that explained everything.

"I thought only boys had girl problems," answered Caleb, chuckling at his own attempt at humor.

When Ruby failed to laugh with him, he answered her question. "It should only take an hour or so. I have a few questions and he mentioned he needed a hand today. He said it was a small task."

It was about then that they came upon the entrance to Samuel's farm. He helped Ruby out of the wagon and walked her to the door. Rebecca answered and let them in. The women seated themselves in the *kich* while Caleb remained standing.

"Can I get you anything? Coffee? Tea?" asked Rebecca, despite the rather uncomfortable look on her face and the large bump in front of her.

Caleb briefly wondered if her arms would reach the cabinet as far away from it as she would need to stand. He was fortunately wise enough not to ask out loud and simply said, "No, thank you."

"I've come to help you for a bit with things. I know you cannot bend so well." Ruby said to her twin.

"Thank you," Rebecca said with genuine relief in her voice. "I have not swept in three days."

Caleb looked about the room. It looked clean to him. He was about to say something when Ruby answered. "This must be driving you mad. I will make sure it is all done today, *schwester.*"

"I need to get going. Please let Samuel know I was here," Caleb said.

Rebecca braced herself to stand and show him out when he stopped her. "Sit and rest yourself. I know the way to the door. I will be back in a bit, try to let Ruby help you, *jah?*"

"*Jah.* I am not able to argue much with her on that. I could not catch up if she ran two steps ahead." Rebecca laughed, rubbing her belly as she spoke.

Caleb made his way to the door, then down the porch stairs into the wagon and gave the horse a quick pull to the side. He was off to see Peter at the clearing.

It was a mere ten minutes later that he pulled into the space next to Peter's wagon and looked around. There was a truck marked "McManus Builders", with men offloading long beams and a bulldozer and backhoe digging a basement where he had seen stakes for the *haus*. It was a beehive of activity. Caleb had not expected this today.

"Peter!" Caleb yelled out, waving his hands to get his friend's attention.

After a minute, Peter's head scanned the work around him and saw Caleb. He called out his name and waved him to come over.

"I did not know you were using *Englishe* to build your home," Caleb said scanning all the work being done around him.

"I have Samuel to thank for that. He knew an *Englishe* builder. They will have the foundation set today, then truck an Amish crew here to build my *haus* in the next four weeks. I will do the painting, the cabinetry, and the floors," Peter replied excitedly. "Better yet, they are building this *haus* and a big shed for me at cost. The owner of the building company came out himself with Samuel and told me about how he owed *Herr* Lapp a debt he could not repay. He told me that it is now my debt to pay forward to another. He seemed a genuine and decent man. I'd think him Amish if I'd not seen him drive up and ... well, those *Englishe* clothes he wore." With this Peter was laughing at the silly way the *Englishe* dressed themselves.

"How can any man work with a cloth rope tied around his neck?" he asked Caleb who shrugged, having wondered similar thoughts.

"So, these men are Amish?" Caleb asked with a frown, looking at the men operating heavy machinery and trucks.

"No, he has the Amish driven here to do the building in a small bus. He does not make them do things that are not right," Peter said. "He said that was something that *Herr* Lapp explained to him and talked of building better *hause* cheaper and faster now."

"Well, I can see the faster part. Now what was it you needed my help with?" Caleb asked after catching up with the goings on.

"Emma has asked me to prepare the soil for a garden for her. I must confess, I'm more a furniture maker than farmer. I was hoping you and I might decide where best to place it and then stake it out to have them dig it. I've no plow or I would do it myself," Peter said, looking somewhat embarrassed to have to ask where to put a garden.

"I am glad you asked me," started Caleb, setting Peter at ease. "It is very easy not to plan this out right and have a garden that will not provide well." With this, Caleb hesitated and looked around figuring east and west, then turned back to Peter. "Where are we building your barn?"

"I have just started to gather timbers for it. I figure it may be a project for next year," Peter replied.

"I would hope we could get it done this year for you, but the question was where not when," came Caleb's reply.

"I have given it a little thought. I will use it mostly for the horses and as my work space. Why do we need decide now where to put it?" Peter asked.

"It will cast a long dark shadow when it is raised. We don't want to have the garden in its shade," Caleb said simply.

"Well, I had thought to make a second cut from the path to the *haus* here." Peter said standing about a third down the path. "I will have occasion for trucks to come to the shop and I do not want them near the *haus.*"

"That is wise," Caleb agreed. "Perhaps you should have the path cleared and the timbers milled into rafters and barn boards. Samuel and I spoke. We would like to help you prepare the lumber and get that built for you this summer after planting is done and before the crops are ready to be harvested."

"That is a tall order," Peter looked his *schwager* up and down a moment, then smiled. "If you think it can be done, I say let us do it." He clasped Caleb's hand, sealing the arrangement. "Now, where to put Emma's garden?"

"With the barn that far off, I'd plant it to the east of the *haus*, fairly close. There will be morning and daylight sun with an afternoon shade from the *haus* to make picking cooler. It also makes easier access once *bobbele* start to crawl about the place." Caleb paused then continued, "Do not have the *Englishe* make the garden with heavy equipment. I will borrow Samuel's plow and turn the soil for you. I just cut Ruby's Saturday. It is that time."

"I cannot thank you enough," Peter started, only to be cut off.

"We are *familye* and neighbors now, Peter. Besides, I might need some furniture built someday. You wouldn't happen to know the craftsman that made my bed, would you?" Caleb said laughing at his now blushing friend.

The two men had spent nearly two hours walking the land and talking. They staked the garden and as they went to ask the men not to drive the heavy equipment on the space, they saw them circled around a bulldozer, now turned off. One man had removed a heavy geared wheel and had called to have its replacement brought out, so they could continue.

While Peter spoke to the men about the garden, Caleb asked the foreman what they would do with the broken part.

"We toss those in the trash. Can't be repaired," came the reply.

"What does it weigh?" Caleb asked.

"A bit over a hundred pounds, I guess. Why so curious?" the foreman asked him.

"I would take it from you, if you would let me," Caleb said.

The foreman shrugged and said, "Sure, if you'd like it. I can have the guys load it in that wagon for you."

"That would be very helpful. Thank you." Caleb shook the man's hand.

Peter finished speaking to the crew and caught up to Caleb. "Why are they taking that broken part to your wagon?"

"That broken wheel will be a new plow blade for you the next time you see it," Caleb said, laughing. "I will teach you how to plow a garden for yourself, if you would let me. Of course, it won't be ready for this season's garden."

"Of course," agreed Peter.

Caleb reached out and grabbed Peter's hand to shake it. "I am sorry. I must go retrieve my wife from Samuel's *haus*. I'll be out later this week to plow that garden for you. Tell Emma I will make it extra big, so she has more weeds to pull."

"I think I will leave that bit of teasing for you," Peter said.

"Maybe the two of you could have dinner with us later this week?" Caleb asked.

"*Jah*, I'd like that," Peter agreed. "I will have Emma come see Ruby tomorrow."

Caleb was surprised that even living on the same farm how little he and Peter's paths crossed. He hoped it would get better now that his visiting rounds were complete, and Peter's were near done as well.

Caleb retrieved his wife, and still got home with enough time to fertilize the garden with the composted cow manure he had piled up the past year. It had not been a pleasant task, but the reward came now when he did not pay to fertilize and still got bountiful harvests.

After spreading the fertilizer, he hand-tilled in the part they would plant with peas. He might be able to get to that tomorrow if he found the time.

Ruby called out to him as he finished to clean up for dinner. Caleb saw that dinner was on the table and there were only two places set.

"Are Samuel and Rebecca not coming?" asked Caleb.

"She said she was not up to even that short ride," Ruby said. "I think her next ride will be with that *bobbel* on her lap. I think it may come sooner than we thought." The last part was said softly with a near palpable longing in her voice.

"A playmate for our *kinder, jah?*" added Caleb, knowing where his wife's thoughts lie.

"*Jah*, Caleb. It is as she and I had always talked about, our *kinder* growing up together." Ruby smiled brightly as she said this.

4

By week's end, the stretch of late February warmth had Caleb itching to get an early start in the fields. He hitched the horses up to the plow and cleared his *mutti's* garden, finished tilling the manure in the rest of his own, and then went out to prepare a field for an early planting of hay. It was his habit to pray before he plowed the fields. He asked for *Gott's* hands to guide him and to fill him with peace.

Today, that peace would not arrive on schedule. As he finished his prayer, he heard his name being called out from a distance. Spinning his head back and forth, he spotted Ruby. She was waving her arms over her head and trying to get his attention. It would have caused him to laugh if he did not see the serious look on her face.

"Caleb, come to the *haus!*" Ruby shouted when in earshot. Seeing him acknowledge her, rather than wait for him, she spun back and walked briskly towards the main *haus*.

Caleb broke into a jog and got there moments after Ruby. His parents' door was open, so he let himself in. As he walked towards the voices, he realized he had not even taken the time to clean his feet. *Mutti* would not be amused.

Caleb got to the great room and was surprised to see both of his twin *schwestere* and their husbands standing together. *Daed, mutti,* and Naomi sat with Ruby. Caleb's entry had the two couples looking at each other and then the group.

"Daed, mutti," started Lizzie then Emma broke in.

"We want to share some news," she said.

"Our *haus* is near finished," added John, Lizzie's husband.

"And ours is but a few more weeks away," added Peter.

Silence ensued. The status of their *hause* was not the type of news that took everyone to hear.

The two girls looked at each other for a moment then towards their parents. Lizzie said, "We hear that the two of you are planning to visit your *enkelkinder.* We trust that will apply to those nearer to you as well as your first two."

A loud gasp and cheer went up from Ana, Ruby, and Naomi. Caleb looked at Jacob and Jacob to Caleb and they let each other know neither knew what was going on.

Ruby caught Caleb's part in this and whispered to him, "Your *schwestere* are going to have *bobbele."*

Caleb shook his head as if clearing cobwebs. His mouth dropped, his eyes opening wide, and he said, "Which one? When?"

"Both of us, this fall," the twins shrieked excitedly.

Caleb jumped up, shook both Peter and John's hands. then gave each of his *schwestere* a big hug. "I need to do this now, while my arms still make it around you two." He laughed, teasing two of his favorite targets.

Caleb did not see Ruby have to force a smile. He was too busy celebrating with his *schwestere*.

Later, after they had eaten a meal cooked by five of his favorite women, Caleb and Ruby walked back to their home hand in hand. Ruby seemed to have something on her mind so Caleb delicately probed.

"Very exciting news, *jah?*" he said, thinking this was a safe spot to start.

"Yes, husband. I am very happy for them," came Ruby's reply, the word 'them' sounding a bit too loud.

"You would also like to be happy for yourself this way?" Caleb asked her, gently.

"We had talked of being pregnant together, raising our *bobbele* together. They have started without me it seems," Ruby said, the sadness clear in her voice. "I am not so young as they are. What if I cannot have *bobbele*, Caleb?" She turned to her husband in near tears.

"*Gott* does things in his own time. He did not give Sarah and Abraham a son until he was ninety-nine," he reminded her.

"We will pray that *Gott* does not have that planned for us, *jah?*" Ruby said trying to joke with her husband.

"Yes, my Ruby. We will pray hard that that is not our future. You have, after all, promised me a houseful of *kinder*. I would not like you to have to do that well into your hundreds," Caleb said this as if he meant it.

Ruby's head spun, eyes wide, then her thoughts caught up with her and she laughed and kissed her husband. Both stopped and looked around sheepishly. They got back to their own home, banked the fire to last the night, prayed and then went to bed.

Caleb awoke late the next morning. Ruby still dozed next to him. She was a determined woman, Caleb reminded himself. It seemed to him she was now determined to be pregnant just as his twin *schwestere* were.

Caleb smiled at his beautiful sleeping wife then got himself dressed and out to do the work of the farm.

Entering the barn, he was surprised to see his *vater* finishing up the day's milking. He walked over to him and thanked him.

"Your *mutti* said you would be late to your chores today. I sometimes wonder how she knows so much," Jacob said to him smiling.

"Ruby and I were up late," Caleb said, then blushing profusely added, "talking."

Jacob did not press further. The two spoke of the herd, upcoming auctions, and Caleb shared the plans to raise a barn for Peter and Emma this summer.

"You are a *gut bruder* and friend, Caleb," his father said, patting him on the back to reinforce his words. "I will help them get ready for it as well. There is much to do before the crowds arrive if it is to go smoothly. I have done this a few times already, but this will be your first, *jah?*"

"I went to the raising of the Broder's barn after the other burned down, but I was too young to do more than carry buckets of nails to the men," Caleb recalled.

"Peter is a craftsman with wood. I am sure he can make the plans for it. We will help him cut the main timbers, so the barn can be raised in a day and finished in a week. I trust you have been making nails with all that banging from your forge these past weeks? We will need many to hold the boards to the side of the barn," Jacob said to his son.

"You know me well, *Daed.* I have nearly three tin pails of them already. I figure to bring five pails of them and give the left-overs to him as a gift," Caleb replied, then added, "He does not use them in his furniture, but every home needs nails eventually."

The two men worked side by side most of the day, prepping fields, spreading more fertilizer in his *mutti's* now doubled garden. At day's end, they put away the tack from the horses, brushed them down, and fed and watered them before going to their own homes to be fed themselves.

As they parted, Jacob said softly to Caleb, "I will get the milking for the next week or so if that is okay with you."

Caleb's blush was visible even in the fading light. "*Jah, vater.* If you long to do it, I will not stop you. Let me know when you tire of it," he said, trying to sound sincere.

Jacob smiled to himself, remembering his life near thirty years earlier and went in to his own bride.

5

This was the pattern for the next two weeks, Jacob got the early start and Caleb joined him later and later in the morning. March had ignored its reputation as a lion and had thawed the ground near fully.

Caleb had already planted two fields of early hay. He wanted to increase the herd further this year. They had five cows expecting and would keep all but bulls that were born. With the use of Samuel's bull next season, he would not need two of his own to keep the cows milking.

Samuel had made use of Caleb's bull and had a couple calves on the way as well at his farm. Spring was arriving with pregnancy everywhere but his own home, it seemed to Caleb. Not that Ruby was not determined, he thought. He would need to speak with her. He was the man on this farm. He could not keep starting his days so late and have it work out well for them all.

That night, over dinner, Caleb spoke with Ruby. She broke into tears again.

"Caleb, you should have chosen a younger bride. I am not pregnant again. I may well be barren." Ruby was talking faster and faster as she went so Caleb stopped her.

"Ruby, you are all of nine months older than I am. We have many years and many *bobbele* ahead of us. You must trust in the Lord's own timing. We cannot continue with me not working the mornings. I will begin to milk my herd tomorrow. We will welcome our *kinder* when *Gott* wills it."

"We will not stop trying, will we?" Ruby asked.

"No, but we must stop trying so hard," Caleb said, laughing. Ruby joined in after a moment.

He surprised Jacob by being up and milking the herd before him. Jacob said nothing of it and went about cleaning out the stalls and throwing new straw down from the loft.

Caleb had barely finished the milking when a wagon he recognized as Samuel's came flying up the path to the *haus*. Samuel jumped out, leaving the horse untethered and ran towards the barn.

"Caleb, grab Ruby. She has someone that wants to see her at our *haus!*" he yelled excitedly.

Caleb let his *vater* know the milking was done and went to get Ruby. When they got to the barn, Samuel and Jacob had hitched a horse to the wagon and it was ready for them. Jacob hid a smile as the two got into the buggy, but let it spread across his face as the young people left.

They arrived at Samuel's farm faster than either ever had made the trip. Samuel rushed into the *haus,* waving for them to follow. When they came into the home, they were greeted by Rebecca, sitting with a baby wrapped in a blanket in her arms.

"Rebecca," shouted Ruby, then caught her voice, and made it softer, but no less awestruck. "How gorgeous! Is it a niece or nephew? Can I hold it?" came her questions without a gap.

"Sit, Ruby. You can hold him. He is fed and burped," Rebecca said with a smile on her tired face.

Ruby did just that, pulling a chair near her twin and taking the *bobbel* as it was handed to her. Her face was glowing. She kissed the newest addition to her extended *familye* on the nose and then turned to Rebecca and Samuel.

"You have yet to introduce us properly," Ruby said to the new parents.

"After much discussion, we have decided to name him Otto Caleb King." Samuel said, looking Caleb in the eyes. "We hope you do not mind."

"Mind? I am honored, my *gut* friend. I am honored," Caleb said, flush with excitement.

"Another Caleb for me to hug and kiss," Ruby said, who then did just that as she explained to the tired newborn how much fun they would have together.

She cuddled that baby right to sleep before handing him reluctantly back to Rebecca, who put him down in a new crib.

Caleb knew from its simple design and great beauty that it was Peter's workmanship. *I will have to ask him to make us one as well,* thought Caleb.

Ruby then took over. "I will have meals brought to you for the next week. I will not take a no, so do not even offer it."

Rebecca had started to resist and was stopped short.

"You need to recover and take care of that precious *bobbel*. We will take turns bringing you meals. I will check in with you daily to help out here."

"No, that won't work at all," Caleb said.

Samuel looked at Caleb and Caleb looked at Samuel, then Samuel spoke. "I've only seen her this way once, Caleb. She got her way then as well."

"Yes, but I am her husband. You will do as I tell you, *jah* Ruby?" Caleb said flatly.

Ruby had never had Caleb speak to her in this manner and thought back to her talk with Naomi. "What is your plan then, husband?" she asked with resentment building inside her, despite her efforts.

"If Samuel and Rebecca can bear it, I'd like you to stay with them for the coming week. I will eat with my parents, then come for you in a week," Caleb surprised her by saying, then his face lost its fake hardness.

"But my garden, my *haus* ..." came Ruby's response.

"I will have Naomi weed the garden. The *haus* is so clean it shines. I will try hard not to make a wreck of it while you are here. This is better for everyone, is it not, my wife?" came Caleb's final word on this as he kissed his wife's brow.

"It would make me very happy," Ruby agreed.

"We cannot thank you enough, Caleb. Are you sure?" asked Samuel.

Caleb looked to the twins now hugging and smiling, "This is where she needs to be, Samuel. You have *familye* here, let us be that for both of you."

Ruby broke her hug with Rebecca and ran to Caleb. "I will never doubt your love for me ever again, Caleb." With that, she hugged Caleb so tight the air went out of him.

"I'm not sure what that means, but if it gets me a hug such as that, I am content," Caleb said, then asked his wife what she would need so he could bring it back to her later in the day.

Ruby made a quick list, then added, "And the cast pot. My *schwester* will teach me that recipe of hers this week, finally."

Caleb laughed, then shook Samuel's hand again and took his leave from the women and the new tot. He smiled to himself as he realized how accustomed he was to having Ruby by his side. This was made all the more plain when he did not feel her sitting beside him on the ride home to share the news.

6

The week flew by. Caleb threw himself into work at the farm and in the evenings, he spent an hour or two at the forge making nails and starting to shape the wheel into a plow blade.

The hardest part of his day was the end of it when he washed and went to an empty bed. On the last night, he prayed for his Ruby. He prayed that she would be happily pregnant or happily not. He prayed for Naomi who had welcomed him back into her life and read with him after dinner. He prayed that she found her way as a woman in church.

He ended his prayers by thanking *Gott* for reminding him how much his Ruby made his life better, and thanking Him again that the week was done, and that he would get her back the next day. Caleb's last thought that night was that he even missed her cold feet.

Ruby's week went differently. She cooked and cleaned and played with little Otto. Rocking him to sleep was to be her favorite new pastime.

She prayed with Samuel and Rebecca, ate with them, and slept in her old room on a bed that she did not recall being this small and this empty. Each night, she thanked *Gott* for bringing her here to Barnville. She thanked Him for her Caleb and putting such a gentle heart into such a sturdy man.

After her prayers, lying in bed, she came to realize that she had not been married as long as Rebecca before she became with child. Realizing that, she found peace and slept well.

By week's end, Rebecca was as caught up and rested as a new mother could be. She had little Otto getting used to his evening routine, and was starting to put her house back in her own order.

As happy as Ruby was to be of help, it was becoming clear she was no longer needed there all day and night. Both Emma and Lizzie had stopped by to meet the newest King family member and agreed to bring meals by at night for the next week. As much as Rebecca wanted to get back to her routine, she accepted the meals with the grace befitting such a kind offer.

Almost a month later to the day, Peter, John, Caleb, Samuel and their spouses packed up Lizzie's belongings and helped her move into the new *haus* on the Beiler farm. The men did the lifting and the women the arranging and planning.

They also talked of restarting their quilting bee and rotating homes. When all was nearly complete, Lizzie looked around and became worried.

"John, what happened to the table? We don't have a table. How can we have a home with no place to eat?" She was in a near panic at this point.

"Lizzie, I am sorry. I must have left it in my wagon," Peter said. "Come, John. Give me a hand with it."

The two men left out the front door, crossing the porch and lifting up a tarp on Peter's wagon. Each man grabbed half and made quick work of bringing it in.

"What is this?" Lizzie asked. "This is not the table we have. Ours only seats four. There is room here for six or eight."

"Eight," confirmed Peter. "John and I spoke. He agreed to let me give you this as a late wedding present."

"No, Peter. It is too much," Lizzie said, eyeing the sturdy oak table.

"If it makes you feel better about it," Peter started, "I feared I would have no place to sit when we came to visit."

Lizzie thought about the small round table she had expected, then looked at the big oak rectangle in front of her.

"We will have room enough for you with this, but I fear you would still have no seat," she said apologetically.

"About that …" Peter said quietly. "Gentlemen …"

The four men left, only to return with two wooden chairs each that matched the table. The end chairs had arm rests while the side chairs were plain.

Lizzie sat to the right, next to the head of the table, her spot. Her hands ran across the thick oak top. Despite loving the table, she knew she could not accept it.

"Peter, the table is too much. This is so much more than we can accept from you." Lizzie looked to John for help with this.

John was about to speak, but before he could, Emma jumped in. "I had asked my husband to make a matched pair of these table and chair sets.

One goes into my home, the other into yours. Would you deny me my set by turning down yours?" Emma accused her twin. "If it is too much for one of us, it is clearly too much for each of us."

John Beiler stepped up and ended the conversation. "Peter, this is a masterful work. It fills a need neither my Lizzie nor I realized that we had. I hope to do the same for you. You are moving into your home in some scant few weeks and have no cows for milk, have you?"

"I'd not given it much thought," Peter confessed. "I have worked so much on the structure of the *haus*, that I have forgotten to make it a home."

"I have a cow and calf that will help you do that. I will bring them to you when we help you to move so that your family never goes without milk," John said. It was clear from his voice it was not a payment, but a gift leaving no room for argument.

"It seems then that you have also filled a need we had not addressed. I am glad to have you as a friend, John Beiler." Peter shook his hand and the question of the table was ended.

It was less than a month later that they moved Peter and Emma into their new home. True to her comment, an identical table and chair set was in their dining area.

Peter had made all the counter tops and cabinets. He had fashioned them to have no knobs and no decorative trim, and they did not lose any of their beauty from lack of adornment.

John and Lizzie arrived with a cow and calf in tow and a wooden crate making such a racket as only spring chicks make.

"It occurred to me that you might like eggs for breakfast, *schwester*," Lizzie said to Emma. "I trust Peter can fashion a coop for them?"

"After our conversation regarding milk, I took the liberty of making a coop. I'd yet to get hens to fill it," Peter said, pointing to a small coop and wired area near the garden.

"What is that white box, Peter?" Lizzie asked about a small white stack of boxes with a roof over it.

"It seems our Peter has himself a hive of bees," John said to his bride. Then to Peter, "Do you plan to have more? We hire a man to bring bees to help our food crops germinate. He brings two or three hives each time."

"I had only thought to have the one for our own use. It was a wedding gift after Emma made some of her honey bread at my uncle's *haus*," Peter explained. "It is not difficult, I was raised with them. I could help you establish your own colonies," Peter offered. "The man that helps your fields no doubt sells the honey made there at market. That is something you could do as easily, *jah?*"

"The money we spend on those bees is well worth it for the extra crops they produce. Having honey from them would be a plus. Once we are done with this move, we should talk more of this," John responded.

Caleb listened to the two men's animated talk with interest. *This is how Amish thrive*, he thought. *This is what Romans 12:4-5 speaks of, "For as we have many members in one body, and all members have not the same office: So we, being many, are one body in Christ, and every one members one of another."*

As they had for John and Lizzie, the group made light work of moving in Peter and Emma. The pregnant twins took turns watching over little Otto, giving Rebecca a chance to work with Ruby, setting up the *kich* and pantry under the watchful supervision of the woman of the *haus,* Emma. By day's end, that work was done as well.

The women had a meal prepared and cooked for their men, and they sat at the big table to eat together. The first of many, many meals this group would share under each other's roofs.

The four couples fell into their own rhythms as spring turned to summer. The women rotated homes every Wednesday and quilted as fast as they spoke.

The men tended their farms, and in Peter's case, his stall and his small shop. As the days grew longer, the men made a habit of getting together one afternoon a week and preparing the lumber for Peter's barn and shop. They felled a couple of the biggest trees on the property for posts and rafter beams, then dragged them into place with rigged horse teams.

Once the major timbers were stacked near where the barn would be raised, they set about cutting the long, wide boards that would be used for siding. Between them, they decided the date to shoot for would be early August. As the weeks turned to months, the stack of wood grew taller and it became clear that the task was clearly attainable.

While the men spent their spring and early summer this way, tending their farms and working together weekly and Saturday afternoons, their wives fell into their own rhythms. They would get together every Wednesday to quilt, and cook in Emma's kitchen Saturday afternoons so the men could get more done.

It was May when the twins began to show their pregnancies. They grew more excited each week asking the now expert Rebecca questions from delivery to diapers.

Ruby smiled through all the excitement. She enjoyed bouncing her nephew Otto every chance she could.

Each time the women met, there was a moment of waiting to see if Ruby had any news to share before they began to pray prior to their quilting bee. Month after month they began with no news from Ruby.

7

July arrived with the lumber ready for the barn raising. Extra chickens ran around Peter's yard, unaware that they were going to be fed to family and the community coming to help.

It was during this time that little Otto had his very first cold. He started with a sniffle and holding his ear, then came the crying, throwing up, and then more crying.

It was on the second day of this that they took him to the *Englishe* doctor who gave Rebecca and Samuel eardrops to use on Otto's ears, and praised their parenting skills for how otherwise happy and healthy their baby was.

By the week's end, Otto was back to his bubbly self. Rebecca, however, had picked up the bug. She in turn shared it with Emma at the next Wednesday quilting bee. As is too often the case with something shared, Emma then shared with both Lizzie and Ruby the following week.

Here the barn raising was days away and both Ruby and Lizzie were miserable. To Ruby, the worst of it was having to avoid Otto for fear of giving it back to him.

Peter's extended family arrived to help, so he had hired a local girl to take orders at his stall so that he could be on the farm. They had all the posts rigged and ready for the crew to show up on the next morning.

Monday arrived with a cloudless sunny countenance. Caleb and John helped line up tables for the women to serve lunches on. The wives brought baskets for their husbands and the single women brought baskets for the single men to try. This was clearly the social event of the year.

At seven-o'clock, the men stood in a circle with their heads bowed. Bishop Yoder spoke to them about community and commitment to each other, and then they prayed.

The men, clad mostly in their light blue shirts, dark blue pants and suspenders, dispersed like an angry ant hill. They began tying rope, preparing poles to help lift, and separated into groups to pull, groups to push, and groups to nail in temporary supports.

The women put out jugs of water and lemonade. Before long, they would walk among the men to make sure they did not grow hot and tired.

First one frame went up, then the second. Boards were strung to space them properly, and then connecting beams were raised. After the first two were in place and solid, the remaining frames went up like dominoes in reverse, each getting secured in place as the next was getting put into position and prepared for lifting.

So much had been readied that by lunch the big pieces of the frame were in place and they were working on secondary and tertiary rafters to hang a roof onto. The barn was teeming with blue-shirted, straw-hatted men with saws, chisels, and hammers.

The air had taken on the sweet smell of freshly cut timber, and wood shavings fell from the newly raised rafters as if it were snowing shaved wood.

Ruby stopped counting when she got to sixty men up on the barn. She did not run out of men to count, but rather none stayed still long enough to get a firm count.

She kept the youngest children busy and out of the way until it was time for all to come down and enjoy a festive lunch. As the men made their way to the tables, they were met with newly poured glasses of cold water, pitchers of lemonade, and a basket lunch.

The younger women passed out the basket lunches that had been made for the workers. It was not unheard of for a certain someone to get an extra piece of chicken or a larger slice of pie from a young lady looking to catch his eye.

The clamor of banging gave way to the laughter and happy chatter from men who had done this job many times and from those who were raising their first barn. All commented on how well-prepared Peter was for this.

After the men had eaten and slaked their thirst, they began climbing back into the rafters. Some added trusses to the roof, others began to side the barn.

This was when some of the younger men got their hands dirty as well. Those too young to climb and lift could still hammer nails to fasten the bottom of the barn boards. Those too young to swing a hammer effectively could carry nails around to make sure none were waiting.

Wayne Troyer grabbed a hammer and walked towards the barn. He looked around to find Hannah Schrock. She was sitting near Jacob Bayler. Jacob was clearly the center of her attention at the moment.

"Hannah," he shouted to be sure she was watching as he flipped the hammer into the air to catch it after it spun around in the air.

Watch it she did, as he timed the release poorly and struck himself in the forehead with the pound of hammer. Wayne Troyer dropped like a sack of potatoes. Hannah, Jacob, and the people with them fell about themselves laughing at him.

Naomi was also watching. She ran from her spot over to him. She was the first thing an embarrassed Wayne Troyer saw when he finally stopped seeing two of her.

"I don't need your help," he said to Naomi.

"Yes, I noticed that all your friends rushed over to make sure you were okay," Naomi replied to him.

At this Wayne turned to where his friends sat, and they were all still there, laughing. Most had turned away from him and gone back to their conversations. He went to lift his head and call to them, but the attempt had his eyes squeezing closed again and his hands rush up to his head in pain.

"Wait here, I will get you help," Naomi instructed him.

Moments later, Ruby and Naomi returned. Ruby put a cold cloth on his head and asked him simple questions to make sure he knew who he was and where he was.

"How many fingers am I holding up?" she started.

"Three," came the correct reply.

"What is your name?" Ruby asked flatly.

"Wayne," came the soft response.

"What is your last name, Wayne?" This time the question had a bit more interest in it.

"Troyer, Wayne Troyer, ma'am," he replied.

Ruby looked to Naomi, asking a question without words. Naomi nodded.

"How did you get this lump on your forehead, Wayne?" Ruby asked him, looking at the knot forming where the hammer had struck.

Wayne's face began to turn a brighter shade of red than even the lump rising from it.

"He tripped and landed on his hammer, Ruby," Naomi offered.

Ruby knew full well that was not the truth of it, but asked Wayne, "So, you tripped?"

"Yes. Naomi tripped me. Silly girl. Always trying to get my attention and now it has led to this," Wayne replied, turning Naomi's kindness into poison against her.

Ruby looked at this boy, then at Naomi, then back to the boy.

"Is your *vater* here? He should hear the truth of this so that you are not punished for what you did not do," Ruby said.

"Naomi, go tell Caleb to bring Jacob to me. You will need to explain this to your *daed* after we speak with Wayne's."

Naomi looked twice struck. She had tried to be nice and not embarrass Wayne and now even Ruby believed him. She stormed her way to Caleb who called their *vater* down from the rafters. The three walked towards where they could see Ruby speaking with a man and a boy.

Jacob walked up to the trio first. "Elmer Troyer, this is your Wayne?" he asked, pointing his thumb towards the youth.

"Yes. Seems only a short while ago these two came into the world, *jah*?" came the reply from an old friend.

"Well, Ruby," Jacob said turning to her. "What dragged me down from my perch?"

"Wayne should explain it to both of you," Ruby said, then all faces turned to Wayne.

"I had just finished my lunch and was going to help with the barn boards, *daed*. And this *girl*," his voice snarled that word out, "ran out and tripped me. I fell upon my hammer and was knocked out. I could have been hurt even worse."

All eyes now went to Naomi who was on the verge of tears.

"Is this true, Naomi?" Jacob questioned, his voice full of thunder.

"Wayne," Ruby said before Naomi could speak. "What I did not tell you when you first said this is that I saw the entire thing. Would you like to think about your description at all?"

All heads pivoted back to Wayne. He was turning red again. "She tripped …" he started.

Ruby's head was slowly turning side to side.

"I tripped …" he started a second time.

Again, Ruby's head moved side to side.

"I lied," he finally admitted. "I was trying to impress someone and hit myself with the hammer." Then his face lit up. "But she lied too. She said I tripped and hit my head," pointing at Naomi.

"So, let me make sure I have this right," started his *daed*. "Even after I told you not to play with the hammer, you did."

Elmer waited for his son to nod agreement.

"Then, you knocked yourself out with the same hammer."

Again, he waited for a nod.

"This young lady came to see if you were hurt and you bore false witness against her?"

"But she lied and said I tripped." Wayne tried again.

"She went out of her way to make you appear less a fool than you acted, and you repaid her in this way?" Elmer had begun to turn red himself at this point.

He grabbed his son by the arm, spun him to face Naomi, and demanded an apology to her and her family.

"I am sorry," Wayne sputtered meekly.

"Jacob, I am sorry, my friend, for the shame my son has cast upon himself and that he tried to cast upon your Naomi," Elmer said, wringing his hands together. "We have a barn to raise. I will not let him come the rest of the days of this. He will also be punished at home."

"He is but a boy, Elmer," Jacob offered his friend.

"No, he is as close in age to being a man as your Naomi is to being a woman. I wish he were as close to his goal spiritually as she is," Elmer said then turned to Wayne. "Go wait in the wagon and pray forgiveness for your sin against this woman." He said this loud enough that all near could see the boy scolded.

Elmer walked back to the barn, shaking his head as he went. Jacob and Caleb stood with Ruby and Naomi.

"Naomi," Jacob turned to his youngest. "Why did you lie?"

"I am sorry, *vater*. This boy had been mean to me at school. I thought if I showed him kindness, he might learn from it. I was wrong thinking it, and wrong doing it," came a matter-of-fact reply from Naomi.

Jacob looked behind Naomi and saw Ruby nodding her head, confirming Naomi's tale. "Naomi, *'The Lord detests lying lips, but he delights in people who are trustworthy.'* Do you know where that is from?" he inquired.

"It comes from Proverbs, *vater,*" came her mild reply.

"You lied today. Had Ruby not been witness to the accident, you would be answering for striking that boy. Do you see the wickedness that comes from lying?" he asked in a voice as serious as he had in him.

"Yes, *vater*. Should I go wait in the wagon as well?" she meekly asked.

"No, you will make yourself useful. You will make the rounds with water for all the young men who are hammering the boards at the base. Make sure not a single one goes thirsty!" Jacob said, wagging his finger at her. "Now, get to it!" He said so loud and quick that she literally jumped to it.

As Naomi ran towards the pail and ladle, three sets of eyes followed her path.

"*Vater* Fisher, are you aware that is the job all of the young girls actually are begging to do?" asked Ruby, her head tilted waiting to see his answer.

"Really? I guess I might have chosen a better punishment then," Jacob said, revealing nothing as he walked back to the frame of the barn and got back to the work of building it.

"Did he know that already, Caleb?" Ruby asked her husband.

"Before coming here today he told me this is his fifteenth barn," came Caleb's reply. He too then turned and walked back to the barn.

Ruby stood there for a moment shaking her head at these Fisher men. The sun beating down on her and the stress of the conflict had the remnants of the stomach bug threatening to bring up her lunch. She walked back to the shade fanning herself as she went.

The sun dropped lower towards the horizon and work stopped for the day. Caleb looked up at the structure. They had raised up all of the frame, gotten one long side completely covered in boards and nearly finished the short side in back. It would take one more day to side it, another to roof it and paint it.

Peter had set up a grill and had dozens of chickens split and roasting on it. Big cast iron pans sizzled with potato casserole and loaves of bread were brought out. Any who wished to eat with Peter and Emma were welcome. Peter said a prayer before the meal thanking the Lord for his neighbors' help.

"Peter, you and your *familye* did an amazing job of having this all prepared and set out today," Bishop Yoder remarked, coming to say goodnight after the meal. "I will be back again in the morning. Let us pray for a cool breeze like today, *jah?*"

"*Jah*, I think we accomplished much today. I am grateful to be a part of this community, Bishop Yoder," Peter replied.

The men had all gathered around the bishop at that point and he led them in a prayer, thanking the Lord for the opportunities life gave them to be there for each other, and for the spirit of willingness that was instilled in these good people. He finished by thanking the women for their part and keeping the men fed and water flowing.

8

In the morning, Ruby's stomach bug returned with a vengeance. She had to ask for Naomi's help with the milking and collecting eggs for breakfast.

"Little Otto seems to have beaten that bug easier than you, Ruby," Caleb said, concern clear for his wife. "Are you well enough to help today? I can explain to your *schwester* and to the twins."

"I will not let a little virus stop me. I will stay out of the sun today and I'll be fine before the day is out, you watch and see," Ruby said, with more determination in her voice than in her eyes.

"I have a hanger bracket for the barn by the forge. I will load it up and meet you by the wagon," Caleb told her.

Ruby had no idea what a hanger bracket was, but used that loading time to wash the breakfast dishes and get herself ready to go. The two rode to Peter's as they always did, snuggled tight together.

There was less heavy lifting on day two. Caleb gave Peter the bracket to mount to the rafter closest to the loft entrance. This would hold the block and tackle that would allow him to lift hay to his loft, or lift anything that was too heavy by itself. They would find uses for it today without a doubt.

Much as the day before, the work started with bowed heads and a prayer. Quickly thereafter, men and ladders made their way to the barn and the sides went up even as the decking was prepared for the tin roof.

Throughout the day, Naomi kept up her penance of having to help the young men keep hydrated. Ruby noticed that a couple of them seemed to need much more water than the others.

Lunch time came, and Ruby came to her. "Naomi, John Miller," she said pointing to one of the thirsty boys, "and Jacob Bayler," pointing to the other, "have asked if you could bring them a lunch basket."

"That is rather forward of them, is it not?" Naomi asked Ruby.

"I could always get another girl to bring them," Ruby said as if she were about to do it.

"No, I can manage," came Naomi's response. "I will, of course, have to tell them I am too young for such things."

For another six months or so, thought Ruby.

Naomi sat between the boys, making them compete for her attention. Ruby got close enough to hear her tell them she was only fifteen and they should be paying attention to the older girls there.

It was all Ruby could do not to laugh out loud as she heard that. Both boys agreed that Naomi was much more mature than most of those girls. Ruby smiled, seeing Naomi had this well in hand, and went back to sit in the shade. Fighting this stomach bug had her tired with only half the day done.

Lunch ended as it started, with a prayer, and the men went back to their work. The barn had taken its form and was much more there than missing at this point. Peter had a small crew start to paint one long side of the barn. It would be dry by the time the roof went up the next day, so the men would have a way up and back down that was not covered in wet paint.

338

Out came the buckets of red barn paint and the building sprang to life in its new color. As day two ended, the siding was done, one wall was completely painted, and the stack of tin panels was dragged into place for the next day.

This night's meal was hamburgers and hot dogs. Caleb sat with Ruby and she ate two burgers and a pile of potato salad.

"I am glad to see you feeling better," he said, nodding at his wife.

"I am glad to be rid of that bug. Now I can go back to playing with my little friend, Otto," Ruby said with a smile on her face and in her eyes.

Otto sat across from her in Rebecca's lap. He was turning crackers into soup by gumming them over and over. He and Ruby both thought it was great fun to be having.

The last morning of the *spiel*, Caleb was woken by his wife jumping from the bed and running to a sink.

"I thought you were over that finally, Ruby," Caleb called into the next room.

He got up and walked to her.

"I am. I think the potato salad went bad in the sun," she said aloud.

"I had nearly as much as you and I did not have a problem," Caleb replied.

Ruby gave him a gentle slap in the stomach and said, "You could eat it after a week in the sun and say nothing about it."

Caleb thought a moment then said, "Maybe two or three days, not a week." Then the pair started laughing.

"We have little left for today. I am sure we can do this without you," Caleb offered his Ruby, who clearly did not survive the potato salad as well as he had.

"I think I will do the milking and then go back to bed," Ruby said. "Tell everyone I am sorry, and I will see them soon."

"I will, and let me give you a hand with the milking before I go so that you can start recovering faster. If you are not better tonight, we will go to the doctor tomorrow. I will not hear any arguments on this," Caleb said.

"I'm sure it will not come to that," Ruby said, and the two got the cows milked and the eggs gathered.

As Caleb was getting ready to leave, Ruby called to him, "Give little Otto a hug from me."

"I will, but I am sure he'd rather have it from the source."

Ruby smiled thinking of her nephew Otto, what a good little *bobbel* he is.

Caleb arrived without Ruby and offered her apologies to all.

The women went to check the temperature in the refrigerator to make sure there was no replay with the potato salad today. The men prayed, then got to painting and raising the roof.

The decision was made to break for lunch with about two hours of work left over.

Naomi was again requested to sit with her pseudo-suiters and drew some rather unpleasant looks from more than one of the girls who were of courting age.

Today, after the lunch break the tables were broken down and loaded into wagons. The pots, pans, and dishes were all washed up and set into baskets to return to their homes.

By the time the men were done with the roof and the painting, there was nothing but trampled grass and a new red barn to tell of what had been going on here for the past days.

Peter made sure to shake every man's hand who had helped and thank them personally. Emma did the same with each of the women. This barn meant that Peter could now move his shop into the barn, saving the money he spent to rent space to build his furnishings.

He had the men work a few corrugated fiberglass panels into the roof as well, so the barn was well lit by the sunshine. Several who saw this agreed that it would happen on their own barns the next time a roof panel needed repairs.

When all the hands were shaken, and all the tools put away, Bishop Yoder led them in a prayer and a song from inside the barn. The empty barn echoed the singing back to them and amplified it. More than one person looked around thinking others had joined them in singing.

After the song, the crew dispersed back to their wagons and homes. Bishop Yoder came to Peter and they agreed to hold a Sunday meeting in the barn in two weeks' time. Peter consented to make the barn and his home part of the regular circuit for prayer meetings.

As the bishop got into his wagon and left, Peter and Emma stood on the front porch of their home. Across the way a bright red barn stood where an empty spot had been last week. Peter's eyes roamed the wooded acres and landed back on the garden near his home, now a symphony of green colors moving gently in the breeze.

He turned to Emma then and kissed her forehead. "We are blessed, Emma. I am more so for having you by my side."

Emma had been idly rubbing her expanding belly while they stood. Hearing Peter's words broadened her smile and she held his hand, leaning into him. "We are equally blessed, Peter."

9

Caleb arrived home to find Ruby asleep on top of their bed. She had not so much as gotten under the covers nor even taken her shoes off. He would have to bring her to the *Englishe* doctor tomorrow, no matter how much she disliked going to them.

He made himself a meal from the leftovers in the kerosene refrigerator and ate alone. He said a prayer for his sick wife and shut the *haus* down for the night.

Morning came, and Ruby was no better. Caleb milked the cows, checked on the hay, determined he had a field to harvest in about a week's time.

By this time, Ruby had gotten herself dressed. Caleb went in to break the news to her that she was going to the doctor, like it or not. He was surprised by her lack of resistance.

Caleb drove the wagon as gently as he could to the doctor's office. They sat, filled out the forms, and had the *Englishe* stare at them like they always seemed to do.

After a short while, a nurse called Ruby's name. Caleb looked to see if Ruby wanted him to come and she assured him she would be fine. About fifteen minutes later, the nurse that had called Ruby's name stuck her head out the door and looked about. Seeing Caleb, she walked over to him and quietly asked him to come with her.

They went through the door, down a hall, and into a room where Ruby lay on a table. An *Englishe* woman doctor pointed to a chair and asked Caleb to sit. His heart was beating in his throat at this point and he began silent prayers for his Ruby's health.

"Mr. Fisher. I am Doctor Carter," the woman began. "I have been speaking to your wife here and we think we have found out why she is not getting over the stomach bug."

Caleb had heard of diseases that took even some as young as his Ruby and he continued to pray hard, gripping the seat cushion beneath him.

The doctor went over to Ruby, and parted the hiked dress from the blanket covering the lower half of Ruby, exposing her stomach. Reaching towards one of the many white box electric machines, she grabbed a flat wand and a tube of something.

Caleb watched as she squirted a blob of a clear jelly-like substance on Ruby's belly, then the doctor rubbed the wand across the jelly, spreading it.

On a screen nearby, a pattern of lines showed up and the room filled with a drumming sound.

Caleb looked at Ruby then at the doctor then back to Ruby. "Is that bad, doctor?"

Both women laughed at him now. The doctor stopped herself and pointed to a spot on the screen where the waves were blurred. "Your wife is pregnant."

Caleb stood sharply, then turned to see Ruby nodding.

"We are going to have a *bobbel?*" he asked excitedly.

"Yes!" squealed Ruby, reaching out to her husband to hug him to her.

"Well, actually no," the doctor said. This stopped their celebration and they turned to her.

"This," she said, pointing to the screen again, "is a baby." She paused then continued. "This is another baby. Congratulations, you are going to have twins," she said, surprising Ruby with the news as well as Caleb.

"Twins? Twins? Twins!" Ruby repeated, getting used to the idea, then excited by it.

"Are they boys or girls?" Caleb asked

"Oh, it is too early to tell that. We can make a follow-up appointment to check in six to eight weeks if you want to know."

Caleb looked at Ruby who shook her head. They would know when they needed to, no sooner. The doctor gave Ruby some instructions and told her to see the receptionist on the way out to set up regular check-ups.

She knew most Amish women only came to her when they were too ill to do their chores and did not hold much hope for seeing this woman again until after the birth.

"The receptionist also has a list of midwives if you prefer to give birth at home," she added.

Ruby's eyes showed more interest in this bit of news than the scheduled appointments.

Caleb and Ruby walked out of the office and he helped her up into the wagon. He climbed in and held her tight as they made their way home. Caleb was trying not to go so fast as to jostle his wife in any way.

"Caleb," Ruby started. "I've not seen you drive so slow since we courted. I will be fine. Now, rush this horse home. We have news to tell!"

Caleb looked at her then nodded, giving a snap to the reins and letting the horse speed up. He gripped his Ruby tighter and smiled all the way home.

They went to his parents first, then to Emma and Peter's, but found the home empty. Then they stopped at Samuel and Rebecca's home. They saw a pair of wagons there already.

When they knocked at the door, Rebecca smiled and said to the room, "Here they are now," and waved them in.

Seated at the table were Emma and Peter, as well as Lizzie and John. Caleb looked to Ruby, smiling. This was a triple blessing. They would not have to drive all the way out to the Beiler farm now to tell them.

"John has agreed to sell me a few more of his herd," Samuel said. "We decided to talk over the details over dinner. Since we were having company, we invited Peter and Emma. I went looking for you two as well, but did not find you home. Do the two of you wish to join us?"

"We have plenty," chimed in Rebecca.

Ruby gave a slight nod to Caleb who then agreed to stay for dinner with their *familye*.

"So, what has you out and about, Caleb?" Samuel asked his friend.

"We are on our way home from the doctor's office. Ruby has been sick far too long for my tastes." Caleb explained the original purpose of them being out.

"Well, we had hoped to ask for some help from you, Rebecca, and the two of you as well," Ruby said nodding at the other twins at the table. "It seems I am to be sick for a while more."

All the faces in the room dropped. Ruby saw the look of love and concern in each of them, then she finished. "Seeing as I am pregnant with twins."

The room exploded with noise and everyone stood to rush in congratulating Ruby and Caleb. The men shook his hand and hugged her, the women hugged everyone.

"Well, no wonder it took you so long, *schwester*. You were cooking up an extra helping." Rebecca laughed at Ruby.

The women got up and went into the *kich*, no doubt to talk more about *bobbele* than preparing dinner. The men talked about their farms and their plans. After an hour or so, the women came back into the room with an early dinner in tow.

Heads bowed, Samuel led them in prayer ending with Psalm 127:3, *"Behold, children are a heritage from the Lord, the fruit of the womb a reward."*

Everyone at the table nodded approval at his words and ate another simple meal made better by good company and conversation.

As he finished his meal, Caleb leaned back and looked around him. In this room alone, he had a dozen members of his family, four of whom he had yet to meet. He quietly prayed thanks to *Gott* for the bounty of his blessings.

After the meal had finished, the closing prayers said, and the dishes all washed, the couples said their goodbyes.

Caleb and Ruby arrived home and prepared for sleep. Before they climbed into bed, they said their prayers and Caleb reached out and drew his wife to him.

Caleb looked up and said wistfully, "If *Gott* blessed us no more than this, Ruby, I will die a happy man."

Ruby smiled at her husband as they lay down to sleep.

Far above *Gott* smiled, knowing that He had many more blessings waiting for Caleb and Ruby.

If you liked this book, please leave a review online where fine paperbacks and electronic books are sold.

Watch for more stories from Barnville, Pennsylvania, Population 1300.

Find out more about Laura and Amos' other books and connect with them at www.LauraJMarshall.com